BLOOD OF THE MOUNTAIN MAN

*Also by William W. Johnstone
in Large Print:*

Law of the Mountain Man
Code of the Mountain Man
Journey of the Mountain Man
The Last Mountain Man
Pursuit of the Mountain Man
Return of the Mountain Man
Revenge of the Mountain Man
Trail of the Mountain Man
War of the Mountain Man
Courage of the Mountain Man

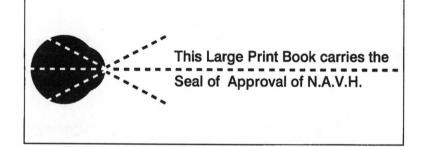

This Large Print Book carries the
Seal of Approval of N.A.V.H.

BLOOD OF THE MOUNTAIN MAN

William W. Johnstone

G.K. Hall & Co. • Waterville, Maine

Published in 2001 by arrangement with Zebra Books, an imprint of Kensington Publishing Corp.

G.K. Hall Large Print Western Series.

The text of this Large Print edition is unabridged. Other aspects of the book may vary from the original edition.

Set in 16 pt. Plantin by Rick Gundberg.

Printed in the United States on permanent paper.

Library of Congress Cataloging-in-Publication Data

Johnstone, William W.
    Blood of the mountain man / William W. Johnstone.
        p.   cm.
    ISBN 0-7838-9487-2 (lg. print : hc : alk. paper)
    1. Jensen, Smoke (Fictitious character) — Fiction. 2. Rocky Mountains — Fiction. 3. Mountain life — Fiction. 4. Montana — Fiction. 5. Large type books. I. Title.
PS3560.O415 B58 2001
    813′.54—dc21   2001024383

Dying is a very dull, dreary affair. And my advice to you is to have nothing whatever to do with it.

W. Somerset Maugham

One

Sheriff Monte Carson swung down in front of the mountain home and petted several of the many dogs that lived around the place. Properly stroked, they scampered off to resume their playing. Monte looked up as the front door opened. The sheriff had never gotten used to how big the man was who stood in the doorway. The man was inches over six feet, and with the weight to go with it. His shoulders were door-wide and hard-packed with muscle. His hips were lean and the muscles in his legs strained his denim jeans.

"Smoke," Monte said.

"Monte," the West's most famous gunfighter said. "You're just in time for breakfast and coffee. Come in."

Monte took off his hat and stepped into the lovely home of Smoke and Sally Jensen. He howdied and smiled at Sally, just as beautiful as ever, and took a seat at the kitchen table. Sally turned to the stove and cracked three more eggs and added another thick slice of ham to the other skillet.

"What's up, Monte?" Smoke Jensen asked, pouring the sheriff a cup of coffee.

"Smoke, how long's it been since you heard

from your sister Janey?"

The question took Smoke by surprise. "Why . . . years. I thought she was dead."

"She is," Monte said bluntly, as was the Western way. He reached into his jacket pocket and took out a telegraph. "This came in early today. It's from the marshal of a little town up in Montana. Right smack in the middle of the Rockies. A mining town called Red Light."

Smoke looked at the man and Sally turned from the stove, arching an eyebrow at that.

Monte smiled. "I know. Strange name for a town. You'd better read the wire, Smoke."

Sally put the sheriff's ham and eggs and home-fried potatoes in front of him and Monte took knife and fork to hand and fell to eating, after buttering a hot biscuit.

The telegraph read: JANEY JENSEN, DIED RECENTLY OF NATURAL CAUSES AND LEFT EVERYTHING TO HER BROTHER. IMPORTANT THAT MR. K. JENSEN COME TO RED LIGHT AS SOON AS POSSIBLE TO LAY CLAIM TO ESTATE, WHICH INCLUDES BUSINESS IN TOWN AND RANCH IN VALLEY.

It was signed, CLUB BOWERS, SHERIFF, RED LIGHT, MONTANA.

"I knew a Club Bowers," Smoke said. "He was an outlaw."

"Same one," Monte said. "I know him, too. That might give you an idea what kind of town it is."

8

"Just where is Red Light?" Sally asked.

"In the middle of nowhere," Monte said. "It's a mining town, and it is isolated. Nearest town of any size is a good hundred miles away. There's talk of changing the name from Red Light to something else, but so far it's just talk."

Smoke sipped his coffee and stared at the sheriff. "Monte, you're walking around something. Come on — what is it?"

"This is one of those freak strikes, Smoke. It's in a place where gold and silver shouldn't be. But they were found, and it's a good vein. It's slowing down some, but it'll probably be producing for a good many years to come. I know about Red Light. I had a friend killed up there a couple of years ago. The town is set up in the mountains, above one of the prettiest valleys you ever put your eyes on. Valley runs for miles and miles. River runs right through the entire length of the valley. The ranchers down there supply the beef for the miners. Tell you the truth, in a situation like that, I'd rather have a ranch than a gold mine. You'd best get up there. If you tarry long, you just might not have a ranch left."

"The other ranchers might take it?"

"You betcha. And you'll notice the wire read 'K. Jensen.' That tells me your sis never let on about your nickname. You bet those other ranchers will try to horn in. They'll be fightin' like coyotes over a scrap of meat."

"I wonder what the business in town is?"

Monte shrugged.

9

"Janey," Smoke said. "All these years I thought she was dead. I would have sworn she was dead. I heard she was." Smoke snapped his fingers. "I *know* she's dead. Then . . ."

"Her daughter, honey?" Sally said, putting his plate in front of him and sitting down with a biscuit and a cup of coffee.

"That all you're eating?" Smoke asked with a frown.

"I'm on a diet. Her daughter?" she repeated.

"Maybe. She did have a daughter by that gambling man she took off with back in Missouri. She pulled out in '64 and I heard she had the child in '67. She wouldn't be out of her teens."

"She had a daughter, Smoke," Sally said. "I remember some of the women talking about it back in Idaho Territory — before I met you. Jenny was her name."

"Monte, can you wire back and see if this is Janey or Jenny who died?"

"Sure."

"I'll be in town this afternoon and stop by your office."

Monte finished his breakfast and headed back to town. Over a second cup of coffee, Sally said, "This is bringing back bad memories for you, isn't it, Smoke?"

"Some." He smiled at her. "But I'll survive them."

"This girl, if it is Jenny, would be no more than a child. Seventeen at most."

"What do you remember about her?"

10

"Nothing. I never saw her. The ladies of the town said that she was at school back East."

"We'll know more after I go into town."

"Saddle my pony for me. I'm riding in with you."

"Sidesaddle, of course," Smoke said with a straight face.

Her reply would not have been printable in those times.

"Here's the whole story, Smoke," Monte said, handing Smoke several pages of telegraph paper. "I wired a sheriff I know up in Montana Territory. He knew all about it."

Smoke opened the envelope. MISS JANEY JENSEN DIED OF FEVER TWO YEARS AGO. WAS PROMINENT BUSINESS-WOMAN IN TOWN. OWNED BUSINESSES AND RANCH IN VALLEY. IS BURIED IN RED LIGHT, MONTANA CEMETERY. HAD ONE DAUGHTER, JENNY. JENNY RETURNED TO RED LIGHT AND IS LIVING ON RANCH. ENTIRE ESTATE LEFT TO JENNY. NO ONE KNEW WHERE TO FIND JANEY'S BROTHER, A MISTER K. JENSEN. UNDERSTAND HE WAS FINALLY LOCATED IN COLORADO AND NOTIFIED. TELL HIM TO BE CAREFUL. DON'T TRUST ANY LAW OFFICER IN COUNTY. K. JENSEN IS RIDING INTO A DEN OF SNAKES. ANY RELATION TO SMOKE? IF SO, TAKE HIM ALONG. JUST

KIDDING. TAKE CARE OF YOURSELF, MONTE.

"Man lays it right on the line, doesn't he?" Smoke said.

"Tom's a good man," Monte replied. "Is Sally going up there with you?"

"No. Not initially. I might send for her later on. Jenny vanished. I don't like the sound of that. Damn it, Monte, she's my only kin. Except for some folks in Iowa that I have never seen and who fought against my father in the war. I understand they harbored such bad feeling toward those Jensens who fought for the south that they changed their name to Jen*son*."

"That war tore up a lot of families, Smoke. Mine included. When are you pulling out?"

"Tomorrow, probably. I'll ride the trains as far as possible. It's been awhile since ol' Buck and I hit the trail. We'll both look forward to it."

"Not taking one of your appaloosas?"

"Not this time. Buck's a mountain horse and better than any watchdog in the world. And meaner, too. I want him to see some more country before I retire him. Lord knows, we have seen some trails together."

"You really love animals, don't you, Smoke?"

"Yes. And I respect them. I don't trust a man who doesn't like animals. There's a flaw in his character . . ." He smiled. "Although some of Sally's highly educated friends say that is not true."

12

"They called you a liar to your face?"

"Only once."

Buck was a mountain-bred buckskin that was just about too big and too much horse for the average man. But Smoke was not an average man. He had gentle-broken the animal and was the only one who could ride it. Truth be known, he was about the only one who *wanted* to ride the mean-eyed animal.

"Now, you change into your suit when you reach the rails," Sally told him, handing him a sack of food for the trail.

"Yes, dear," the most famous gunfighter in all the West replied.

"And you button your collar and fix your tie properly."

"Yes, dear."

"And if your suit is rumpled, you have it brushed and ironed at the nearest town."

"Yes, dear."

"And as soon as you are settled up there, send for me."

"Yes, dear."

"And you will *not* let anyone know that you are Smoke Jensen unless it becomes absolutely necessary."

"Yes, dear," he said with a smile, towering above her outside the house. He closed his big hands around her arms and gently picked her up with all the ease of picking up a pillow. He kissed her lips and set her back down, then chuckled.

"What is so funny?" she demanded.

"Knowing my sister, what if it turns out the business she owned in town is a whorehouse?"

Sally narrowed her eyes. "If that is the case, *Mister* Jensen, you are in a world of trouble."

"Yes, *ma'am!*"

Two

Smoke Jensen was a known gunfighter, though not by choice. Dozens of books — penny dreadfuls — had been written about him, ninety-nine percent of them pure crap and nonsense. Songs had been sung about him, and at least one play was still being performed about the life and times of Smoke Jensen. Smoke had read some of the books, or as much of them as he could stand, and he usually used them afterward to light fires in the stove or fireplace. The songs were terrible and the play was worse. But for all his fame and notoriety, relatively few people knew what he looked like. He seldom left his horse ranch, called the Sugarloaf, in the mountains of Colorado, and when he did venture out, it usually was not for long. So many would-be toughs and gunslingers had taken to wearing their guns as Smoke wore his, that trademark was no longer a giveaway.

Smoke rarely buckled on two guns anymore, doing so only when he knew he was riding into trouble. He was content to wear one gun, right side, low and tied down.

He was a ruggedly handsome man, but not in the pretty-boy way. His face was strong, his jaw firm, and his eyes cold as winter-locked fjords.

15

He loved children and animals, and attended church on a regular basis, even though the preacher at the town of Big Rock, Colorado, knew Smoke would never pay much attention to the New Testament, since he was strictly an Old Testament man.

He raised appaloosas on his ranch, running only a few head of cattle now.

His wife, Sally, was of the New England Reynoldses, and enormously wealthy. She was a strong-willed woman, not one to mince words and certainly not someone to ride over. Sally was a strong supporter of women's rights, was very outspoken on the subject, and would not back down from a grizzly. She had strapped on pistol and picked up rifle and sent more than one thug to Hell in her time. She was also a loving mother and a faithful companion to her husband and a sweet person . . . just as long as you didn't mess with her man.

Smoke rode to the rails and boarded the train. At rail's end, he signed the hotel registry as K. Jensen and no one paid any special attention to him, except for the men commenting on his size and the ladies on how handsome and how well mannered he was.

Smoke had stabled Buck, curried him, and told the boy to grain him and not mess with him. It was doubtful Buck would hurt a child; he never had, but one never knew. The horse was a killer, and he bonded only with Smoke.

Smoke carefully bathed and shaved, and

dressed in a dark suit, white shirt, and black string tie. He belted his gun around him and tied it down, slipping the hammer thong free of the hammer. It was something he did from habit, like breathing.

The large hotel, fairly fancy for the time, had a separate bar and dining room, connected by a door that was guarded on the saloon side by a man who looked like he ate wagons for lunch. Smoke entered the bar and ordered a whiskey. Not much of a drinking man, he did occasionally enjoy a drink before dinner, sometimes a brandy after dinner, and a beer after a hard day's ride.

Saloons were a meeting place, where a man — women were not yet allowed — could find out road conditions, trouble spots where highwaymen lurked, the best place to buy horses or cattle, what range was closed, and where good water could be found. Smoke leaned against the bar, sipped his whiskey, and listened.

"I heard Smoke Jensen got killed down in Mexico," a man said. "Gunfighter name of Jake Bonner got him."

Smoke hid his smile.

"What'd he do, back-shoot him?"

"Outdrew him."

Smoke tuned them out. Jake Bonner was a two-bit punk who had been making brags for several years that if he ever came upon Smoke Jensen, he was going to kill him.

"Bonner's in town." That remark brought

Smoke back to paying attention to the gabby citizens.

"And he's sayin' he killed Jensen?"

"He's talkin' big about it."

"Well, by God. I knew he'd been gone for several months. I heard he hired out his gun. Say, now, this is news."

"Says he's got proof. Says he's got Jensen's boots, just jerked off his dead body. Fancy, engraved boots. Got the initials SJ right on the front of each one."

"You don't say?"

By this time, twenty men had gathered around and were listening to the bull-tossing.

"Say, stranger."

Smoke realized the citizen was talking to him, and he turned slightly. "Yes?"

"Didn't you come in on the 4:18 train?"

"That's right."

"Thought so. Did you hear anything about Jake Bonner killing Smoke Jensen?"

"No. I haven't heard anything about that."

"Funny. Seems like the news would be all over."

"If it's true," Smoke replied, sipping a bit of whiskey.

"Mister, you're a big'un, but I'd not call Jake Bonner a liar if I was you. Jake's a bad one."

"Every town has one."

"Not as bad as Jake. The man's cat-quick with a gun. Why, he's got five notches carved in his gun handle."

"Tinhorn trick," Smoke said.

"You callin' me a tinhorn?" the voice came from the boardwalk batwings to the saloon.

Smoke turned slowly. The man facing him from about thirty feet away was young, no more than twenty-two or -three. He wore two guns, pearl-handled, in a fancy rig. His coat was swept back, his hands by his side.

"Anybody who carves notches in his gun-handles is a tinhorn," Smoke said, placing his shot glass on the bar. "If that fits you, wear it."

"I'm Jake Bonner. The man who killed Smoke Jensen. And you'll take back that remark, mister. Or you'll drag iron."

"What if I decide to do neither?"

"Then you're a yeller dog."

"I've known some nice dogs in my time. As a matter of fact, I've known a lot more nice dogs than nice humans."

Back in a corner of the big room, a faro dealer sat with a smile on his lips. Of all the men in the room, he alone knew who the big man in the black suit was. He'd seen him several times, once in action. And he knew that if Jake Bonner didn't close his mouth and do it real quick, he was either dead on the floor or stomped into a cripple.

Jake walked closer to the bar, his fancy spurs jingling. "Mister, I think you're a liar and a coward. What do you have to say about that?"

"I think you'd better go home before I decide to change your diapers."

The bar cleared, the men leaving as of one mind. Only the faro dealer remained in the direct line of fire. He knew that if Bonner was dumb enough to draw — or attempt to draw — he'd never get a shot off. The faro dealer figured he was in the safest spot in the saloon.

"Before you *what?*" Jake's words were almost a scream.

Smoke was getting angry, but his was never a hot anger. It was a cold fury. "Are you deaf as well as stupid?" He knew he was pushing, but punks infuriated Smoke. Especially one who walked around making the claim that he'd killed him.

Jake walked closer, and Smoke knew then that Bonner was no gunfighter. No gunfighter wanted action this close up. The odds were too great that both men would take lead.

"You're a dead man, mister," Jake hissed the words.

"No," Smoke said slowly. "But you're sure a hurt one." He backhanded Jake with a hard right that knocked the man spinning. Jake fell against a table, the table collapsed, and Jake landed on his butt on the floor in a state of confusion.

Things weren't supposed to work out this way. Every time he'd try to get up, the big stranger would knock him back down. Jake felt his lips pulp and knew he'd lost a couple of teeth. The big man hauled back a huge fist and busted Jake right on the nose. Jake screamed in pain as his beak busted and the blood poured. In a fog of hurt, Jake felt himself being jerked to his feet and hurled through the air. He crashed against a wall and the air left him.

When Jake could catch his breath, he reached for his guns, but his holsters were empty. He blinked a couple of times and saw his guns, on the bar, in front of the big stranger. The stranger was calmly sipping at his whiskey.

Smoke unloaded the matched .45s and lined up the cartridges on the bar. "Children shouldn't play with guns," he said. "You might hurt yourself, Booper."

"The name is Bonner," Jake gasped.

Smoke nodded gravely and finished his drink. "You all through trying to play tough boy, Bonehead?"

Jake struggled to his feet and stood swaying for a moment. Then, with a curse, he reached behind him and jerked out a knife.

"I really wish you hadn't done that," Smoke said.

"Jake!" the faro dealer shouted. "Don't do it, boy. You don't know who you're messin' with."

Jake sneered at the dealer. Smoke stood facing the bar, both hands on the polished mahogany.

"I'm gonna gut you like a fish, mister," Jake panted, the blood dripping down from his busted nose and smashed lips.

The batwings flipped open and a man wearing a star stood there. "Put it down, Jake," he ordered. "Do it now, or I'll shoot you where you stand."

Jake slowly lowered the knife. The Marshal walked around to face the young would-be tough. "What the hell ran over you, Jake? A beer wagon?"

Jake refused to answer.

"Put the knife up, Jake. Right now."

Jake sheathed the big blade and with something that sounded like a sob, abruptly turned and lurched from the saloon.

"These are his guns, Marshal," Smoke said. "I took the precaution of unloading them."

The marshal walked up to Smoke and the counterman placed a cup of coffee in front of him. "Jake's a pretty salty type, mister. Not many men around here would have tried to disarm him."

"He's a two-bit loudmouth," Smoke replied. "Nothing more."

"You got a name?"

"Doesn't everybody?" Smoke turned and walked out of the bar and into the dining area. He was seated and a menu was placed in front of him.

The marshal was irritated and his face showed it. He turned to follow Smoke and the faro dealer said, "Leave him alone, Jeff. He's a good, decent man who was pushed, that's all. Believe me when I say that is the *last* man in the world you want to crowd."

"You know him, Sparks?"

"I've seen him a time or two, yes. He just wants to have a meal and a good night's sleep, that's all."

Jeff thought for a moment, and then nodded. "All right, I'll take your word for it. But you know Jake's not gonna stand for this."

"His funeral, Marshal."

"Yeah, that's what I'm afraid of."

Smoke ate his meal and had coffee, then stepped out onto the porch for a cigarette and a breath of night air. He had not forgotten Jake Bonner. That would have been a very unwise thing to do. For the Jakes of this world, once humiliated, would never forgive or forget, and Smoke was careful of his back.

He looked across the street and saw the marshal sitting on the boardwalk, watching him.

The marshal knows Jake isn't going to forget what happened in the saloon, he thought. And he's thinking Jake just might decide to do something tonight.

Smoke sat down in a chair that was shrouded in darkness and finished his cigarette. He was tired, but not sleepy. He knew he should go on up to his room and lie down, but he didn't want to do that. He was more irritated than restless. He would have liked to walk the main street of the town. But to do that would only bring him trouble. Hell, he thought, sitting here will probably bring me trouble.

In my own way, I am a prisoner.

Come on, Jake, he reasoned, his thoughts suddenly savage. Come on. If you're going to do something foolish, do it now and get it over with.

The marshal stood up and walked to his office.

He stood for a moment in the open door, then stepped inside and closed it behind him.

I'm a stranger here, Smoke thought. I'd better have witnesses.

He stood up and walked through the hotel lobby to the bar, a tall, well-dressed man in a tailored suit. In the saloon, he ordered coffee and stood by the bar, waiting for it to cool. The place was doing a brisk business. But when Smoke elected to stand at the bar, the long bar cleared, the men choosing tables instead.

That amused Smoke, in a sour sort of way. He was conscious of the faro dealer watching him. I've seen that man somewhere down the line, Smoke thought.

The batwings pushed open and Jake Bonner stood there, his bruised face swollen now. He'd found him more guns and his holsters were full.

"I'm callin' your hand, mister," Jake said, his voice husky with emotion. "Now turn around and face me."

Smoke turned, brushing back his coat as he did. "Go home, Jake Bonner. There is no need for this."

"Do what he says, Jake," the faro dealer called. "He's giving you a chance to live. Take it."

"Shut up, gambler!" Jake yelled. "This ain't none of your affair. I'm the man who killed Smoke Jensen. No two-bit stranger does to me what this one done."

"You didn't kill Smoke Jensen, Jake," the

24

dealer said. "Smoke Jensen is standing in front of you."

The saloon became as hushed as a church. Jake's face drained of blood and he stood pale and shaken.

"Go home, Jake," Smoke told him. "Go home and live. Don't crowd me."

"Draw, damn you!" Jake screamed, and grabbed iron.

Smoke's draw was perfection, deadly beauty. As Jake's hands closed around the butts of his guns, he felt a hammer blow in the center of his chest. He stumbled backward and fell against the wall, then slowly slid down to sit on the floor. His guns were still in leather.

"No," he said. "This ain't . . . this ain't right. This ain't the way it's suppose' to be."

"But it is," the faro dealer said.

"You go to hell!" Jake Bonner screamed.

It was the last thing he said.

Smoke holstered his gun and stood by the bar. He picked up his coffee cup with his left hand and took a sip. Just right.

"Jesus God!" a man breathed. "I seen it but I don't believe it. It was a blur. Hell, it wasn't even that!"

The marshal stepped in, gun drawn. He looked at Jake, then at Smoke, and holstered his .45. "I knew it was going to happen," he said. "I thought about lockin' Jake up until mornin'. Now I wish I had."

"Jake called him and drew first," a man said.

"Or tried to. That's Smoke Jensen, Marshal."

"The poor dumb fool," the marshal said. "Not you," he was quick to add, looking at Smoke.

"You have any questions for me?" Smoke asked.

"Only one. When are you leavin' town?"

"First thing in the morning."

"Good. Somebody get the undertaker and get Jake fitted for a box." The marshal looked at Smoke. There were things he wanted to say, but he was wise enough not to say them. It wasn't that he blamed Smoke, for he was sure that Smoke had been pushed into the fight. "Good night, Mister Jensen," was all he had to say.

Smoke nodded and left the room.

He was gone before dawn the next morning.

Three

Smoke had a long ride ahead of him, but it was one he was looking forward to. He had wanted to provision up at the town that was now miles behind him, but felt it best to move on. There might be more like Jake Bonner in town.

He shot a rabbit and had that for lunch, then caught several fish and had them for his dinner. The next day he rode up to an old trading post and after looking it over from a distance, decided to provision there. He stepped inside and knew immediately he had walked into some sort of disagreement. There were six men besides the owner in the dark and smoky room that served as a bar — cowboys, from the look of them. Three stood facing three, and their faces were dark with anger. The owner or manager or whatever the hell he was stood behind the rough plank bar.

"Beans and bacon and flour and coffee," Smoke said, walking up to the bar.

"Mister, this ain't a real good time for doin' no grocery shoppin'," the man told him.

"It's as good a time as any," Smoke replied. "Fill the order."

"I reckon Dupree hired you, too, mister," a

cowboy said to Smoke.

Smoke looked at him. "Nobody hired me to do anything. And I never heard of any Dupree. Just passin' through is all. You boys carry on with your business and let me do mine." His gaze returned to the man behind the bar. "And toss in a box of .44s while you're at it."

One of the cowboys had looked out the window at Smoke's horse. "I never seen that brand before."

"Now you have," Smoke replied. "A can of peaches, too," he added to his order. "You have any food cooked?"

"Beans and beef," the man said. "Mister, ride on. This ain't no time for . . ."

"Dish me up a plate of it. A big plate. I'm hungry."

"Are you hard of hearin'?" a cowboy asked. "You was told to ride on."

All in all, Smoke thought, this trip is turning out to be a disaster from the git-go. "Buddy, I don't know what your problem is. But I do have a suggestion. Leave me the hell alone and stick to your own knittin'!"

The cowboys, obviously working on opposite sides of the fence, and probably arguing over range or strayed beef or water rights, looked at one another and silently decided to band together against this stranger who it appeared was not taking either side very seriously.

The bartender shoved a plate of food at the tall stranger and Smoke stood at the bar and went to eating, ignoring the cowboys.

"Well, if that don't beat all!" one said. "Just turns his back to us and starts feedin' his face."

"Fill the order," Smoke told the man behind the bar.

The man sighed.

"You fill that order, Smith," a puncher said, "and you'll get no more business from the Lazy J."

"And none from the Three Star," the other side warned.

"Fill the order," Smoke told him.

"Man," the bartender said. "You have put me in one hell of a bind. You know that?"

"It's a free country," Smoke told him. "If you don't want to sell me the goods, then do so of your own choosing. Not because of threats from this bunch of saddlebums."

"Saddlebums!" one of the men shouted.

Another walked to the bar and leaned against it, staring hard at Smoke. He took a closer look at the man nonchalantly eating his meal. Feller sure was big. He looked at the man's wrists. Bigger than most men's forearms. But he figured the six of them could handle him without much trouble.

"Mister, I think we'll just clean your clock."

Smoke turned and hit him with a left that seemed to come out of nowhere. The impact sounded like a melon hit with the flat side of an ax. The man's boots flew out from under him and he was slammed to the floor, flat on his back. He did not move.

"Now leave me the hell alone and let me finish my meal," Smoke said, without looking at the remaining five.

They looked back at him, then at the motionless puncher on the floor. One side of the man's face was rapidly swelling and they knew his jaw was broken.

One punch. One broken jaw. No one among them seemed especially eager to step up to the bar.

"Close your mouth and fill my order," Smoke told the man behind the bar.

"Yes, sir," the man said softly.

"You as good with that gun as you are with your fists, mister?" a cowboy from the Lazy J asked.

"Better," Smoke told him.

"You just might have to prove it," he said.

"Then that makes you short of sense," Smoke replied. "I'm passing through, nothing more. You boys are on the prod, not me. You pushed me, not the other way around. Think about it."

The man on the floor still had not moved, except for his swelling jaw.

"You got a name?"

Smoke put down his fork and turned, facing the five. It was then that several of them noticed the hammer thong had been slipped from the big stranger's six-gun. No one had seen him do it, so that meant it was done when his boots left the stirrups and hit the ground. All of them noticed that he was facing five-to-one odds and showing no fear, no excitement, nothing except dead calm.

"Smoke Jensen."

The bartender slowly sank to the floor, behind a beer barrel. Somewhere within the confines of the trading post, a clock ticked loudly.

Of the five punchers, one found his voice. "Feller down the way claims to have killed Jensen in Mexico."

"He lied. Jake Bonner is dead. I killed him night before last. I didn't want to. But he crowded me. Just like you're doing."

"I ain't crowdin' you," a Three Star rider said. "I'm sittin' down and stayin' out of this."

"Me, too," a Lazy J man said.

"That makes three of us," another one said.

The men moved out of the line of fire and sat down and very carefully put their hands on the rough tabletop. It was by no means an act of cowardice. It was just showing exceptionally good sense.

"Sit down, Luke," one of the three said. "You, too, Shorty. This is stupid. The man ain't done us no harm. I'm big enough to admit we was out of line and pushy."

"I ain't takin' water from no killer," Luke said stubbornly.

"Me, neither," Shorty said. "And I ain't real sure this is Smoke Jensen. I think he's a tinhorn."

"I'll turn around and finish my meal," Smoke

offered an honorable way out of a bad situation. "You boys sit down and have a beer on me. How about that?"

"I say you go right straight to hell," Shorty said, his voice thick.

"It won't be me who takes that trip today, boys," Smoke told them. "Think about it."

"You can't take both of us," Luke bragged.

"Yes, I can," Smoke said quietly and surely. "But I don't want to."

"Now I *know* he ain't Smoke Jensen," Shorty said. "He's yeller."

The front door opened and two men stepped in. Both quickly sized up the situation.

"Shorty," one said. "Sit down."

"Luke," the second man said. "You do the same. Right now."

"This tinhorn braced me, Boss," Luke said.

"No, he didn't," one of the men seated said. "We all started this. Dixie there," he looked at the man on the floor, "he stuck his face in the stranger's and got stretched out with one punch."

"This hombre says he's Smoke Jensen, Boss," Shorty said.

The men, obviously the owners of the Lazy J and the Three Star, stepped between Smoke and the two riders. One faced the punchers, the other faced Smoke.

"Is that right?" Smoke was asked.

"That's right. I came in here for a meal and supplies. Nothing more. And I'll ride if given the chance. But no more mouth from your boys."

"We pay the men for work. What they do or say on their own time is their business."

"Then I hope you have room in your cemetery for two more." Smoke was blunt.

The bartender had stood up. "Jensen's tellin' the truth. He didn't do nothin' 'cept come in here and ask for supplies."

"I think you better ride," the rancher facing Smoke said.

"Is that an order?"

The rancher's smile was thin. "Just a suggestion, Mister Jensen."

Smoke nodded his head. "Sack up my supplies," he told the man behind the bar. "And total up my bill. I'll be moving along."

"Just like I said," Shorty popped off. "Yeller."

The ranchers stepped out of the way. That was the final straw and they both knew it. No man would stand for that.

Luke sat down.

Smoke looked at Shorty. The man was scared and sweating. He had worked himself into a corner and didn't know how to get out of it. Shorty was probably a pretty decent sort; it was not a crime to be young. Smoke took a chance and took a step toward the puncher.

Shorty looked confused and stood a step back, bumping into a table. Smoke kept walking toward him.

"Are you crazy?" Shorty said, a shrill sound to his words. "Hold up, man."

Smoke kept walking.

The others in the room wondered what in hell Jensen was up to.

Smoke walked right up to Shorty and jerked his six-shooter from leather. He tossed the gun to a puncher seated at a table. The puncher caught the .45 and held it like he was holding a lighted stick of dynamite.

"Sit down, Shorty," Smoke said. "And I'll buy you a drink. The trouble is over."

Shorty sat, then looked up at the man. "That took guts, Mister Jensen. I acted the fool."

"We all do from time to time. You sure don't hold a corner on the market."

Smoke walked the room, introducing himself and shaking hands with all the men. Whatever friction might have been between the punchers had vanished. The men had gotten Dixie to his boots and the man wobbled over to the table and sat down. Turned out his jaw wasn't broken, but it damn sure was badly bent.

"I had a mule kick me one time wasn't that hard," Dixie mush-mouthed.

The ranchers sent their men back to home range and they sat and had coffee with Smoke.

"So Jake Bonner finally got himself six feet," Three Star said. "It's overdue."

Lazy J said, "You lookin' for land up this way, Smoke?"

"No. I'm heading for a place called Red Light. Can you tell me anything about it?"

"It's a damn good place to stay away from,"

Three Star replied. "It's a den of snakes and they're all poison."

"It's a hard four-day ride from here," the other rancher said. "Figure on six unless you want to wear your horse out. But," he added with a smile, "if that's your buckskin out yonder, it don't look like he ever gets tired."

"He's a good one," Smoke acknowledged. "And the best bodyguard I ever had."

"I can believe that. He gave me a look that caused me to give him a wide berth," the rancher said. "Thanks for givin' Shorty a break. He's a good boy, but hot-headed. This might cool him down some."

The men chatted for a time, the ranchers telling Smoke the best way up to the rip-roaring mining town of Red Light, and then Smoke packed his supplies and rode north.

"I always figured Smoke Jensen for a much older man," one rancher said.

The other one bit off a chew and replied, "Killed his first man when he was about fourteen. Then he dropped out of sight for a few years. Raised by mountain men. Ol' Preacher took him under his wing. When Jensen surfaced a few years later, he was pure hell on wheels with a gun. Nice feller once you get to know him."

The West was being settled and tamed slowly, but it was getting there. Smoke avoided the many little towns and settlements that were cropping up all over the place. Most would be

35

gone in a few years, some would prosper and grow.

At the end of the third day, Smoke was beginning to feel a little gamy and wanted a hot bath, a bed with clean sheets, and a meal that someone else had cooked. He topped a ridge and looked down at a small six-store town, about a dozen homes scattered around the short main street. He rode slowly down the rutted road. As he entered the town he was conscious of the eyes on him. He swung down in front of the livery and told the man he'd stall and curry Buck himself.

"I damn sure wouldn't touch that hoss," the liveryman said. "That beast has got a wicked look in his eyes."

"Gentle as a kitten," Smoke said.

"What kind of a kitten?" the man asked. "A puma?"

Smoke smiled and spent the next few minutes taking care of Buck while the big horse chomped away at grain.

Taking his kit and his rifle, Smoke walked across the street to the combination saloon, cafe, and hotel. It was mid-afternoon and the town was quiet. He registered as K. Jensen and went to his room. Taking fresh clothing, he walked to the barbershop and ordered hot water for the tub while he had himself a shave.

"Passin' through?" the barber inquired.

"Yup," Smoke told him. "Seeing the country. Thought I'd head up to Red Light and see what's up there."

"Trouble," the barber was blunt. "That's a bad place to head for, mister."

"Oh?"

"Yes, sir. You're a hard day and a half from Red Light. Over the mountains. Used to be a decent place. Lots of small miners. Then Major Cosgrove moved in with his pack of trouble-hunters and before you knew what had happened, he owned the whole kit and caboodle. Them that tried to hold on to their claims suddenly got seriously dead. They tried to get their dust out, and they was robbed. I ran a shop up there for a few years. I made good money, but man, it got chancy, so I pulled out and settled here. The money ain't so good, but the peace is nice. Except when Red Lee and his boys come to town."

"Red Lee?"

"Owns a ranch east of here. Likes to think he owns everybody around here, too. Know the type?"

"Sure."

"A couple of his boys is over to the saloon now. You'd best walk light around them. They like to start trouble, and they fancy themselves gunslicks."

"I'll certainly take that under advisement," Smoke said.

He bathed carefully and then ordered more hot water to rinse off in. Dressed in clean clothes, while his others were being laundered, Smoke walked back to the hotel and into the saloon for a whiskey to cut the trail dust. It was just a little early for supper.

He ignored the three men sitting at a table and walked to the bar. But he immediately pegged the men as rowdies and trouble-hunters. Nowhere had he seen any sign of a marshal or a marshal's office in the small town.

Smoke was beginning to have bad feelings about this trip. All he'd set out to do was settle his dead sister's affairs, and so far all he'd had was trouble. He really wished he was back on the Sugarloaf, with Sally.

"Whiskey," he told the bartender. "From the good bottle."

"Well, now," one of the rowdies said. "Looks like we got us a dandy come to town, boys. *From the good bottle,*" he mimicked mockingly.

Smoke looked at the bartender as he poured the whiskey. There were warning signs in the man's eyes, but Smoke ignored them. He was tired from the trail, wanting only a drink, a hot meal, and a warm bed. He was in no mood to be pushed around by the likes of those at the table.

He despised that type of man and always had. He'd helped Sheriff Monte Carson run more than one of 'em out of town, and he'd personally killed his share of 'em over the years. They were, as the good folks in the Deep South called them, white trash.

Smoke took a sip of his whiskey and carefully sat the glass down. He turned to face the men. "You have a problem with that, loudmouth?"

The men fell silent, their mocking smiles suddenly gone from their faces. The bartender moved back, away from the tall stranger. Two locals at a table looked at each other and wished they were somewhere else.

"Are you talkin' to *us*, mister?" one of the trio said.

"I don't see anyone else in the room who stuck his lip into my business."

"You just bought yourself a whole mess of trouble, mister," another of the three said.

"You got it to do," Smoke told him. "Fists or guns. It doesn't make a damn bit of difference to me. Step up here and toe the mark."

Four

The three looked at each other and smiled. "You know who you're about to tangle with, drifter?" one asked.

"Three braying jackasses."

The men flushed as anger overtook them. "You want him, Carl?" one asked.

"Let's put a rope on him and drag him," another suggested.

"Fine idea, Shell."

Smoke looked at the third man. "You have a name, or did your mother just throw you out with the garbage and forget about you?"

"Why, you! . . . Yeah, I got a name. Ned."

"Well, come on, Ned. Don't be shy."

The men again exchanged glances. They'd been riding roughshod over people for years. At no time had they ever run up on anybody like this tall stranger.

The locals were doing their best to hide their smiles. And it did not go unnoticed by the three rowdies.

"You think it's funny now, citizens," Shell told them. "But when we finish with this yahoo, we'll settle your hash, too."

"You won't be able to do anything in about

five minutes," Smoke told him. "None of you. Now either shut your damn mouths or step up here. What's it going to be?"

Ned cussed and walked up to the bar. Smoke hit him in mid-stride, his left boot still off the floor in a half-step. Smoke hit him with a solid left that pulped the man's lips and knocked him flat on his butt on the floor.

Shell and Carl rushed him. Smoke turned, picked up a chair, and splintered it across Shell's face. The blood flew and Shell joined Ned on the floor.

Carl's eyes widened and he did some fast back pedaling, but it was too late. Smoke stepped in and began hammering at the man with both fists, the lefts and rights landing like small bombs, and sounding like them.

Carl swung a wild blow and Smoke grabbed the man's forearm and tossed him over the bar. He landed on the ledge amid dozens of bottles of whiskey. The mirror jarred free of its braces and fell on him, shattering in hundreds of pieces. Ned was staggering to his feet just as Smoke grabbed him by the neck and the seat of his jeans and propelled him toward one of the big front windows. Ned started hollering as soon as he realized what Smoke had in mind. His bellering was cut short as Smoke tossed him through the window. Ned sailed over the warped boardwalk and impacted against and wrapped around a hitchrail. Ned did a little acrobatics around and around the rail and

41

landed on his back in the street, the wind knocked from him.

Carl was staggering around behind the bar, trying to figure out what had happened. Smoke cleared it all up real quick by grabbing the man by the bandanna and brutally hauling him over the bar. Carl's eyes were bugged out and he was making choking sounds. Smoke began spinning him around and around in a circle, Carl impacting with tables and chairs and knocking them in all directions. Smoke released his hold on the bandanna and Carl went sailing across the room, right through the second large window and out into the street. Carl was thrown up against a horse and the animal reared in fright and kicked out with its hind legs. The steelshod hooves caught Carl right in the butt and the would-be tough went sailing across the street. He landed on his face in the dirt, out cold.

The citizens in the saloon were enjoying every minute of it, wide eyed and smiling.

"Oh, hell!" Shell said, getting to his feet and facing a mean-eyed Smoke Jensen.

Smoke smiled at him and then reared back. Shell bounced off a wall and very unwillingly came toward Smoke. Smoke stepped to one side, grabbed the man in the very same manner he'd done with Ned, and threw him out into the street. Shell landed in a horse trough and wisely decided to stay there.

A very startled Red Lee and his foreman had just ridden up and stared in amazement at the sight before them.

"Who is that out there?" Smoke asked the locals who were still sitting at a table.

"Red Lee and Jim Sloane," he was told. "Big rancher and his foreman."

"Is that right?" Smoke said. He found his whiskey, downed what remained of it, and walked out to the boardwalk, using the batwings, about all that was still intact at the front of the saloon.

Smoke stood on the boardwalk and looked at the two men for a few seconds. The big, rough-looking man with red hair returned the stare.

"I suppose you're Red Lee," Smoke said.

"That's right. What the hell is going on around here?"

"Some of your boys decided to get lippy. One of their suggestions was to rope and drag me. I didn't like the idea."

"Damn shore didn't," Shell muttered from the water trough. "It was a really bad idea."

"Shut up," Red told him. He returned his gaze to Smoke.

Smoke said, "You obviously enjoy the notion of your hands riding roughshod over people. So that makes you responsible for whatever happens. The saloon needs to be swept out and straightened up. You do it."

The whole town had turned out. At least thirty-five people now stood on the boardwalk, silent and listening and watching.

Red's expression was priceless. It took him a

43

moment to find his voice. "You want me to do *what?*"

"Swamp out the saloon."

"When Hell freezes over," Red said.

"Oh, it'll be before then." Smoke's hand flashed and his .44 came out spitting fire and lead. The bullets howled and screamed around the hooves of Red's horse. The animal panicked and reared up, dumping Red on his butt in the street. The foreman was frantically fighting to get his own horse under control.

Smoke could move with deceptive speed for a man of his size. He was off the boardwalk and in the street in the blink of an eye. He jerked the foreman out of the saddle and threw him down in the dirt on his belly, momentarily addling the man. He turned and planted a big fist smack on the side of Red's jaw. The rancher went down like a brick.

Smoke jerked their guns from leather and tucked them behind his own belt. Jim got to his boots just in time to feel a hard hand gripping his neck and another hand gathering up denim at the seat of his pants. The foreman felt himself propelled out of the street, up on the boardwalk and then through the broken window. He slid on his face for a few feet before his face came to rest against a full cuspidor.

Jim looked up to see his boss come sailing through the other broken window. Red Lee landed hard on his belly and slid a couple of yards, coming to an abrupt halt when his head banged against the front of the bar.

The bartender had long since exited out the back door and hastily beat it over to the barbershop. He and the barber were standing by the front window, watching.

"Who is that man?" the bartender asked.

"Damned if I know," the barber replied. "But he's sure a one-man wreckin' crew."

Over at the saloon, the bulk of Smoke Jensen filled the pushed-open batwings. His hands were filled with guns taken from the still addled hands of Red Lee. "Find some brooms and dustpans," he told the men on the floor. "And get busy."

"You're a dead man," Red Lee said, his voice harsh and filled with hatred.

Smoke tossed him a pistol. The six-shooter landed on the floor, inches from the rancher.

"You want to try your luck, be my guest," Smoke told him.

Outside, Ned had climbed out of the water trough and was slopping around. The liveryman ran over and whispered in his ear, and Ned damn near fainted. He squished up to the boardwalk and over to a busted window.

"Boss? Dyer just read the brand on that stranger's horse. That's Smoke Jensen, Boss."

The saloon had never been so clean. Ned, Shell, and Carl pitched in and the five of them worked at it until it shone. Smoke sat at a corner table and ate supper while the men worked.

"I'll be back through here from time to time,"

Smoke said, having no intention of ever returning to this town. "Chances are you won't know I'm around, but I will be. If I hear of you or your men ever crowding another citizen or drifter, I'll hunt you down and kill you, Red."

"This wasn't none of your affair, Jensen," Red said sullenly, pushing a broom across the floor.

"Not until your men started crowding me. That made it personal."

"They was just havin' fun."

"I didn't see the humor in it."

Other area ranchers and farmers had drifted in and were enjoying the scene. The saloon was nearly full. Red and his men had been throwing their weight around for years, and payback time was long overdue and much appreciated.

Smoke was under no illusions about what Red was going to do. Just as soon as Red got a chance, he was going to try to kill him. Ned and Shell and Carl were cowboys, not fast guns. They rode for a rough brand, but they were not killers.

But Jim Sloane was another matter. Smoke felt he would side with his boss when it came down to the nut-cuttin'.

Red finally threw down his broom and turned to face Smoke. "That's it, Jensen. No more."

"Your choice," Smoke told him, a fresh pot of coffee on the table before him.

"You'd kill me over a bunch of people you never laid eyes on before today?"

"I don't want to."

"That don't answer my question."

"You figure it out."

"I come in here first, Jensen. I fought . . ."

"I don't want to hear that crap!" Smoke said harshly. "I'm sick of hearing it from men like you. Yes, you fought Indians and outlaws. Yes, you settled this land. But it's 1883 now. And time has passed you by. The old ways are all but gone. It won't be long before this territory will become a state. With a state militia and maybe even a state police force. You think they'll put up with the crap you've been pulling? The answer is no, they won't. Look around you, Red."

Red did, and saw a half a dozen ranchers and their foremen, all armed, all staring back at him. Suddenly, all because of one man, Red knew his days of being top dog were over. The people had become united against him. And he hated Smoke Jensen for that.

"You still lookin' for hands out at your spread, Mister Jackson?" Shell asked a rancher.

"Still lookin', Shell. You interested?"

"I sure am."

"Me, too," Ned said.

"And me," Carl was quick to add.

"You're all hired."

"You yellow bastards!" Red told his former riders.

"You'd best watch your mouth, Mister Lee," Shell told the man. "You can insult me all you like, but leave my family out of it." He looked at his friends. "Let's get our gear from the ranch.

See you 'bout dark, Mister Jackson."

"The grub will be hot and waitin' on you, boys."

The three punchers left the saloon . . . after nodding respectfully at Smoke.

Red Lee cursed the men until they were out of sight. Smoke waited, well aware that the man was hovering near the breaking point.

"Go home, Red," another rancher told the man. "Go home and cool off."

"Don't you tell me what to do, you goddamn rawhider."

"We all were rawhiders when we first came here, Red," another rancher said. "Even you. So you got no call to insult us."

"I'll do just as I've always done," the man popped back. "And that is whatever I damn well please."

"Them days is over, Red," a farmer spoke up. "You're the only rancher in the area that don't buy my vegetables and bacon and hams, and whose men still ride roughshod over my place. It'll not happen again. I tell you that face to face."

Red pointed a finger at the farmer, dressed in overalls and low-heeled boots. The finger was shaking and his voice was thick with barely controlled emotion. "You don't talk to me like that, Jergenson. I don't take lip from a goddamn squatter."

Smoke sat and listened. With any kind of luck, he would not have to draw on the hair-trigger-tempered rancher. He felt that the locals were

48

just about to deal with Red Lee. And maybe he'd been wrong about the foreman, Jim Sloane. The man was slowly edging away from his boss, occasionally looking pleadingly in Smoke's direction.

Smoke sat drinking coffee, waiting. He hated two-bit tyrants like Red Lee. He'd had a gut full of them as a boy, back in Missouri, working their hard-scrabble rocky farm from can-see to can't-see while his daddy was off in the war and his mother lay dying.

Red suddenly stopped his cursing and shouting and turned on Smoke. "Stand up, gunfighter," he said.

"Don't do it, Red," Smoke told him. "Just settle down and be a good citizen from now on. Can't you see that the others are willing to forgive and forget?"

"I said get up, damn your eyes!"

"Try me, Red," the rancher named Jackson said.

Red turned, disbelief in his eyes. "You, Jackson? You want to try me?"

"I reckon it's come to that, Red," the rancher said calmly, standing with his feet spread and his right hand close to the butt of his six-gun.

"I'm out of this," Jim Sloane said. "Red, man . . . come on. Let's go home."

"You're fired, you son-of-a-bitch!" Red shouted.

"You're hired," a rancher told Sloane. "You're a good cowboy, Jim."

"Draw, damn you!" Red shouted to Jackson.

"I'll not start this," the rancher said.

Red's temper exploded and he grabbed iron. He got off the first shot, the lead splintering wood at Jackson's feet. Jackson didn't miss. His shot took Red in the center of his chest and the man staggered back, an amazed look on his face.

"Why . . . you shot me," he said.

Smoke poured another cup of coffee.

Red tried to speak again but his mouth was suddenly filled with blood. He slowly sank to his knees on the fresh-mopped floor and his gun slipped from his fingers to clatter on the boards. Red knelt there, looking at the pistol.

"It didn't have to be," Jackson said.

"Yes, it did," another rancher disagreed.

The words were very faint to Red Lee as the world began darkening around him. This just couldn't be happening to him. Not to him.

"I tried to tell him," Jim said. "Over the past months I've tried and tried to talk sense to him. He just wouldn't listen."

"I know you have," Jackson said.

"The day of the tyrant is over," Jergenson said. "I knew it had to happen."

"You be sure and save me a couple of them hams come this fall," a rancher told the farmer. "They was mighty fine eatin'."

"I will," Jergenson said.

"Hams?" Red Lee gasped.

"Has he got any kin?" the barber asked.

"Not that I know of," Jim Sloane replied. "His wife took the kids and run off years ago. Right after he beat her real bad."

"She had it . . . comin'," Red said.

Jackson punched out the empty and loaded up. "I don't have much use for a man who'd beat a woman," he said.

Red Lee fell over on his face.

"Hell, now I got to mop the damn floor," the bartender said.

Five

Smoke rode out just as the sun was beginning to peep over the ragged crags of the mountains. He had not looked forward to this trip in the first place, and so far his feelings had certainly proved accurate.

He was glad to put the little no-named village behind him as he rode north toward the mining town of Red Light.

By the end of the day, he was deep in the mountains and climbing higher through the twisting and winding passes. He'd been here before, back when he was a boy, roaming the wilderness with the mountain man, Preacher. He remembered a quiet little stream and was looking for it. Smoke loved the high country. It was here amid the splendor of the mountains that he felt most at home, most at peace with himself and his surroundings.

He did not dwell on the death of the rancher, Red Lee. To Smoke's way of thinking, the deaths of bullies and those who took from society more than they gave were no more meaningful than the hole a man leaves after sticking his finger into a quiet creek. Nothing.

Smoke Jensen did not know how many men he

himself had killed. He knew the figure was very high. If he never had to draw a gun on another man, it would suit him just fine. But if he had to kill again, a bully, a rapist, a murderer, a man who rode roughshod over the rights of decent people, it would not cause him to lose a second's sleep.

Courts were fine and dandy. A needful thing, he supposed, to protect those who could not protect themselves. Smoke needed no such protection. He could take care of himself, his loved ones, his property. And if anyone violated anything he loved or protected or owned, they would have to face him, and courts be damned. His was a simple code, one if followed by all men would make the world a simpler place in which to live: You leave me alone, I will leave you alone. You have a right to a personal opinion, just as I do. But no more than I do. If you violate my space, you will have to fight me. Smoke knew he was an anachronism. He knew that courts and lawyers and judges were responsible for making the world a safer place, but a much more complicated one. And he felt it didn't have to be.

Smoke rode his own trails, followed his own code of conduct, and tried to live a good life. And he did not give a damn whether others liked it or disliked it.

He found the spot where he and Ol' Preacher had camped so many years ago, and to his delight it had not been disturbed by the destructive hand of man. He made his camp and fished for his supper and was just washing up the skillet when a man halloed the camp.

"I'm friendly," the man called. "I done et, so you don't have to feed me, but I sure would like a cup of that coffee I smell."

"Come on in," Smoke called.

The man was not young, probably in his late sixties, Smoke guessed. A miner, to judge by the equipment his mule carried. Smoke pointed to the coffeepot and the man squatted down and poured himself some, using his own tin cup, which had certainly seen better days.

"Leavin' Red Light," the miner volunteered. " 'Tain't no fit place to be no more. Done gone lawless and mean. If you're headin' that way, mister, I'd suggest you give it a second thought."

"I was thinking about checking it out."

The miner shook his head. "Then you're headin' into trouble." He eyeballed Smoke. "Although I'd allow as to say you look like a man who could handle 'bout anything that was throwed at you." He looked at Smoke's Colt. "That ain't new," he remarked. "But it's seen some use," he added drily.

"Some."

"I ain't never gonna go back up yonder, so I can tell you who to look out for and what's wrong with the place," the miner said. "And that's easy. Everything is wrong. Don't trust the sheriff or none of his deputies. They're all in the pocket of Major Cosgrove, who's a thief and a murderer and an all around no-good. He talks fancy and lives in a fine home. But he's no-'count. Red Light's a boomin' town now, and mean to the core. Must be seven, eight hundred people all crowded up there. It'll stay that way 'til the gold is gone. Then there won't be fifty people left. Jack Biggers is the big rancher in the area. He's just as mean and no good as Sheriff Bowers and Major Cosgrove. As are the men who work for him. It's just not a good place to tarry, son. I'd give it some thought."

"How about other ranchers in the valley?"

"You know about the valley, huh? They ain't but two other ranchers. Jack Biggers and Fat Fosburn. Jenny Jensen and an old man named Van Horn is holdin' the kid's ranch agin' long odds. The powers that be want the girl's ranch. The other ranchers was burned out, run out, or killed. I fear for the girl's life, I do. For them men would as soon kill a girl as shoot a snake. She come into all her ma's property. But most of it ain't fitten for a decent girl to be associated with."

"Oh?"

"No, sir. It ain't. All but the ranch. It's a beautiful little ranch in that valley. And my, my, it do have good water and graze. But Jack Biggers wants that property for him. And what Jack Biggers wants, he gets." He finished his coffee and stood up, moving toward his horse and mule. "Well, I thank you for the hospitality. I got me a favorite place 'bout three, four miles down the way. But I smelled that coffee and got to

55

salivatin'. See you, young feller."

Before Smoke could ask another question, the miner had swung into the saddle and was gone. Smoke went to his pack and began removing what he felt he might need, including a ten-gauge Colt revolving shotgun that he had had for many years. He had sent it back to the factory in Hartford to have it reworked and refinished and they'd done a bang-up job. It was originally a 27-inch barrel and he'd sawed that off to within a few inches of the forestock. At close range it could clear an entire room of all living things. The cylinder held five rounds, and Smoke had loaded them and a sackful of other shells himself.

He took his pistols and cleaned them carefully, loading them up full. For the time being, he would not wear his left hand holster but instead tuck the second pistol behind his gunbelt. He had a hunch — unless somebody recognized him, he could, for a time, ride in and be known as K. Jensen with nobody the wiser. At least it was worth a try.

He cleaned and loaded his rifle and rolled up in his blankets and went to sleep. He wondered what kind of business his sister might have had that would not be "fitten" for a young lady to go near.

Smoke topped a rise and looked down at the town of Red Light. He took an immediate dislike to the place. The streets were crooked and twisty and narrow, the buildings all jammed up against one another. Like most boom towns, it was a mishmash of buildings and tents and wagons. Even from where he sat above the town he could hear the shrill and false laughter of hurdy-gurdy girls, busy separating miners from their gold dust and nuggets, and behind it all the banging of tinny-sounding pianos.

Smoke had deliberately not shaved his upper lip since leaving the ranch, and his mustache was nearly grown out, since he had a naturally heavy beard. The mustache made him look several years older and a hell of a lot meaner. The mustache was beginning to droop down toward his chin and made Smoke look like he'd just come off the hoot-owl trail.

"All right, Buck," Smoke said. "Let's go check out this dump."

The livery was on the edge of town and Smoke reined in and swung down. A young boy of about thirteen came out and pulled up short at the sight of the huge, mean-eyed horse.

"I got a stall for you, mister, but you're gonna have to handle that hoss yourself."

"What's the matter, Jimmy?" a loudmouth hollered from a boardwalk so new some of the boards had not yet lost their sawmill color. "You want me to show you how to handle a hoss?"

"Nick Norman," Jimmy whispered. "He's a really bad one, mister. A bully."

"Tell him if he thinks he's man enough to handle this horse, come on and try," Smoke returned the whisper. "Don't worry about him coming back at you. He'll be so stove-up he won't be able to walk for six months. If he lives."

"Well, why don't you come show me, then, Nick," Jimmy called.

"I'll do that," the loudmouth said, stepping off the boardwalk. "And then I'll give you a thrashing for being smart-mouthed with me."

Nick looked at Smoke and said, "Get out of the way. I'll larn your horse some manners."

Smoke smiled and pointed at the dangling reins.

Nick jerked up the reins hard and said, "Come on, you ugly son-of-a-jerk."

Buck bit him, clamping down with his big teeth. Nick screamed as the arm was lacerated and the blood flowed. Nick jerked out a pistol to shoot the horse and Buck butted him, knocking the man to the ground, the pistol sliding away in the mud. Nick grabbed up a heavy board and got to his feet. He reared back to strike Buck and Buck reared up and came down with both shod feet. One hoof made a terrible mess of Nick's face and the other smashed a shoulder, the sound of the breaking bones clearly audible. Nick lay in the mud, badly hurt and unconscious.

A man came running up, pushing through the gathering crowd. He wore a star on his chest.

Smoke pointed to the bloody and broken Nick and said, "You'd better get your resident loudmouth to a doctor, deputy. He's hurt pretty bad."

The deputy started to say something about the best thing to do would be to shoot the damn horse. But he bit back the words and closed his mouth. He didn't like the look in this big stranger's eyes. And to make matters worse, that damn big horse was looking at him, too, ears all laid back and wall-eyed mean. The deputy had seen a few killer horses in his time, and this was definitely one of them.

Smoke petted Buck for a few seconds and then picked up the reins, starting inside the huge barn.

"Where do you think you're goin'?" the deputy called.

"To stable my horse," Smoke called over his shoulder. "You have any objection?" Before leaving town, Smoke had wired a friend of his, a judge down in Denver, and asked if his Deputy U.S. Marshal's commission was still valid.

"That was a lifetime appointment, Smoke. You think you might need that badge soon?" he'd asked him.

"Maybe," Smoke wired back.

"You have the full weight of the United States Government behind you, my boy," the judge had wired.

"All the weight I need I carry on my hip," Smoke closed the key.

"By God, I might!" the deputy hollered, losing his temper. "I don't like your attitude, mister."

Smoke dug in his saddlebags and pinned on the badge before stripping off saddle and bridle

59

and pouring grain into a feed trough.

"Did you hear me, damn it?" the deputy yelled, as the crowd outside the livery swelled, the small mob making no effort to assist the unconscious Nick Norman. "I said," the deputy shouted, "do you hear me, you damn saddlebum?"

Smoke hesitated for a moment, then took off the U.S. Marshal's badge and put it in his pocket. Might be more fun without it, he thought.

"Git out here and look at me!" the deputy shouted, now reenforced by two other badge-toting men.

Smoke made sure his second gun was hidden by his coat and then he walked out of the gloom of the livery to face the three so-called lawmen.

"All right," Smoke said, as the mob of men and painted women fell silent. "I'm looking at you. But if I have to look at you for very long, I'll lose my appetite." He glanced at the other two. "And that includes you, too."

The three men looked at each other, not quite sure how to handle this situation. As deputies under Sheriff Bowers, they were accustomed to bullying their way around the area, and having people kowtow to them. But this stranger didn't seem a bit impressed by their badges.

They didn't realize that Smoke immediately knew that the three of them combined wouldn't make a pimple on a good lawman's butt.

"We're deputies," one of the three said.

"Wonderful," Smoke told them. "Go get a lost cat out of a tree."

Jimmy the stableboy could not hide his grin.

One of the deputies noticed it and flushed. "I'll slap that smirk offen your face, boy."

"You'll do it when Hell freezes over," Smoke told him.

The deputy cut his eyes to the big stranger. "You don't talk to me lak 'at, mister. I got me a notion to put you in jail."

"Why don't you try?" Smoke said softly.

"All right!" a voice shouted from behind the crowd. "Get out of the damn way and let me through."

The crowd parted and a big man stepped into the small clearing in front of the livery. He was about the same size as Smoke and did not appear to have an ounce of fat on him. He was clean-shaven and smelled of cologne. He wore a very ornate star pinned to his coat and at first glance appeared to be a man used to getting his own way. He wore two guns, low and tied down.

"I'm Sheriff Bowers," the man said, fixing his gaze on Smoke. "What's going on here? What happened to Nick?"

"Nick got rough with my horse," Smoke told him. "My horse didn't like him or the treatment and let him know about it. Then this loudmouth piece of crap wearing a badge showed up and I don't like him. He threatened this boy here." He pointed to Jimmy. "That tells me what type of sorry trash he is. So, Sheriff, if you own him,

you'd better put a leash and a muzzle on him."
Smoke was feeling the old wildness settle on
him. It was a cold sensation. He had felt the
same emotion when he'd entered the old silver
camp years back, hunting the men who had
raped and killed his wife and killed his baby son.
Smoke had left some fourteen-odd men dead in
the streets.

This trip had turned sour from the git-go and
Smoke was feeling more and more of the old
wildness fill him.

Sheriff Bowers read the warning in Smoke's
eyes and took in the man's boots and clothing.
The boots were handmade and expensive. The
coat was handmade to fit the man's huge shoulders and arms. The .44 he wore at his side was
old, but well-cared-for, and it had seen a lot of
use. It was not fancy, and that spoke volumes to
the sheriff.

There was something about this big stranger
that was unnerving to the sheriff. He did not like
the sensation. "A few of you men carry Nick to
the doctor's office. The rest of you people break
this up and go on about your business."

"That son-of-a-bitch called me trash," the
deputy in question said. "I'll not stand for that."

"Shut up, Patton," the sheriff said harshly.
"Just close your mouth and keep it closed." He
turned his attentions back to Smoke. "You mind
walking with me?"

"Not at all, Sheriff," Smoke said. "You object
to my checking in at the hotel?"

"Not a bit. We'll talk on the way over there."

Patton stepped toward Jimmy. "I'll take a buggy whip to you, boy. Teach you to sass me. I'll strip the hide right offen your back."

Smoke hit the man, sudden and unexpectedly. The blow made an ugly *smushing* sound in the air. Patton's boots flew out from under him and he landed on his back in the mud, his mouth leaking blood. He did not move.

The sheriff, the deputies, and the crowd stood in shocked silence. Smoke looked at Jimmy. The boy's clothing was patched and his shoes were held together by faith and rawhide. Smoke handed the boy two gold double eagles. Jimmy stood in open-mouthed shock.

"You go get you some new clothes and boots, boy. Then come back here and take care of my horse. If any of these badge-wearing trash bothers you, you come get me. They won't bother you again. All right?"

Jimmy looked at the money in his hand. More money than he had ever seen. "Yes, *sir!*"

"You come over to my store, Jimmy," a merchant called. "I'll fit you right up and treat you fair."

Smoke looked at the man. "You be damn sure you do just that." He started walking toward the hotel.

"Somebody carry Patton to the jail and lay him on a cot," Sheriff Bowers said, his voice suddenly filled with weariness. He had just noticed the pinholes in Smoke's shirt, made by the badge. Invisible warning lights flashed in the sheriff's head. Something was all out of whack here. Go easy on this, he cautioned himself. Real easy.

Patton moaned in the mud and sat up. Smoke stopped and turned around, his right hand close to the butt of his gun. Patton cursed him and struggled to his knees in the mud. He pulled out his pistol and jacked the hammer back. Only then did Smoke draw.

No man or woman in the crowd had ever seen such a draw. Most didn't even see it, it was so fast. A blur of speed and a report of fire and gunsmoke. Patton fell back, a hole right between his eyes.

"Smoke Jensen!" a man shouted. "I knowed I'd seen him afore."

"Oh, my God!" Sheriff Bowers said. "That's Janey's brother."

Six

It was all out in the open now, so Smoke registered at the hotel using his real name. The desk clerk stood goggle-eyed as he wrote his name.

"I want the best room you have," Smoke told the man.

"Certainly, sir! I'll give you the Eldorado Suite. And may I say it's a pleasure having you here? We'll do everything we can to make your stay as relaxing as possible."

"Fine. While I have a cup of coffee in the restaurant, you make sure the sheets are changed on the bed and a tub of hot water drawn. I want lots of towels and a fresh bar of soap."

"Oh, absolutely, sir. Right now."

Smoke turned to look at the bulk of the sheriff, standing in the door. "Have some coffee with me, Sheriff?"

Sheriff Bowers nodded. Damned if he knew just what to do about this situation. Jensen guns down one of his deputies, then calmly turns and walks off without even so much as a fare-thee-well.

Club Bowers opened his mouth to speak, but Smoke was already walking into the dining room. Getting more irritated by the second,

Club followed along behind and flopped down in a chair when Jensen finally chose a table in a corner of the room and called for coffee.

"Do you understand that you just killed one of my deputies?" Club blurted.

"*He* was trying to kill *me*," Smoke replied. "Is there a law in this town against defending yourself?"

"Patton was an officer of the law!"

Smoke said a very ugly word and smiled sarcastically at the sheriff. "But not much of one."

"What do you mean by that?"

"The way I get it, Bowers, is that you and your men are in the pocket of Jack Biggers and a Major Cosgrove."

"That's a damn lie!"

Smoke smiled up at the waiter. "I'd like some pie, too, please. Apple, if you have it. Sheriff?"

"No. I don't want any damn pie! Who told you that crap, Jensen?"

"A fellow I met along the trail. He wasn't very complimentary toward you and your department. Or Cosgrove and Biggers, for that matter."

"Who was he?"

"I didn't ask his name. Who's the attorney handling my sister's estate?"

"Dunham. His office is over the assayer's place." He leaned back in his chair. "I didn't know Janey had a brother."

"Where is her daughter?"

"Jenny? Out at the ranch, I suppose. When

66

you see her, tell her to sell. She's bucking a stacked deck."

"Biggers want the spread?"

"It butts up against his. Hell, Jensen, Jenny's just a kid. She can't run the place."

Smoke ate his pie, conscious of the sheriff's eyes on him.

"You worn a badge from time to time, Jensen?"

"I've worn one before."

"I should remind you that you're way out of your jurisdiction here."

Smoke smiled at him and pushed his pie plate to one side. "I have a lifetime U.S. Marshal's commission, Bowers. And Judge Francis Morrison knows I'm here and *why* I'm here. Don't crowd me. Don't crowd my niece. And above all, don't interfere in my business. You got all that?"

Never in his life had Bowers been talked to in the manner in which he was now being addressed. For a few moments he could but sit and stare at the man across the table from him. He was under no illusions about Smoke Jensen. He knew all about the man, or thought he did. Jensen operated under his own strict code of ethics. And no matter how the law read, he did not deviate from them. Less than ten minutes had passed since Jensen had shot one of his deputies right between the eyes, and now the man sat calmly, finishing up his apple pie. Incredible.

Bowers would be the first to admit he was no

match for Jensen when it came to gunplay. The thought of facing Jensen eyeball to eyeball and dragging iron had not even entered his mind. He did not think there was a man alive that could match Jensen's speed and unbelievable accuracy with pistol or rifle. Few men were as strong as Jensen. And Bowers also knew that Smoke Jensen's courage was matched by few, if any.

Bowers knew all the stories about the legendary gunfighter. He'd heard them for years, no matter where in the West he happened to be. He'd been raised by mountain men, killed his first man when no more than a towheaded boy. Had faced alone up to twenty men and emerged victorious. His exploits were known worldwide. Books had been written about him. Songs had been sung. Plays had been staged. But he didn't know how much was true and how much was pure balderdash.

He suspected it was all true.

Club Bowers was unable to find his voice. He shoved back his chair and stood up, still staring open-mouthed at Smoke. He knew he should say something, but he didn't know what. He shook his head and walked out of the dining room. At the archway he stopped and turned, looking back at Smoke Jensen. The man was rolling a cigarette while the waiter filled his cup with coffee.

"Incredible," Club muttered.

Smoke slept well that night and awakened refreshed and ready to face the day. He dressed in jeans and a black-and-white checkered shirt. Since his identity was known and there was no need for any charade, he'd shaved off his mustache and strapped on both pistols, the left hand pistol worn high and butt-forward. Sally made his shirts for him, since store-bought shirts were usually too tight across the shoulders and too small for his massive arms. He usually carried four or five extra shirts. He made sure all the loops in his gunbelt were filled with .44s and then checked his big-bladed Bowie knife. It was razor-sharp. He stepped out to meet the day.

After breakfast, he strolled over to Lawyer Dunham's office, the townspeople giving him a wide berth as he walked, his spurs jingling.

Smoke pegged Dunham as a shyster immediately. And he suspected that Dunham knew he had, for the lawyer attempted no tricky legal maneuvering when Smoke told him to produce the will.

"Since Jenny is young," Dunham said, "Miss Janey left everything to you until the girl comes of age. I . . ."

"Where is my sister buried?"

"Just outside of town, sir. It was a lovely funeral. The headstone has just been set in place. Quite an elaborate monument, I might add. The local minister and some of the good ladies of the town were, ah, upset at the inscription, but Miss Janey was quite clear as to what she wanted on the stone."

Smoke stood up. The lawyer was obviously in awe at the bulk of the man. "You get all the papers in order. I'll be back after I pay my respects to my sister."

"Certainly, sir. I shall have them ready."

At the livery, Jimmy was decked out in new duds and boots. A nice-looking boy. He'd even had his hair trimmed. "I got money left, Mister Smoke," Jimmy said.

"Keep it. As long as I'm in town I'll pay you to look after my horse."

Smoke saddled up and rode to the windswept and lonely graveyard. Janey's monument was the largest in the cemetery. He was amused at the inscription, and could see why the local, so-called "good ladies" might be offended at the words.

Carved deep in the expensive stone, under Janey's name and date of life and death, were the words, I PLAYED LIFE TO THE HILT AND ENJOYED EVERY GODDAMN MINUTE OF IT.

"There never was any love lost between us, Sis," Smoke spoke the words softly. "But I understand you raised a good girl. I'll see to it that she makes out all right."

He put his hat back on his head and walked out of the graveyard. A time-weathered old cowboy was waiting at the entrance to the cemetery.

"I'm Van Horn," the man said. Smoke guessed him to be in his late sixties or early seventies. But tough as wang-leather and no backup in him. "I worked for Miss Janey at the ranch. Miss Jenny is there now. She's waitin' to see if you're gonna throw her off the place."

"Why would I do something like that? I don't want the ranch or any of my sister's property. It all goes to Jenny when she comes of age. I intend to see that it does."

Van Horn grunted. "I figured Miss Jenny was being fed a line by Biggers and Cosgrove and Dunham. I know your reputation for being fair and told Miss Jenny what them others was sayin' was all a pack of lies."

"Ride with me," Smoke said. "Let's go settle this at the lawyer's office."

Smoke read the documents carefully and then signed the papers. He then stared at Dunham so long the man began to squirm in his chair. "Did you tell my niece that I was going to throw her off the ranch and take all of the property?"

"Why, ah . . ."

"Do you represent Biggers and Cosgrove?"

"Why, ah . . ."

"Did you encourage her to sell to Biggers all the while knowing that she could not legally do so?"

"Why, ah . . ."

Van Horn stood leaning against a wall, enjoying the lawyer's discomfort. He didn't know what Smoke Jensen was going to do, but whatever it was, he wasn't going to miss a second of it.

"You are a lowlife shyster son-of-a-bitch lawyer," Smoke told the pale and shaken barrister. "Playing both sides against the middle and trying to cheat a young girl out of her inheritance."

"You can't talk to me like that!" Dunham protested.

"I just did." Smoke reached across the desk and got a fistful of Dunham's shirt. He hauled him over the desk and then proceeded to throw him out of the second-story window. Dunham went squalling and shrieking through the glass. He bounced off the awning and fell into the mud of the street, landing squarely in a big pile of horse droppings. He wasn't badly hurt, except for his dignity, which was severely bruised.

Sheriff Bowers stood on the boardwalk in front of his office and shook his head at the sight.

The hearse carrying the body of Deputy Patton rattled by, heading for the cemetery. Doc White had told Club that he didn't know if Nick Norman was going to make it. That killer horse of Jensen's had fractured the man's skull. Jensen was going to have to be dealt with, but damned if Club knew how to go about it. Biggers and Cosgrove were due in town this morning. He'd lay it all in their laps.

Club watched as Smoke and Van Horn mounted up and rode out of the town, heading for the ranch out in the valley.

"You own that, too," Van Horn said, pointing to a two-story house on the edge of town. It was a fancy and well-kept place. The sign on the lawn proclaimed it to be The Golden Cherry.

"What is it?" Smoke asked.

"You don't know?" the old cowboy asked.

"No."

"It's a whorehouse."

Jenny Jensen was quite the young lady, very pretty and petite and well mannered. She seemed in awe of her Uncle Smoke.

Smoke put her at ease quickly and Van Horn left them alone in the house. As she made coffee and set a platter of doughnuts on the table, she smiled at Smoke shyly.

"I can't do much," the girl admitted. "But I can cook. That's one of the things taught us at finishing school in Boston."

The girl was lovely, with a heart-shaped face and a figure that would turn any man's head. Smoke smiled at her. "How long have you been out here, Jenny?"

"About a year. I came out when I learned of my mother's death."

"How did she die, Jenny?"

"There was an outbreak of fever. Mother and her . . . girls nursed the sick miners. Mother caught the fever and died. It took Lawyer Dunham almost a year to find me."

"He knew where you were, Jenny. He was just stalling for time. He and Biggers and Cosgrove couldn't figure out a way to cheat you out of your inheritance, that's all. Then I entered the picture and that really shook them up. What do you know about this ranch?"

"More than most men think I do. I *really* have a very good education and understand business. I've gone over the books and the ranch is paying its way. I don't have many cowboys left, not nearly enough to efficiently run the ranch. And no one will come to work for me."

"I'll get you hands, Jenny. Don't worry about that. Do you want to stay out here?"

"Oh, yes. I love it. I've had entirely enough of cities."

"Then here is where you'll stay. Do you object to my moving in here?"

"Oh, no! Not at all."

"I'm going to send one of the hands to the nearest telegraph office and get my wife up here pronto." Smoke smiled. "I'd better let her know that I now own a, ah, house of ill repute."

Jenny laughed and it was a good laugh, full of life and good humor. "The Golden Cherry. Yes. And the Golden Plum, too."

"What is that? The will only stated that I owned all of Janey's businesses in town and the ranch."

"A saloon in town. A very profitable one. I've never been inside either establishment. Van Horn won't let me. He's the foreman. He's really a nice man."

"Do you ride?"

"Oh, yes. But when I came out here I swore I would never again ride sidesaddle. It's not very comfortable. I'm afraid I shocked some of the so-called good women around here by wearing a split skirt and riding astride."

"You and my wife will hit it off, Jenny. You both think very much alike. Can you shoot?"

She shook her head. "I never fired a gun in my life until a few months ago. Van Horn is trying to teach me. But I'm afraid I'm not very good."

"We'll work on that." Smoke rose from the table and walked through the house, and it was a nice home, the rooms large and airy. The place was a bit too feminine for his tastes, but since a woman had owned the ranch, he didn't find that unusual.

Smoke paused at a gun rack and took down a double-barreled twenty-gauge shotgun. He checked it and handed it to Jenny. "You practice with this, Jenny. My wife will be here in about a week, and the two of you can target shoot together. Can you trust all your hands?"

"Absolutely. Van Horn ran off those he felt were not loyal. Even the younger men are afraid of him."

Smoke nodded. "They should be. He was one of the very first gunfighters. I remember my mentor speaking of him. Can you get me some writing paper, please?"

He sat down at a desk and wrote: Sally, you'd better get up here fast. Among other things, I just inherited a whorehouse. See you soon.

Smoke called for Van Horn, handed him the note and some money and said, "Give this to your most trusted hand and have him ride for the nearest telegraph office. Wait for a reply."

The old gunfighter read the note and smiled. "Be good for the girl to have a decent woman to associate with. I'll get a rider out now. You going to stay out here on the place?"

"Yes. I'll want to see the spread first thing in the morning."

"I'll see to your horse." He turned to go, paused, and looked back. "Preacher done a good job with you, Smoke. I'm right proud to have you here. The girl might stand a chance now."

Van Horn gone, Smoke said, "Let's take a look at the books, Jenny. That's something I hate to do, but it has to be done. Then we can sit down and you can tell me about your mother."

"I don't know that much."

"Whatever you know is more than I do. I've only seen her a couple of times since she ran off back in '64 or '65." Smoke smiled. "She tried to have me killed both times."

Seven

The spread was not a huge, sprawling one, but it was certainly large enough to provide a family with a very good living. The graze ran from ample to lush and the water was plentiful. The cattle were fat and sleek.

"Any problems with rustling?" Smoke asked.

"Once," Van Horn replied. "I caught two of Biggers no-'count hands usin' a runnin' iron and shot them both."

Smoke noticed but made no comment about Van Horn's strapping on two Remington hoglegs and tying them down. If just half of what Preacher had told him about Van Horn was true, the old man was a pure devil in a gunfight. Preacher had said that Van Horn had once faced six men in a trading post down in Colorado and when the gunsmoke had cleared, Van Horn was the only one standing, and he had four bullet holes in him.

"Fat Fosburn owns the spread north of this one," Van Horn said as they rode. "He's the mayor of Red Light. Biggers owns the land south. They got us boxed for a fact."

"Fosburn? That name is familiar."

"Used to be an outlaw. Rode with Bloody Bill

back in the sixties. He's as mean as a hydophoby skunk and will stop at nothin' to get what he wants. He's said that if he has to, he'll kill Jenny to get the land."

"Real nice fellow."

"Yeah. Just dandy. Yonder comes Ladd. He's been ridin' the south fence. Good boy."

Ladd was a man in his early twenties, stocky and with a go-to-hell look in his eyes.

"Ladd," Van Horn said. "This here's Miss Jenny's uncle, Smoke Jensen."

Ladd's eyes widened.

"He's gonna be with us for a time, seein' that Miss Jenny gets her due. You go on to the house and get you some breakfast. Then you and Ford stay close to home."

"Yes, sir," the young puncher said. "Pleased to meet you, Mister Smoke."

"Now you've met all the hands we got," Van Horn said. "Ladd, Ford, and Cooper. We need at least three more."

"We'll get them. Parcell has a cabin some-where in these mountains."

"Wolf Parcell?"

"That's him."

"Hell, Smoke, he's older than me, and I'm near 'bout as old as God. I didn't know he lived around here."

"Over there," Smoke said, looking toward the towering mountains. "I'll find him. And there is a kid in town at the livery, Jimmy. He'll do to take care of things around the house."

Van Horn smiled. "Little Jimmy Hammon. His folks had a small spread west of here. Biggers and Fosburn burned them out and killed the boy's parents 'bout seven or eight years ago. You're right. Jimmy's a good boy."

"We need one or two more good men."

"You got anything against Mexicans or Indians?"

"Not as long as they do their work. Knowed some fine Mex punchers in my time."

"There's one in town. I saw him."

"Pasco? He come in here as a sheepherder. No rancher will hire a sheepherder."

"I will. I know Pasco's cousin. He's a gun-fighter. Carbone. He spoke highly of Pasco. One more."

"There's a half-breed Injun roams the valley. But he's a surly one. Don't seem to like nobody."

"Has anybody ever given him a chance?"

"You do have a point."

"What's the Indian's name?"

"Bad Dog."

"We have a crew."

It took Smoke two days to find the cabin of Wolf Parcell. The old mountain man was standing in the door when Smoke rode up.

"I heard you was in the area," Wolf said. "Figured you'd be about, pesterin' me." The old mountain man was still rock-solid tough and had a mean look in his eyes. He wore two pistols belted outside his buckskins and a huge Bowie knife. "I'll have to say that Preacher done well with you. What do you want?"

"Get your kit together, you worthless old coot. You're going to work for me."

"Work! Wagh! I ain't worked for nobody but myself in fifty year."

"I need you," Smoke said simply.

"That's good enough for me," Wolf said. "Light and set. Coffee's hot and strong. I'll be a few minutes."

Fifteen minutes later, the two men rode out.

That afternoon, with Wolf leading the way, they rode to the camp of Bad Dog, a half-breed Cheyenne.

"Dog," Wolf said, "this here is Smoke Jensen. His little niece is in trouble down in the valley, and I aim to help her."

Bad Dog looked up at Smoke. "Heard of you. My people say you are a fair man. You fight Biggers and Cosgrove and Fat?"

"Yes."

"Me, too."

And the three rode out.

Van Horn had sent Ladd into town, and he returned with Little Jimmy and the Mexican, Pasco.

"You got any objection to working with cows?" Smoke asked the Mexican.

"If it means a fight with Biggers, Cosgrove, and Fat, I'll work for the devil," Pasco replied.

"I've been called that," Smoke said.

"So I've heard," Pasco smiled his reply.

"Stow your gear in the bunkhouse."

Over coffee, Jenny said, "That is the most disreputable-looking crew I think I have ever seen. Except for Jimmy."

"They'll stand to the last man, Jenny. They're tough as rawhide and meaner than pumas. Right now, I want you to bake a half dozen pies and fry up a tubful of doughnuts. Then I want you to bake a dozen loaves of bread and cook up the thickest stew you ever made in your life. Can you do that?"

"You bet I can, Uncle Smoke."

"After this evening's supper, Jenny, you won't be able to drive those men off with a shotgun."

The men spent the rest of that day getting set up in the bunkhouse, mending shirts or socks, looking over the remuda, and loafing. Young Jimmy Hammon was in for a quick education, bunking with these salty ol' boys, but most of what he would learn would be vital and stand him in good stead for the rest of his life. And Smoke also knew that the older men would look after the boy.

Soon the aroma of baking began to fill the house and Smoke had to leave before his mouth got to watering so bad he'd look like a drooling fool.

He got a couple of carrots and an apple from the kitchen and walked to the corral and picked out a horse to ride, sparing Buck. The horse was a big black with a mean eye. He and Smoke took to one another right off.

Van Horn strolled up and leaned against the railing. "He's a bad one, Smoke. Nobody rides Devil. He's a pure killer."

Smoke smiled and whistled softly. The big black came right to him, the other horses giving him a wide berth. Smoke had quartered the apple and the black took the pieces as gently as a baby.

"I knew one man tried that and lost part of a finger," Van Horn said.

"We understand each other," Smoke said, rubbing the velvet of Devil's nose. "We're alike and he senses it."

"He ain't been cut, Smoke. He's dangerous."

"No, he isn't. He's just misunderstood, that's all." Smoke stepped inside the corral and walked around, the big black following along behind him, just like a puppy, occasionally reaching out to nibble at Smoke's shirt, but with only his lips, not his teeth.

The other hands had gathered around the railing, watching Smoke and the big horse. After a time, Smoke put a blanket on him and walked him around, then saddled him and the black took the bit with no fuss.

"Damnedest thing I ever did see," Van Horn said.

"Open the gate," Smoke called, swinging into the saddle, and he and the black went out of the corral at a gallop. The black loved to run, and Smoke let it go until it tired. Several miles from the house, the big black slowed and Smoke reined up and swung down, letting the animal blow.

"We're going to get along just fine," Smoke told the horse named Devil. "I might even buy you from Jenny and take you back with me."

Smoke looked all around him, in this valley surrounded by mountains. Fine spread, he thought. I can see why the others want it. But they're not going to get it . . . not the way they plan, anyway.

Back in the saddle, he walked Devil back to the ranch. Rather than risk Jimmy getting hurt, he rubbed the black down himself and turned him into the corral. He forked some hay for the animals and finished just as Jenny started ringing the supper bell. The men started lining up and Smoke smiled at them as Jenny waved them into the house.

"We all eat together, gentlemen," the girl informed them. "So come on and fill your plates."

And fill them and eat they did, all of them with one eye on the mound of doughnuts she had fixed and covered with a cloth. Then she started taking apple pies out of the oven and Smoke thought the men were going to stampede the stove.

The hands drank at least two gallons of coffee, and were so stuffed with stew and fresh baked bread and pies and doughnuts, Smoke hoped the ranch was not attacked that night. None of the men seemed capable of moving, much less fighting.

He gave them an hour to rest after so much food and then walked over to the bunkhouse. "You boys get enough to eat?"

Bad Dog rubbed his belly and smiled. "The young lady has a cowboy here forever, if she chooses."

"Same goes for me," Pasco said. "For one so young, she sure knows her way around a kitchen."

Wolf Parcel was stretched out on his bunk, sound asleep and snoring softly. Jimmy was also asleep.

But Smoke wasn't fooled about Wolf. The old mountain man would come awake instantly at the first sign of trouble, a pistol in one hand and a razor-sharp Bowie in the other, cutting and slashing and shooting. Smoke knew from experience and observation that young trouble-hunters who tangled with old men usually came out much worse for wear, for old men have no illusions about fair fighting: they fight to win.

Smoke was raised by old mountain men, and he shared their philosophy: there is no such thing as a fair fight. There is only a winner and a loser. If you're in the right, it doesn't make any difference how you win or what you use to win in defending yourself. Just win.

Van Horn came out of his small private quarters into the main bunkhouse and said, "All right, boys. Wake up and listen up. By now,

Biggers, Fosburn, and Cosgrove will know we've hired a crew. Up to now, they haven't made any raids on our property. But that might change. What you boys can expect is for their hands to try and catch you off this spread and stomp you or shoot you or drag you." His eyes touched young Jimmy. "And that includes you, boy. For the time being, Jimmy, your job is take care of the ranch grounds and the barn and so forth. You're mighty young to be totin' a six-gun, but no younger than me or Smoke here. So startin' tomorrow, you pack iron like the rest of us. I'm gonna put a rifle in the barn, the shed, and the outhouse. There'll be an ammo belt with each one. Things are gonna get real bad real quick, I'm thinkin'. Try not to do no lone ridin'. Always buddy up if you can. We got to have supplies, so tomorrow I'm gonna send a wagon into town. Smoke here said he'll ride in with it. Ladd will drive, Cooper will ride flank. One of us will always be here on the ranch, or no more than five minutes from it. Jimmy will be here all the time. The next day we start a cattle count, as close as we can, that is, and brandin'. We got to sell about five hundred head, and that means we got to move them into Red Light to the holdin' pens. Smoke, when are you expectin' your wife to arrive?"

"In a couple more days, three at the most. I've arranged for the Pinkertons to escort her up from track's end."

"Good move. She'll be safe along the way,

then," Pasco remarked. "No one around here wants to get the Pinks down on them."

"I'm counting on that. With Sally here, that will free another man to work the herd. My wife will put lead into a man faster than you can blink. And she'll have Jenny shooting well in a few days. One thing we have to do tomorrow is stock up on ammunition. Enough for a siege. I suggest we take two wagons into town and stock up enough staples to last several months."

Smoke eyeballed the men. "Might as well tell you now, Jenny wants to ride into town with us."

Van Horn started cussing.

Smoke let him wind down. "I don't like it either. But she's a young woman and she wants to pick up some lady-things and just shop for a time." He smiled. "Besides, she is the boss."

Wolf Parcell belched, grinned, and patted his belly. "Damn shore is that."

Eight

Sheriff Monte Carson had handed Sally the telegram and stepped back while she was opening it. He was expecting Sally to explode, and she didn't disappoint him.

"A *whorehouse!*" Sally yelled.

"Now, Miss Sally," Monte said. "It ain't as bad as . . ."

"A *whorehouse!*" Sally yelled. "My husband owns a whorehouse!"

"He says you better get right on up there."

"You can bet your boots and spurs I'm going up there." She went to the door and yelled for the foreman. He came at a flat run.

"Yes, ma'am?"

"Get my horse ready for travel. I'm pulling out first thing in the morning. You run things here until we return."

"Uh . . . yes, ma'am."

Sally turned to the sheriff. "When you get back to town, you get me passage on the train. Rent a car. I'll alternate between passenger car and staying with my horse."

"Uh . . ."

"Do it, Monte!"

"Right! Consider it done, Sally."

87

The sheriff gone, Sally packed swiftly. Just a couple of dresses; mostly jeans and work shirts and an extra pair of boots. She paused. And a pair of shoes for the dress, if she elected to wear a dress. She tossed in a gunbelt and her .44. Walking to the gun cabinet, she took down her .44 carbine and put it in the saddle boot.

"A *whorehouse!*" she said.

The next morning she was on the train, heading north.

Not yet trusting Devil around people he was not familiar with, Smoke saddled up Buck for the ride into town. Jenny climbed up beside Ladd and off they went, rattling down the road.

Just before leaving, Smoke told Van Horn, "I'm expecting trouble in town. It's just a feeling I have in my guts."

The old gunfighter nodded in agreement. "So do I." He toed out his cigarette butt. "Ladd and Cooper are good boys. They'll stand. Don't worry about things here. You just be careful. We don't have many friends in Red Light."

That was evident when the man at the big general store insulted Jenny and refused to sell her anything. Ten seconds later, after looking into the cold eyes of Smoke Jensen and almost soiling his drawers, he apologized profoundly for his remark and began filling the large order as fast as he could work.

Several cowboys appeared in the door. Smoke had seen the Biggers brand — a Triangle JB —

on a dozen horses lining the narrow street. "Shopkeeper, you was told not to sell to them," one of the men said.

"It's a free country," Smoke replied, turning from the counter to face the men. "And who the hell asked you to stick your mouth in this matter?"

"Jensen," the spokesman for the group said, "you may be a big wheel down where you come from. But around here, you ain't jack-crap. I'd bear that in mind, was I you."

"You're not me," Smoke told him. "Now why don't you just shut your face and wander back to wherever the hell it is you came from?"

"That's all!" Sheriff Bowers said, walking up and stepping into the store. "Seems like you can't even come to town without startin' trouble, Smoke."

"I didn't start this. But I will finish it, if I have to. We came into town for supplies, that's all. These yahoos tried to stop the store owner from selling to us. Now, what do you have to say about that?"

Club Bowers was silent for a moment. Everything would have been real easy if Smoke Jensen hadn't a showed up. Everything was working out to plan . . . until he rode into town. Now everything was all fouled up. Taking a ranch away from a seventeen-year-old girl and an old has-been of a gunfighter was one thing. Pulling iron against a U.S. Marshal was something else. Especially when that marshal was Smoke Jensen.

He knew the Marshals' Service had a nasty habit of avenging their own. And they didn't always do it according to a law book. What the powers that be in the town didn't need right now was for a bunch of U.S. Marshals to come riding in, hell-bent for revenge. But, Club thought, if I ain't in town, I can't be held responsible for what happens.

"You boys go on back to the saloon and cool down," Club told the JB riders.

"The boss said to . . ."

"Did you hear me?" Club's question was loudly and harshly spoken. "Move." When the men had gone, Club turned and walked swiftly to the livery.

"He's ridin' out," Cooper said.

"Well, we're in for it now," Smoke said.

"That was Dick Miles doin' all the talkin'," Ladd said. "He's a bad one, Smoke. All of Biggers' men are drawin' fightin' wages."

Smoke smiled. "I forgot to tell you boys — so are you."

The punchers smiled. That extra money would go a long ways toward a new saddle or a gun or a handmade pair of boots to wear on special occasions.

"There go the deputies," Cooper said. "All of them. Hightailin' it right after Club."

"And here comes Dick and a whole bunch of others," Ladd added. "They ain't even waitin' 'til the law gets out of town."

Smoke walked to the gun racks and took down

three double-barreled shotguns, tossing one each to Cooper, Ladd, and Jenny. He broke open a box of shells and said, "Load them up. I'm going to open the dance. Stay inside and when I yell, if I yell, open fire."

"Mister Jensen?" the shopkeeper said. "I heard that Major Cosgrove has offered a thousand dollars to anyone who kills you."

"Is that all?" Smoke asked. "That's an insult. I've had a hundred times that amount on me." Smoke pulled both guns and stepped out onto the high boardwalk, cocking the .44s. He'd been doing this since he was a boy, and Preacher had taught him that when somebody's huntin' you, why hell, just take it to them and open the dance.

"Is it a good day to die, boys?" Smoke called, lifting his .44s.

"Jesus!" one of JB hands said, a rifle in his hands and the words drifting to Smoke. "This ain't gonna be no tea party."

"You can believe that," Smoke said, and opened fire without warning.

The street was suddenly filled with rolling thunder, twelve rounds fired so close together it sounded like one long, ragged volley. Smoke jumped from the boardwalk and jerked his rifle from the saddle boot. But there was no one left standing in the street, only a bloody pile of dead and dying and badly wounded Triangle JB hands.

Cooper and Ladd and Jenny stood in the store

91

and stared open mouthed at the carnage before them. Smoke calmly punched out empties and reloaded, holstering his .44s. A half dozen men, all with guns in their hands, had come after Smoke Jensen. Only two would live past that bloody morning in Red Light, Montana. Dick Miles had taken a round in his rifle butt, the slug's impact driving the stock into his belly and knocking the wind from him and putting him on the ground, otherwise unhurt. His ridin' buddy, Highpockets Rycroft, was only slightly wounded. But neither of them wanted any more of Smoke Jensen on this day.

A doctor ran out into the street and began ministering to the wounded as best he could, but their wounds were fearsome ones, all belly and chest shots.

Dick struggled up on one elbow. "You won't get away with this, Jensen," he called. "This is one time when your fancy name don't mean nothin' to nobody."

"Yeah?" Smoke said. "Why don't you carve that on the tombstones of your buddies?"

"I tell you, boys," Cooper said, relating the day's events to the crew, "I ain't never seen nothin' like it in my life. Smoke just walks out on the boardwalk, says, 'Is it a good day to die, boys?' and started tossin' lead."

"That's the only way to do it," Van Horn said. "If you know somebody's comin' after you, don't give 'em no breaks. Just plug 'em."

"I wish I'd a seen it!" Jimmy said, sitting wide-eyed on his bunk.

"You'll see a lot more than that 'fore this battle's done, son," Van Horn promised. "Jack Biggers will pull out all the stops now. He don't have no choice in the matter. This is gonna be a fight to the finish, and Smoke knew it today. That's why he done what he done."

"Well," Wolf Purcell said, rising up from his bunk. "That's four gunhands we won't have to deal with. Let's go have some of Miss Jenny's grub. I'm hongry."

Jack Biggers couldn't believe his eyes or ears. Four of his best men had been brought back to the ranch tied across their saddles. Dick was out of it for a few days because of a horribly bruised stomach, and Highpockets had lost the use of his left arm for a time.

"Jensen just opened fire?" the rancher asked. "He just started shooting? Why, that's against the law!"

The two survivors exchanged glances at that comment. "He asked us if it was a good day to die, and started shootin'," Dick said.

"I don't think any of us even got off a shot," Highpockets admitted. "I never heard a man work no .44s like that. This wasn't no fast draw. Jensen had his hands full of iron when he stepped out of the store. And I never in my life seen no man that rattlesnake cold."

"Oh, I have," Biggers said. "I know several of

them. I'll send a wire and have them here within a week. If this is the way Jensen wants to play it, I'm just the man to show him a thing or two."

The two toughs again exchanged glances. Maybe so, maybe not, they were thinking. But you might change your mind if you ever see Jensen in action.

"I'll have that girl's spread," Biggers said, after shouting for a rider to get the hell over to the house. "And I'll have it soon."

Highpockets thought: I wouldn't count on that, was I you. I really wouldn't.

Sally rode into town, accompanied by three Pinkertons who looked as though they would relish the idea of a little trouble, just to liven things up. No one bothered them, for the word had spread from track's end.

Deputy Brandt called for Club as soon as he saw the three men and one woman ride in.

"Leave them alone," Club said. "Trouble with Pinks is the last thing we want." His eyes appraised Sally as she swung down from the saddle. Quite a looker, he thought. But something told him that Smoke Jensen's wife would be just about as tough to handle as Jensen himself. Sally was one hundred percent a lady, Club had no doubts about that. It was evident in her bearing. But she also had a pistol strapped around her waist and a short-barreled carbine shoved down in a saddle boot. Club had no doubts as to her ability, and willingness, to use both weapons.

Club decided to play the gentleman. He walked over to the group and introduced himself, being sure to take off his hat.

"If I may be so bold, ma'am," Club said. "Are you Mrs. Jensen?"

Sally turned to put cool eyes on him. She was a lovely lady, Club thought again, and she sure do fill out them jeans. But them eyes is remindful of the eyes of Smoke Jensen. This woman would kill a man just about as quick as her husband would. Biggers, he mused, you better back off and rethink your plans. All of you better do that.

"I am," Sally said.

"I'm Sheriff Bowers, ma'am. Pleased to meet you, I'm sure. The Circle Cherry is just a few miles outside of town. That's where your husband is. Take the right fork at the end of town and you'll ride right to it."

"The Circle . . . *Cherry?*" Sally gasped.

"Yes, ma'am," Club replied. "Like the little fruit with a circle around it. It's kind of an . . . unusual brand."

"I saw the Golden Cherry riding in."

"Ah . . . yes, ma'am. But that's something that's not fitten for a man to discuss with a good woman."

"You mean it's a whorehouse, don't you?" Sally laid it out bluntly.

The three Pinks all looked everywhere except at Sally. The blue of the sky suddenly held a lot of interest for them. Club had not blushed since childhood. But blush he did now. "Ah . . . yes, ma'am. You are certainly right about that."

The mayor, Fat Fosburn, walked up to take a better look at this beautiful woman dressed in men's britches.

"Mayor," Club was quick, "this is Smoke Jensen's wife."

Fat looked first at Sally, then at the three heavily armed men with her, and then swept off his hat.

"My escorts," Sally said, lifting a gloved hand toward the Pinks.

"Gentlemen," Fat acknowledged.

"We'd better be riding, Miss Sally," one of the Pinks said.

"Yes," Sally said. She nodded at Club and Fat and swung into the saddle. Looking down at them, she said, "I'm certain we'll be seeing each other again. My husband and I plan on spending a great deal of time around here. Good day, gentlemen." She lifted the reins and was gone down the street.

"It just keeps gettin' worser and worser," Club said glumly.

"It's a game to Jensen," Fat said. "He's played this out before. I know about Sally Jensen. Comes from one of the wealthiest families in New England. Railroads and banks and newspapers and all sorts of businesses. She could buy this whole damn town if she wanted to. She could have a hundred of them damn Pinks in here if she wanted to. Five hundred of them. Send one of your men with a message to Biggers and Cosgrove. We've got to have a meeting. Tonight. At my place. What started out as something simple has suddenly become very complicated."

"It might be too late to stop it," Club said, nodding his head toward two men riding slowly into town.

"What do you mean?"

"Yonder comes Whisperin' Langley and Patmos. Biggers told me he was hirin' him some guns."

"All hell's fixin' to break loose around here," Fat said.

"Yeah," Club said. "Everything's complete now."

Fat looked at him.

"The Devil's already here. His name is Smoke Jensen."

Nine

Sally and Jenny hit it off immediately and before the afternoon was over, they were good friends. The Pinks stayed the night and were gone the next day. One more hand was hired, a quiet man in his late forties or early fifties who came riding up. Van Horn had hired him on the spot.

"Name's Barrie," Van Horn said. "I hadn't seen him in years. Used to be a town-tamer down in the southwest."

"I've heard of him," Smoke said. "I thought he was dead."

"Nope. He just got tired of it. But he's pure hell with that .45. He's a cowboy at heart. I heard that there was a big meetin' at Fat's house night before last," Van Horn abruptly changed the subject. "I got me two, three sources in town. Club Bowers wanted Cosgrove and Biggers to back off and leave us alone. But they wouldn't hear of it."

"What's so special about this ranch, Van Horn?"

"That's a good question, Smoke. There sure ain't no gold. It's up yonder in the mountains. It boils down to greed, I reckon. Pure and simple. But it ain't just the ranch. Red Light will boom for six months, a year, maybe two years. Then it will quiet down or just maybe die out, like a lot of other gold and silver towns out here. They just want it 'cause it's here and they can't have it. Then, too, as long as the town booms, the, ah, house of ill repute and the saloon will bring in tubfuls of money from the miners."

Smoke had arranged with the local banker to make sure that Jenny's money was deposited daily from the "businesses" in town. And even though Cosgrove owned the bank, he knew better than to dicker around with the girl's money. With Sally now in town, and being from one of the oldest and most respected banking families in all the nation, Jenny could consider her money as secure as if it had been surrounded by a division of armed guards. Cosgrove was wealthy, but he knew that Sally Jensen could have him ruined with no more than a stroke of a pen. And he also knew that she would not hesitate to do so. All parties aligned with Major Cosgrove were in a bit of a quandary. Biggers had arranged for hired guns to come in, over the objections of Sheriff Bowers and Fat Fosburn. But so far, Smoke had not left the ranch since his wife had arrived. And attacking the ranch was not in anyone's plans . . . yet.

"We're bein' watched," Van Horn said, as the men leaned against the corral railing and smoked.

"Yes. I know. I plan on doing a little hunting tonight. Pull all the boys in and keep them close until I get back."

"You goin' alone?"

"All by myself."

Just as it was getting dark, Smoke stepped out of the rear of the house after kissing Sally goodnight. He was dressed all in black, with moccasins on his feet and a dark bandanna tied around his head. He carried a length of rope wound across his chest, and precut lengths of rawhide tucked behind his belt. He carried no rifle, just his six-guns and a knife.

"Don't wait up for me, Sally," he spoke from the darkness of the backyard.

"I won't. But I'll leave coffee on the stove for you."

"And a piece of pie, too."

"Maybe. You're getting a little chubby around the middle."

Smoke chuckled. There wasn't a spare ounce of fat on him, but that was a standing joke between them. Smoke disappeared into the gloom of early night.

"Don't you worry about him, Aunt Sally?" Jenny questioned.

"No. I'll worry about him if he starts visiting that whorehouse in town."

The teenager giggled. She knew there was no danger of her Uncle Smoke ever doing that. Sally and Smoke were in love, and it was evident to anyone with eyes.

"Times are slowly changing out here, Jenny," Sally told the girl, as she cut slices of pie and placed them on the table for any hands who might want a late snack, and they all would. Then she covered a platter of doughnuts with a cloth. She placed both on a counter by the back door so the cowboys could find them without waking the whole house. "But for now, in many areas, the lawless rule. Men like Smoke are the only thing that stands between those who would obey the law, and those who would make a mockery of it and stamp on the rights of the just and the decent."

"It's changing back east."

"That is one of the reasons why I left. It isn't changing for the better. People will tell you it is, but it isn't. Instead of the lawless being put in an early grave, many courts are now handing down very light sentences and the criminal element is back on the street within a year or two. And most of them are just as savage, or more so, than when they went behind bars. Prisons without adequate rehabilitation facilities are no more than a college for the lawless. And it will worsen, Jenny. Even my own family, who, even though they are bankers and monied people, are champions of the downtrodden, agree with that. I shudder to think what it will be like for our great-grandchildren."

"What is Uncle Smoke going to do out there tonight, Aunt Sally?"

Sally smiled and put up the dish that Jenny had just dried and handed to her. "I suspect he's going to make life miserable for those working against you, Jenny."

"Kill them?"

Sally shook her head. "Not unless they get hostile with him. Those men in town approached him — us — with drawn guns in their hands. Their intentions were perfectly clear. Tonight is different." Again, she smiled. "To Smoke, it will be fun. To those spying on us here at the ranch, it will not be fun."

The gun-for-hire, who had hired on with Jack Biggers' Triangle JB, felt himself suddenly jerked from the saddle and thrown hard to the ground. He landed on his belly and the air whooshed from him, rendering him, for a moment, unable to move. A gag was tied around his mouth and his hands were tightly bound behind him by what he assumed, correctly, was rawhide. Then someone possessing enormous strength picked him up and toted him off like a sack of grain. A few hundred yards later, he was dumped to the ground, on his butt, his back to a tree.

"Shake your head for no, nod your head for yes," the big man said softly. "Do you understand?"

The gunhand nodded quickly.

"In a moment I'll remove the gag and you can whisper. Do you know what I'll do if you yell?"

The gunhand again nodded. He didn't know for sure, but he had a pretty good idea.

Smoke asked him a few more simple questions

and then removed the gag. The hand spat a time or two and then looked at the bulk of the man squatting before him in the darkness. No doubt in his mind who this was. Jesus, the guy was big.

"How much is Biggers paying you?"

"Seventy-five dollars a month," the hand whispered.

"That's a lot of money to wage war against a seventeen-year-old girl."

"Seventeen?"

"Yes. My niece, Jenny. She's seventeen. You must be real brave to want to kill a young girl."

"I don't want to kill any kid!" the hand protested. "Nobody said nothin' to me about no kid."

"Who did you think you were fighting?"

"You. If you're Smoke Jensen."

"I am. But why are you fighting me? What have I done to you?"

The question seemed to confuse the hand. "Well . . . I guess nothin'. Except you're squattin' on land that belongs to Jack Biggers."

"He told you that?"

"Yeah."

"Now let me tell you the truth. My sister died. She owned this spread, all legal and proper. She left it all to her daughter, Jenny. I'm here to see that Jenny keeps it. That's the top, bottom, and middle of it all. You ever heard of a man named Wolf Parcell?"

"Who hasn't? Mean old bastard. He'd as soon shoot a man as look at him."

"That's him. He works for me. You ever heard of a man named Barrie? B-A-R-R-I-E."

"Hell, yes. Town-tamer from down in the southwest."

"He works for me, too. There's an old gunfighter called Van Horn. Ever heard of him?"

"He's near abouts as famous as you."

"Well, he's foreman of my niece's spread. How about a breed called Bad Dog?"

"Sure. Don't tell me he's workin' for you, too?"

"Yes, he is. Now, you're not a real gunslick. You're a cowboy drawing fighting wages. Have I got you pegged right?"

"You have. I ain't no fast gun. I just ride for the brand."

"How many more like you over on the JB?"

"Maybe . . . four or five. The rest of them comin' in are hired guns, some of them out-and-out killers. Back-shooters. They damn sure ain't cowboys."

"Name them."

"Patmos. Val Davis. Dusty Higgens. Bearden. Whisperin' Langley. Ned Harden. Kit Silver. I damn shore ain't in their class. I damn shore don't *wanna* be."

"You know a man name of Will Pennington, down in Wyoming?"

"Heard of him. Runs the Box WP."

"That's him. He's hiring men. You and your buddies pull out and ride down there. Tell him I recommended you. Do that, or stay here and die. What's it going to be?"

"I'm gone first light. But I ain't alone out here this night, Mister Smoke. There's others that I don't know their names. Just Jack and Paul and Red and Blackie and so forth. But they ain't punchers, I can tell you that."

"Known guns?"

"They think they are."

Smoke untied the man and helped him to his feet. He gave him back his gun. The cowboy looked at it, then grinned and slipped it into his holster. "I never was worth a damn with it noways. As soon as the main house goes dark, me and the others will be gone to Wyoming, Smoke. Much obliged."

"Take off and good trip."

"They're waitin' on you, Smoke."

"Good. I sure wouldn't want to disappoint them."

Smoke waited for a full sixty count after the hand had gone. Then he began following the wide creek toward the south end of the spread. He felt sure the hand would leave as he said he would. Smoke wanted no innocent to be caught up in this battle, and a battle it was about to become. He also had him a hunch that when the cowboy he'd talked to laid it on the line to his friends, they would all soon be gone. Since it was near the first of the month, they had been paid, so there was nothing to keep them around.

He saw his second rider of the evening over on the other side of the wide creek. In some parts of the country, it would be called a river. Smoke picked up a rock and gave it a chunk, the stone hitting the horse on the rump and frightening it. The horse reared up suddenly and started bucking. The rider fought to stay in the saddle. While he was bucked and jumping and snorting, Smoke crossed the creek and knelt about thirty feet from the horse and rider. Then Smoke coughed like a puma and the horse had had quite enough of that area. He put his rider on the ground and took off.

"You hammer-headed no-'count!" the rider now on foot yelled. "I'll take a club and a chain and beat you bloody when I catch up with you."

That made things easier for Smoke. He had no use for a man who would abuse any animal.

Smoke slipped up behind the man and tapped him on the shoulder.

The man spun around, a hand dropping to the butt of his gun. Smoke smacked him in the mouth with a gloved fist and the man dropped like a rock, stunned but not out. Smoke reached down, hauled him up by the front of his shirt, and popped him again, this time on the side of the jaw. The man's eyes rolled back in his head and he was out.

Smoke stripped him down to the buff and tossed his clothes and boots into the creek and left him lying on the dewy grass. The man's drawers needed a good washing anyway.

He heard another rider before he could spot him. "Dewey?" the rider called in a hoarse whisper. "I got your horse, man. What's the trouble?"

Smoke waited.

"It's Frankie, Dewey. Answer me, boy."

Smoke suddenly screamed like a panther, and Frankie's horse went crazy. Frankie left the saddle and landed on his back in the grass. Smoke could almost hear the air leaving his lungs at the impact. Smoke was all over the man before he could even think of recovering. One savage blow to the jaw put Frankie in dreamland for a while. Then Smoke gave him the same treatment he gave Dewey, slinging the man's gunbelt over one shoulder. He caught up Frankie's horse and talked to the animal for a moment, calming it. He looped the gunbelts over the saddle horn and rode south, toward the Triangle JB. He hadn't gone half a mile before he was hailed.

"Frankie! Over here. It's Teddy. Let's have a smoke." He was going to have a Smoke, all right —but not the kind he was hoping for. "Have you seen Dewey?"

Smoke rode right up to him and hit him with the coiled-up rope he'd brought. Fifty feet of stiff rope is a formidable weapon, and the rider was knocked out of the saddle to the ground, his mouth and face bleeding. Smoke stepped down and popped him. Teddy sighed and went to sleep.

When Teddy woke up, he was buck-assed naked and a good eight miles from the ranch.

Ten

Jack Biggers was mad to the core and his face beet red as he stood in front of Club Bowers' desk. "Now, damn it, Club. I ain't gonna take no more of this. Three of my top guns come staggering up in the middle of the night, nekked as the day they was borned, feet all bleedin' and cut, and you're sittin' there tellin' me you ain't gonna arrest Smoke Jensen?"

"Settle down, Jack," Club told him. "If we pull a district judge in here, he's gonna want to know how come your men, on a night with no moon, so black it was like a mine pit, could identify Smoke Jensen. Now, Jack, times are changin'. He'll turn Jensen loose — providin' I ever get him to jail in the first place — and put your hands in jail for perjury. Times ain't like they used to be. Them days are over."

"Now what?" the voice came from the front door.

Riggers turned around to face Major Cosgrove. The man was approximately the same size as Jensen, but carrying just a bit of fat around the jowls and belly. He was in his mid-forties. Behind him stood his mine foreman, Mule Jackson. A huge bear of a man, with arms and hands and shoulders even more heavily muscled than Smoke Jensen, and a cruel face.

Jack, slightly embarrassed, told Cosgrove what had happened.

Major (that was his real name, not a military title) shook his head in disgust and said, "Forget about bringing charges. Any judge, even a bought one, would have to throw it out. Were the men on Jenny's property?"

"Well, yeah. Just like we agreed to do."

"That land is posted. Forget it." Major sat down. "Coffee, Mule."

Mule lumbered across the floor and poured his boss a cup, carefully sugared it, and set the cup on the desk.

Major sipped the hot brew cautiously and said, "We have to proceed very carefully on this, gentlemen. Jensen is a rich man in his own right. Very few people know that he has a freak vein of gold on his ranch, the Sugarloaf. But it's a deep vein. He could tap into that anytime he wished and hire an army. His wife, Sally, has more money than the King and Queen of England. Her family is the richest in all of New England."

"So what do we do?" Biggers demanded. "Give up?"

Major shook his head. "No. We just wait. Only we four and Fat know those mountains on the west side of Jenny's spread, which she owns — or rather, Smoke does, until she comes of age — contain the richest ore deposits of this strike. No, we do what we should have done from the outset. We act like civilized men and buy her spread. Not for the paltry sum we originally offered, but for what it's worth plus the cattle on it. Whatever amount we offer, there is a hundred, a thousand times that in gold in those mountains. That much money will set the girl up back East and we'll be rid of her. Sally Jensen is a businesswoman, very sharp, very astute. She will see the sense in our offer. Bet on it."

"Riders comin', Mister Smoke!" Jimmy yelled from the yard. "Three riders and a buggy. It's Major Cosgrove in the buggy."

Smoke stepped outside, buckling his gunbelt around his waist. Sally stood by a window, her short-barreled carbine at the ready.

Major stepped down from the buggy and knocked the dust from his dark business suit. He smiled at Smoke. "Sir, I am Major Cosgrove, owner of the Cosgrove Mine Company. Might I talk some business with you?"

Smoke looked at the huge man on the huge mule. Mule Jackson and Smoke Jensen took an immediate dislike to each other.

Smoke knew the type well. A bully, a head-knocker, a man who liked to hurt people. A man who was stupid and didn't know it.

"Certainly, Mister Cosgrove," Smoke told him. "Come on in the house. We have fresh coffee."

Seated in the living room, Cosgrove sipped his coffee and complimented Jenny and Sally on its flavor. The women smiled and said nothing.

"I'm afraid," Major said, "I have been cast in a bad light by some people. As a businessman, I must make a profit to stay in business. But not at the expense of innocent people. Jenny, you have had some trouble out here on your ranch, but none of that trouble came from me. You may believe that, or not believe it, but it is the truth. It is no secret that I wish to buy your ranch. But only at a fair price, both to you, and to me."

Smoke had ridden the ranch and knew approximately how many cattle were on the spread. He knew the price of beef and the price of land this lush. And so did Sally. They both listened to the offer Cosgrove made, and both knew it was a fair one.

Mule waited outside, squatting like a great ape by the buggy. Hands came and went and his eyes took them all in. There was not a man among them who would last a minute with him in a fight. Not even Smoke Jensen.

But Major Cosgrove, no stranger to toe-to-toe fighting, thought differently. Jensen was quite another matter. Major had seen eyes like that before, but not often. They were the eyes of a man who walked through life with supreme confidence. A man who took no water from any man. Mule was bigger and stronger than Jensen, but in a fight, Mule would lose because Jensen was smarter and would play on Mule's stupidity.

Major wondered if he could take Jensen in a

fight. It would be interesting, at best. At worst, he would get his brains kicked out by the gun-fighter many called the last mountain man.

"That certainly is a fair offer, Major," Smoke said. "And I assure you that Jenny will give it some thought. But I must tell you that at the present time, she is not interested in selling the ranch."

Major Cosgrove smiled. Thinly. He had been sure they would jump at the offer. He kept his anger under control, but it was with an effort. He was a man accustomed to getting his own way. All the time. Failure was not a part of his plans.

Too much money, Sally thought. I've gone over the books carefully and know what this place is worth. He's offering too much money. Why? She cut her eyes at Smoke and he nodded in understanding and agreement.

"Well," Major said, carefully placing his cup and saucer on a table. "It's been an enjoyable first meeting and I hope a mutually profitable one. Will you two be staying long?" He directed the question at Sally.

"Just as long as it takes," she replied.

And that didn't set well with Major Cosgrove either. This Sally Jensen was an uppity woman who needed to be slapped down into her place. This was a man's world, and women didn't be-long in business. Before this was all over, he felt he just might have to show Sally Jensen a thing or two.

After Cosgrove had left, Sally said, "His offer was far too high. He offered nearly twice what the place is worth."

"Yes," Smoke said. "But Van Horn tells me there is no gold on the spread." He got up and walked to the window and stared out at the mountains to the west. "It's up there," he said softly. "Bet on it. Just like back on the Sugarloaf. The veins are spotty but run deep." He went to the desk and got out the deed to the ranch, going over it carefully. "No question about it, Jenny. You not only own those mountains to the west, you own the mineral rights as well."

"You mean there is gold there?" the girl questioned.

"Yes. Probably a lot of it. But up there, it would take a lot of capital to get set up. Cosgrove has that capital. One person, working alone, could probably dig out enough to make a fair living. No more than that. That's just my opinion."

"So what do we do, Uncle Smoke?"

"Sit back and wait. But while we wait, we round up some cattle and sell them to get some money to operate on."

"Not that we don't have ample funds," Sally added. "And that's something you can bet Cosgrove knows."

"True. Which is why he won't wait too long before making his next move."

"And that will be?" Jenny questioned.

"Unpleasant," Smoke said flatly. "And soon."

"Are you certain you want to do this?" Smoke asked Sally.

The morning after Major Cosgrove had visited the ranch and made his offer, Sally was putting the finishing touches to her dressing, tying a bandanna around her throat.

"Positive."

"I wish I could talk you out of it."

"No way, husband dear."

"Don't you trust me?"

"With all my heart. I just don't trust those chippies at the Golden Cherry." She shook her head. "What a name for a place like that."

Smoke turned his head to hide his smile. But Sally caught it.

"You find something amusing, dear?"

"Not a thing, dear."

"Who runs this . . . establishment?" Sally asked.

"Van Horn tells me the madam is a lady called Clementine Feathers."

Sally muttered something under her breath. Smoke did not ask her to repeat it. He really was not looking forward to meeting his . . . employees, so to speak. "Jenny wants to ride into town with us."

Sally gave him a look that would wilt cactus.

"Ah, right!" he said brightly. "Not a good day for her to do that."

"Van Horn and Barrie will be riding in with us," Sally said, pulling on her gloves. "Barrie says he wants to look over the town. Get a taste of us, in his words."

"That warhoss wants to check out any possible troublemakers and mark them down in his mind," Smoke said. "But I sure wonder why, all of a sudden, he showed up here."

"Van Horn is mysterious about that, too," Sally said. Her slight anger was gone. "But I get the feeling that they both might be hiding something. And before you ask, no, I have no idea what it might be." She smiled. "Ready to ride for town?"

Smoke always worried when that smile appeared, for Sally was not a woman bound by the dictates and constraints of the time. She did what she damn well wanted to do, whenever she damn well wanted to do it.

And Smoke had him a hunch that today she just might decide to do something.

To surprise him.

The town had a feel to it that they all sensed when riding in. The streets were deserted, with not so much as a dog nor a cat present. All the horses had been stabled, and the hitchrails were all vacant.

"Something's up," Van Horn said.

"We been watched," Barrie said. "Those that want the ranch has got people constant on all sides. I was tempted to shoot one out of the saddle the other day. I resisted the temptation," he added drily.

Since it was a miner's boom town, there were

as many saloons as other stores on both sides of the twisting street. And the four riders were very much aware of eyes on them as they rode up the street.

"I ain't felt a friendly eye on me since we rode in," Van Horn said. "I'm gettin' the feelin' I ain't welcome in this place." He spat a stream of tobacco juice. "I just can't imagine why that would be."

Smoke was riding Buck today, since the big horse had nearly torn down his stall in his irritation over Smoke daring to ride another horse.

The unknown voice, calling from concealment in a whisper, reached them. "It's a setup, Smoke. Watch out."

"Miss Sally," Barrie spoke with hardly any lip movement. "I hate to say this, but the safest place for you just might be in the Golden Cherry. And we're right here on it."

"Go, Sally," Smoke said firmly. Softening his tone, and with a smile, he added, "Just remember, what's mine is half yours."

Both Van Horn and Barrie struggled to suppress a chuckle at that. They couldn't contain it.

Sally noticed the expression on the men's faces and smiled. "Just for that, I might bar you men from entering this pleasure palace."

Van Horn laughed. "Ma'am, at my age, that ain't no threat at all."

"Be careful," Sally said, then turned her horse into the half-circle drive of the Golden Cherry.

A henna-haired woman stepped out onto the

116

porch of the two-story home. "Honey, you get in here quick. Moses will take care of your horse. This damn town is about to explode."

Sally stepped out of the saddle and handed the reins to the huge, heavily muscled black man with an easy smile on his lips.

"You go on up to the house, Mrs. Jensen," he said. "You'll be as safe here as in a church."

"I'm Clementine Feathers," the bottle-redhead said, taking Sally's arm. "I run this joint. That husband of yours is some man, ain't he?"

"He is that," Sally said, looking around her. "My showing up here should give the good women of the town something to talk about, shouldn't it?"

Clementine laughed. "Honey, when the lamps are turned down and the covers pulled back, there ain't no such thing as a good woman."

Sally smiled. "Would you by any chance have some tea?"

"Honey, I've got the best tea this side of 'Frisco. Come on in and meet the girls. We've all been wondering when you'd show up. Jenny is a fine little lady. We all like her."

"That there's a hell of a woman you got, Smoke," Barrie said. "She'll do to ride the river with."

"Believe me, I know. Let's head over to the Golden Plum and have us a beer. I need to look the place over."

"You haven't been there yet?" Barrie asked.

"No. But I think now is a dandy time to visit. I

117

feel like there must be a hundred guns pointed at me."

"Cosgrove didn't wait long, did he?" Van Horn asked, as the men reined up in front of the saloon and swung down.

"I guess he figures it would be a lot easier to deal with Jenny than with me," Smoke replied, stepping up onto the boardwalk.

About a dozen locals were seated around tables, and five men stood at the far end of the bar. Smoke knew only one of them, a hired gun out of Utah who called himself Stoner.

The interior of the saloon was as fancy as anything Smoke had ever seen, with heavy drapes and polished brass spittoons. The long bar was gleaming. Gambling tables of all descriptions were spaced across the floor. The place was unusually quiet for this time of day.

"Remember me, Barrie?" one of the five men at the bar asked. He had an ugly-looking knife scar running down one side of his face.

"Can't say as I do," the ex-town tamer replied. He looked at the barkeep. "Beer."

Smoke ordered coffee and Van Horn asked for rye.

"You gunned down my brother in New Mexico Territory some years back," Scarface said.

"Do tell. I don't remember it, so he must not have been very hard to handle. Or very important," he added.

Barrie was on the prod and Smoke wondered about that. Everything he had ever heard about the man added up to the picture of a careful man, not one to push or crowd.

There's more here than I know, Smoke concluded.

"Hey, old man," another of the five called to Van Horn. He was young, not more than twenty-four or -five, and very foolish if he was seeking trouble with Van Horn. Van Horn was as much a legend as any man who ever strapped on six-shooters.

"There's one in every crowd," Van Horn muttered.

"The famous Smoke Jensen," Stoner said, sarcasm thick in the words.

"What's your interest in this affair, Stoner?" Smoke asked. "Other than making war on seventeen-year-old girls, that is."

"You ain't no seventeen-year-old girl."

"You want to make war on me, Stoner?" Smoke lifted the coffee cup with his left hand and took a sip.

Stoner stepped away from the bar, both hands hovering over his guns. "I never did believe all that crap folks say about you, Jensen. You can die just like any other man."

"But not this day," Smoke said, then shot the man in the belly.

Eleven

Stoner folded over and took a step backward. He straightened up, a terrible look on his face, and managed to pull one .45 from leather. Smoke gave him another .44 slug and the man sat down in a chair, the .45 clattering to the floor.

"Now, Barrie!" Scarface hollered.

Everybody pulled iron, the bartender hit the floor, the locals flattened out under tables, and the Golden Plum erupted in gunfire.

The loudmouth who just had to try Van Horn didn't even clear leather before the old gunfighter's Remingtons roared fire and smoke and lead. The kid took two in the heart and was dead before he stretched out in front of the bar, his eyes wide open in death.

Smoke put one in a tall, lanky gunhand and the man sat down hard, hollering in pain.

Van Horn and Barrie finished off the remaining two and the saloon began quieting down.

Outside, somebody began beating on a bass drum and another person started tooting on a trumpet.

"The local temperance league," Van Horn explained, reloading. "Led by Preacher Lester Laymon and his wife, Violet. But she ain't no violet. She's got her a mouth that'd put a champion hog caller to shame."

"Forward into the fray, brothers and sisters!" a woman shrieked. "Into the den of sin and perversion we shall march."

"That's her," Van Horn said.

"Hell, I'd rather put up with another gunfight than have to listen to her," the barkeep said, standing up and brushing off his apron.

"I need a doctor," one of the gunhands moaned.

The sounds of marching feet hammered on the boardwalk. The batwings were flung open and a crowd of men and women marched in. A tuba had joined the bass drum and the trumpet.

"Good God!" Smoke said.

Violet Laymon was slightly over six feet tall and rawboned. She looked like she could wrestle steers. She marched up to Smoke and damn near met him eyeball to eyeball. The man beside her was maybe five-feet-five and about as big around as he was tall.

"Help!" one of the gunmen on the floor hollered.

"Are you saved, you poor misguided wretch?" a woman hollered at the man. "Have you been washed in the blood?"

"Hell, he's got it all over him," Van Horn said.

"Shut up," the woman told him.

"Yes, ma'am."

The tuba player oom-pahhed, the bugler tooted, and the drummer pounded the skins.

121

Club Bowers and one of his deputies stepped into the saloon. "I'll handle this!" the sheriff said.

"You shut up, too," a woman told him.

Violet Laymon looked Smoke square in the eyes and thundered, "Are you the infamous Smoke Jensen, the man who has cold-bloodedly killed five thousand men and who had a place reserved in Hell by the time he was fifteen years old?"

"I really don't know how to respond to that," Smoke told the woman.

"I do!" Sally yelled from the batwings. She stepped inside, followed by Clementine Feathers and half a dozen other Soiled Doves from the Golden Cherry. "That's my husband, and a better man you'll not find anywhere!"

"Cover yourself with proper attire for a lady," Violet yelled at the jeans-clad Sally. "You shameless hussy!"

"Oh, hell," Smoke muttered.

"Somebody get me a doctor!" a wounded gunhand moaned weakly.

Doc White came pushing and shoving through the crowd, followed by Major Cosgrove, Jack Biggers, and the mayor of the town, Fat Fosburn.

The band started up again, a sort of ragged rendition of "A Mighty Fortress." "Sing it with vigor!" Preacher Lester shouted.

A dozen voices lifted in song.

Smoke looked at Van Horn. He was holding his glass of rye in one hand and leading the choir with the other, humming along.

Another badly wounded gunhand lifted himself up on one elbow and pointed a shaking finger at Cosgrove. "You said . . . you said it would be . . ." He fell back and died, his statement unfinished.

"I hope you didn't tell him it would be easy," Van Horn said, over the singing of the choir.

"I didn't tell him anything," Cosgrove snapped. "I never saw that man before in my life."

"Of course, you didn't," Barrie said. "He surely mistook you for someone else."

"Yeah," Van Horn said. "Maybe he thought you was some sort of an angel."

"Jeff," Madam Clementine Feathers said, "get the swampers in here and clean this place up."

"Yes, ma'am."

Cosgrove cut his eyes and found the eyes of Smoke Jensen hard on him. It was not a particularly enjoyable sensation. Major turned abruptly and left the saloon.

"Knock off this damn singin'!" Sheriff Bowers hollered. "This ain't no church. Brandt, Reed, get these people out of here. Where the hell is the undertaker?"

Violet Laymon huffed past Sally, still standing near the batwings, and hissed, "Hussy!"

Sally replied with a smile. Her reply sounded similar to "hitch."

"Well!" Violet threw back her head and

marched out, her husband, the choir, and the band right behind them. Oom-pah-pah, toot, boom!

"What the hell happened in here?" Club Bowers asked, when the place had quieted down.

"We'll never know from this side," Doc White remarked, standing up. "The last one just died."

At the Golden Cherry, Smoke and Sally sat in the comfortable and spacious kitchen and drank coffee and ate pie. Van Horn and Barrie sat in one of the "receiving" rooms, talking with a group of Soiled Doves.

"Some of the girls don't do anything more than talk to the men," Clemmie said. Clementine was too formal, she told Smoke and Sally. "A lot of these miners are happily married, with families hundreds of miles away, and they just want to talk to a woman. But those girls still get tarred with the same brush as the others, unfortunately."

Sally had quickly gone over the carefully kept books and found that the Golden Cherry and the Golden Plum did a fantastic business. Jenny was a very well fixed young lady.

"I'm known from 'Frisco to St. Louie," Clemmie said with a smile. "And I'm known for running the cleanest and the most honest places to be found anywhere. No shanghaiing allowed. No foot-padders allowed. No rough stuff with the girls. You seen Moses? Believe me, not even

124

Mule Jackson wants to mess with Moses. Nobody gets rolled in any of *my* places. And nobody gets cheated. The wheels at the Plum are honest, and so are the dealers. I find out they aren't, they're gone."

"How much of a cut does Sheriff Bowers get?" Smoke asked.

Clemmie smiled. "He gets his share."

"Not anymore. Divide what you used to give him among the girls and yourself here, and among the employees at the Golden Plum," Smoke told her. "All payoffs have ceased. You ladies stay here and chat. I'll go tell Bowers personally."

Van Horn and Barrie tagged along.

Smoke saw Jack Biggers and Major Cosgrove leave the sheriff's office, both men walking with their backs stiff with anger. Cosgrove's shadow, Mule Jackson, looked back and spotted Smoke. Major and Jack stopped and turned around. They watched as Smoke entered the sheriff's office, while Van Horn and Barrie waited outside.

Club and his four deputies were sitting around the office. Smoke was met with very unfriendly glances from the five men. "All payoffs to you from Jenny's estate have now ceased," Smoke told the man. "Try to shut down the businesses and I'll kill you. Try to force more money from Clemmie and I'll kill you. If the establishments mysteriously burn down, I'll kill you. If the employees are hassled by you or your men, I'll kill you. Do you understand all that, Club?"

Club Bowers was so mad he could not speak. He and his men were salting away a good bit of protection money each week from the Golden Cherry and the Golden Plum. Now all that was over.

Brandt stood up, his face mottled with fury. "Why, you goddamn . . ."

Smoke took two steps forward and hit him. The blow took the crooked deputy right on the side of the jaw and the man dropped like an anvil. Brandt lay motionless on the floor, a slight trickle of blood coming from his mouth.

Club Bowers sat behind his desk and stared hate at Smoke. But he was wise enough to keep his hands in plain sight and his mouth free of threats or cussing.

The other deputies, Reed, Junior, and Modoc, sat quietly. They were not afraid of Smoke. They knew that if they all pulled iron together, some of their bullets would nail Jensen. But they also knew that the odds of any of them coming out of it unscathed were very, very slight. At best, two or three of them would die under Smoke's lead. At this range, the carnage would be terrible.

Club Bowers, beneath all his anger, knew that Jensen could not stay in this area forever. Even if all the imported gunfighters that were here and still on their way did not kill the man, he had to leave sometime. He and his wife both had businesses to run back in Colorado. Taking a deep breath to calm himself, Bowers slowly nodded his head.

126

"That was just common business practice, Jensen," the sheriff said. "It goes on from New York City to San Francisco. But if you want it stopped, it's stopped."

"Fine," Smoke said, then turned his back to the men and stepped out onto the boardwalk. Biggers and Cosgrove were still standing on the boardwalk, Mule Jackson a few feet from the men. Fat Fosburn had joined them. Smoke walked up to the men.

"The payoffs to the sheriff and his men from the Cherry and the Plum have just stopped," Smoke informed the men. "One of them had something to say about that. He's still out on the floor. Do any of you have objections to that?"

"I do," Mule said. "I just flat don't like you, Jensen. And I think I'll tear your meathouse down right now." He stepped forward, and for a big man, he was surprisingly swift.

But of all the men present on the boardwalk, Smoke had suspected Mule would be the one to offer up a fight. Smoke sidestepped, then stuck out a boot, and Mule tripped. A little shove from Smoke and the huge man fell off the boardwalk and landed face-first in the mud of the street.

Smoke unbuckled and untied, handing his guns to Van Horn. He pulled leather riding gloves from his back pocket and slipped them on while Mule was cussing and spitting out mud and dirt and getting to his feet. Mule was spewing and spitting out just what he was going to do to Smoke. None of it was pleasant.

"You watch that brute," Van Horn cautioned. "He's killed men with those fists."

"So have I," Smoke replied.

Clemmie and Sally came at a run, as did most of the town's citizens, many of them climbing onto awnings and running up to second-floor landings to get a glimpse of the upcoming fight. Mule Jackson had never been bested in a fight, and while Smoke Jensen was a known gunfighter, and a very well-put-together man, most believed he stood no chance at all against a wicked brawler like Mule.

"Five hundred dollars on Mule!" Fat Fosburn hollered.

"I'll take that bet," Clemmie Feathers shouted.

"Fifty dollars on Smoke," Van Horn said.

"You're on," Club said.

The betting became hot and heavy.

Violet and her band of followers raced up, pushing and shoving through the crowd. "This is disgraceful!" Violet shrieked, while her husband was jumping up and down, trying to see what was going on. He finally perched on top of a water barrel by the corner of a building.

Store owners locked their doors and hung CLOSED signs on the doorknobs. No one wanted to miss this fight.

"One thousand dollars on Mule Jackson!" Major Cosgrove shouted above the din.

"I'll take that bet!" Sally yelled. "And go five times more. Five thousand dollars on Smoke.

You want to put your money where your big fat mouth is, Cosgrove?"

Major's face flushed a deep crimson as his eyes met Sally's. She and Clemmie and a couple of the Golden Cherry's soiled doves were standing in the bed of a wagon.

"I'll take that bet, Little Lady," Major yelled.

Sally nodded her head. "I'm a lady most of the time," she said to Clemmie. "But I can be just about as mean as my husband when I choose to be."

"I don't doubt that for a second, honey," Clemmie replied.

"Come on, you lard-butt!" Smoke yelled to Mule, still slipping and sliding in the mud of the street. "Are you going to fight or dance all day?"

With a roar of rage, Mule charged.

Twelve

Mule slopped up onto the boardwalk, muddy and wet to the skin and mad to the bone. Before he could get set, Smoke hit him flush in the mouth with a straight right that snapped the man's head back and bloodied his lips. Mule stood for a couple of seconds, shaking his big head. Before he could clear out all the little chirping birdies and ringing bells, Smoke crossed a left that landed on the side of the man's jaw and buckled his knees. Mule covered up and took a staggering step back. The bully knew at that moment he was in for the fight of his life. Smoke Jensen was no ordinary man, and he could punch like a sledgehammer! There was a roaring pain in his head that Mule had not experienced since childhood. He was going to have to end this brutally and quickly, and he knew he was going to have to kill Smoke Jensen. He could not let the man beat him. His reputation would be ruined and he'd be a laughingstock. He couldn't let that happen. All that went through his mind in the course of two seconds. When the third second ticked past, Smoke followed him in and hit him twice in the stomach with a left and right that hurt.

Smoke pressed and clubbed the man on the

neck with a balled fist, then stepped back, out of reach of Mule's powerful arms.

Deputy Modoc stuck one boot out to trip Jensen. He felt the muzzle of a pistol jam into his ribs and he pulled back his boot and cut his eyes. He was staring into the cold eyes of the town tamer, Barrie. "Do that again," Barrie said, "and I'll kill you."

Club Bowers looked over at Sally. She had taken a rifle from someone's saddle boot and was holding it, hammer back. He sighed and shook his head. He'd never before met a man like Smoke or a woman like Sally. They were made for each other.

Mule screamed like an angry bull and ran at Smoke in an attempt to lock his arms around the man and crush the life from him. And Smoke knew the man was capable of doing just that. Smoke stepped to one side and smashed a right into Mule's face, flattening the man's nose and sending blood spurting. Mule stopped as if hit with an iron stake, his boots flying out from under him. He landed on his back on the board-walk, the breath momentarily knocked from him.

"Stomp him, Smoke!" someone in the crowd yelled. "He'd do it to you."

"You shut your damn mouth!" Major yelled, his eyes searching the crowd for the citizen.

"You go to hell, Cosgrove," the citizen yelled.

Smoke let Mule slowly lumber to his muddy, low-heeled lace-up boots. Mule could not believe this was happening to him. He had yet to land a punch on Smoke Jensen. The damn man just stood there waiting.

"Stand still and fight!" Mule said, blood leaking from his mouth and nose.

"Well, come on," Smoke told him. "I'm right here." Smoke was under no illusions. He knew he had been awfully lucky so far in this fight, and that just might be subject to change at any time if he got careless.

Mule lifted his big fists and came at Smoke slowly. The man had seen the error of his ways and realized that brute strength alone would not win this fight. Smoke had hammered him some terrible blows, and those blows had taken some of the steam out of Mule. He could not recall ever getting hit as hard and as many times as he'd been hit this day.

Mule had never had to rely on fighting skills to win fights. He could take a punch with the best of them, and if he ever got his hands on a man, the fight was over. Mule liked to crush bones, to hurt men, cripple them. He'd killed a dozen men with his hands over the years, and made cripples out of twice that number. And he had no doubts about the outcome of this fight.

But he should have.

Mule flipped a left at Smoke and Smoke ducked it and went under, driving his right fist into Mule's belly, about two inches above his belt buckle. The air *whooshed* out of the man and Smoke followed that with a jarring left to the side of Mule's jaw that damn near crossed Mule's eyes. Smoke smashed a left and a right to Mule's ribs and then slammed a big right fist over Mule's heart.

Mule staggered back, hurt.

Major Cosgrove cut his eyes to Sally. She was looking straight at him, smiling.

Damn the woman! Major thought. Damn her! She'd never had a doubt about who would win the fight. And damn Smoke Jensen, too.

Club Bowers watched the fight and thought: Mule is finished. Smoke is going to maul him, humiliate him, and maybe bust him up real bad.

Those citizens who supported the power structure in Red Light had fallen silent. They all knew that some professional fighter could probably whip Mule, someone like Jem Mace or that new up-and-comer John Sullivan. They could have beaten Mule, fighting by the rules. But to have some gunfighter come in and do it . . . that was, up to this point, unthinkable.

"Give it up, Mule," Smoke told the man. "Just give it up. I don't want to have to kill you."

"You, kill *me*?" Mule was visibly shaken. "Why, you two-bit gunslinger. I'll tear your head off!" Mule bored in, and that got him a left and right to the face, the left smashing his already flattened nose and the right pulping his lips.

Screaming in rage and pain and almost total frustration, Mule plowed ahead, roaring curses at Smoke, slamming lefts and rights at him. Smoke backed up and took the blows on his arms and shoulders, and they hurt, but did no damage. When Mule grew arm weary and out of breath, he stepped back, and Smoke jumped in close. Mule thought he was swinging for his head and covered up. Smoke instead back-heeled the huge man, sending him crashing to the boardwalk.

When Mule tried to get to his feet, he made the mistake of momentarily presenting his big backside to Smoke, and Smoke couldn't resist it. He planted one boot on Mule's butt and shoved, sending the man off the boards and sprawling into the mud. Mule landed with a mighty splat and buried in the mud.

"Now, that's it, Mule," Smoke called. "The fight is over. If you get up, I'm going to hurt you. Stay down, man."

"A thousand dollars if you'll get up and fight, Mule!" Major shouted. "A thousand dollars, Mule."

Smoke looked at the man, contempt in his eyes. Cosgrove was even sorrier than Smoke had first suspected. He returned his gaze to Mule Jackson.

The man was struggling to get to his feet.

"Don't do it, Mule," Smoke called. "Stay down."

But Mule was furious, that rage shining in his eyes. There was a maddened look on his muddy face. He pulled himself out of the mire and crawled back up to the boardwalk. Slowly, he lifted his fists.

Smoke did the same.

The crowd was now totally silent, so quiet that Mule's ragged breathing could be heard.

Then Mule made the worst mistake he could possibly make. He grinned at Smoke and said, "When I finish stompin' you, gunfighter, I'm gonna snatch that wife of yours out of that wagon, tote her to a bed, and peel them jeans offen her down to her shinin' bare butt. Then I'll show her what pleasures a real man can give a woman."

Killer and no-'count that Club Bowers was, he could but shake his head at that remark. Fat Fosburn put his hands to his face and stifled a moan. Jack Biggers' mouth dropped open. And Major Cosgrove gasped at the stupidity of the man. Men had been hanged for saying less.

Smoke's eyes turned as cold as the frozen Arctic. He slowly walked the distance between them and kicked out with one boot, the point of the boot catching Mule square in the balls. Mule screamed and doubled over. Smoke brought his knee up and the crowd could hear the bones crunch in Mule's face.

Grabbing the man by his long greasy hair, Smoke straightened him up and began battering the man's face and body with savage fists. He smashed the man to the boards, now slick with Mule's blood, half a dozen times, each time dragging him back up and smashing him down again.

"He's unconscious, baby," Sally called from

the wagon, just as Smoke drew back his bloody-gloved fist to strike again.

Smoke let Mule fall. He stood, this big last mountain man, his huge chest heaving with exertion and his eyes savage with killing fury. He turned and took a step toward Major Cosgrove.

"You hit me and I'll sue you!" Major yelled.

The crowd exploded in laughter and Major's face drained of blood, then filled to a high crimson of embarrassment.

Smoke nodded his head and stripped off his gloves. "You bet my wife five thousand dollars on this fight," he panted the words. "Pay her. Right now, Cosgrove."

"I don't have that kind of money on me!"

"Then get it, you son-of-a-bitch!" Smoke shouted at him.

"You can't . . . call me that!" Major said.

"He did," Van Horn said. "Mayhaps you'd better strap on iron, Cosgrove. And just in case Smoke don't feel up to meetin' you, I'd be glad to take his place."

"Look at me, Cosgrove!" Sally said.

Major cut his eyes. Sally's rifle was to her shoulder, the muzzle pointed straight at Cosgrove's chest. "Send someone for my money or you're a dead man."

"Whoooeee!" Clemmie hollered. "Sally, you are my kind of woman." She cocked her head. "Well," she amended that. "Sort of."

Thirteen

Sally was five thousand dollars richer when she swung into the saddle and the four of them rode out of Red Rock to the cheers of most of the citizens of the town. Van Horn and Barrie had money in their pockets from betting on the fight, and all of them were still smiling over the public humiliation of Major Cosgrove. Mule Jackson still had not regained consciousness when the four rode out of town.

"It's going to be all-out war now," Smoke said, putting a damper on the high humor. "Cosgrove will have to come out fighting if he's to regain any of his power."

"I should have shot him," Sally said.

"You're mighty right about that," Barrie said.

"Don't encourage her," Smoke said with a smile. "She's getting as notorious as I am. She'll start packing two guns tied down if this keeps up."

Sally smiled at the good-natured kidding. But she knew her husband was right about Major Cosgrove; he would have to come out fighting if he was to maintain any semblance of his old power. Now, more than ever, Jenny was in danger. But there was no way the girl would consider leaving for her safety. She had that Jensen strain of courage coursing through her veins. And stubbornness, Sally added.

"I hate Mule Jackson," Jenny said, after sitting enraptured, listening to the news of the day. "He gives me a spooky feeling, the way he looks at me."

"He won't be doing much looking for at least a month," Sally said. "I have never seen a man beaten that thoroughly."

"But he'll be more dangerous now," Smoke said, soaking his hands in warm salted water to keep down the swelling. "He'll be carrying a powerful grudge against me."

In the bunkhouse, Barrie was holding the floor. "I never seen nothin' to compare with it," he told the hands. "Mule didn't even get one good lick in on Smoke. Smoke tore him down and whupped him to a fare-thee-well."

"Mule had it coming," Pasco said, sitting on his bunk, mending a tear in a shirt. "He killed a friend of mine with his fists. Killed him for no other reason than that he was Mexican."

"Boys, this is shapin' up to be a bad one," Van Horn took the floor. "Up to now, it's been mild. Now it's gonna turn rough. You all ride with a spare six-shooter in your saddlebags and extra ammo. And you ride wary at all times. Cosgrove has got to come back at us for this day. So we might as well get ready for it."

"You reckon he'll hire more gunslingers?" Ford asked.

"Bet on it. He can't afford to lose. If he does, he'll have to leave the country."

"Smoke really called him a son-of-a-bitch?" Ladd asked.

"Flat to his face."

Ladd shook his head. "Smoke musta really been mad."

"You could say that," Van Horn's reply was drily offered.

Doc White stepped out of his small clinic into the outer office and faced Sheriff Club Bowers. "Mule Jackson has received the most thorough beating I have ever seen given a man. It's a miracle the man isn't dead. While he was unconscious, I had the dentist come over and extract several teeth that were broken off. He is very nearly a total bruise from his face to his waistline. He has several cracked ribs, and if he didn't sustain some type of internal injuries, I'll be very surprised. I put so many stitches in his face I lost count. Oh, one other thing: that man who was kicked in the head by Jensen's horse? He's dead."

Muttering under his breath, Club walked back to his office to find a very angry Major Cosgrove and an equally angry Jack Biggers there. The mayor, Fat Fosburn, sat calmly drinking coffee.

"Five thousand dollars!" Major stormed. "That damn uppity woman took five thousand dollars from me. At gunpoint. And you didn't do a damn thing to stop it, Club."

139

"Half the town heard you make the bet, Major," Club told him. "It would have been worser had you tried to welch on her."

Cosgrove did some more cussing and stomping around, then finally sat down. He threw his expensive hat on the floor. "And the man dared call me a son-of-a-bitch," he wound down.

"Nick Norman just died," Club told the men.

"Who cares?" Biggers replied. He stared at the sheriff. "I got Lonesome Ted Lightfoot ridin' in this week. He's bringing some of his friends with him."

"I didn't know Lightfoot had any friends," Club said. "But thanks for telling me. Who's comin' with him?"

"Les Spivey, for sure. Maybe Curtis Brown."

Club nodded and turned to the window facing the muddy street. He had had a good deal working here. Plenty of money and plenty of power. But he could sense that it was all coming to an end. It didn't make any difference how many gunslicks Major and Jack and Fat brought in. Not any difference at all. The big three, Cosgrove, Biggers, and Fosburn, were beaten men. They just didn't know it yet. But they were whipped.

The best thing for me to do, Club thought, is just pack up and pull out. Just get the hell gone from here. If I stay, I'm going to die.

"What are you thinking about?" Fosburn spoke to the sheriff's back.

"Pullin' out," Club said honestly.

"Pulling out!" Major said, jumping to his feet. "Have you lost your mind? We've got a gravy train here. In a few years we can all be enormously wealthy men."

Club turned to face the town's power group. "We don't have a few years. I don't 'magine we have even a few months. Not if we continue buckin' Smoke Jensen."

"Jensen won't be around in a few weeks," Biggers said, sticking out his chin belligerently. "I got twenty-five of the best guns in these parts on my payroll with more coming in. There ain't no way Jensen can survive all that."

"Jensen's had a hundred men chasin' him before," Club said, "includin' friends of mine who will swear to this day they'll never tangle with Smoke Jensen again. You forgettin' a couple of years back when all them people were chasin' him up in the mountains. He must have killed fifty of them, and Sally Jensen put lead in ten or twenty. You 'member last year, I think it was, that German feller, Count something-or-the-other, hired all those gunslingers to help him hunt down Smoke Jensen? Well, they hunted him until he got tired of it and made his stand. Do you know how many men died durin' that foul-up? You couldn't stack their bodies in these two rooms here and all them cells yonder. Listen to me, people. I know Smoke Jensen. He probably don't remember me, but I *damn* sure remember him. Let me name you some men who had the bad judgment to brace him. Slick Finger

Bob, Terry Smith, Tom Ritter, One-Eye Slim, Warner Frigo, Canning, Felter, Kid Austin, Grisson and Clark, Curly Rodgers, Curt Holt, Ed Malone, Boots Pierson, Harry Jennings, Blackjack Simpson. Richards, Porter, Stratton. Smoke Jensen killed *nineteen* men by himself in a ghost town over in Idaho. Then there's Greeny, Lebert, and Augie. There was Dickerson, Brown, and Necker. Joiner and Wilson and Casey. There was Jack Waters and his three brothers. Then there was Lanny Ball and four of his friends. I think their names was Woody, Dalton, Lodi, and Sutton. Dad Estes had himself and his whole gang wiped out by Jensen. Cat Jennings and Barton and Mills and no-'count George Victor. Utah Slim — *everybody's* heard of him — faced Smoke one day. That was the last thing he ever did. Pig-Face Phillips and a gunhand named Carson called Jensen out. They died in the dirt. You want me to name some more? Hell, I ain't even scratched the surface yet!"

Club Bowers walked the floor, eyeballing each man there. "People, understand something: Smoke Jensen was raised by mountain men. He don't fight like nobody you or me know. And when you get Smoke Jensen riled — and I've seen him riled — he's like . . . well, a whole room full of grizzly bears. He's . . ."

Jack Biggers waved him silent. "You're lettin' your imagination run away with you, Club. Jensen is a tough man. We all saw that when he fought Mule. But he's still just a man. He ain't got no supernatural powers."

"Injuns say he does," Fat Fosburn said. "I used to have some Injuns ridin' with me in my gang, both breeds and full redskin. They were all scared slap to death of Smoke Jensen. You see, Smoke was sort of raised up by a mountain man called Preacher."

That got everybody's attention.

"Yeah," Fat said with a smile. "Preacher hisself. The most famous mountain man of them all. Mean as a snake and tough as an oak tree. And he brought Smoke Jensen up to be just like him. And done a damn good job of it, too. Now you know why he's so damn mean. Club's right about Jensen to some degree. What we got to do, I'm thinkin', is get us a good back-shooter in here."

"You know one?" Major asked.

Fat smiled. "I've already sent for him."

The man Fat had contacted despised Smoke Jensen with a hatred that bordered insanity. Preacher had killed his father with a knife back in the mid-fifties, after he'd caught the man trying to steal one of his horses. Peter Hankins had been a boy in his teens when it had happened. A boy who was already an accomplished thief, liar, pickpocket, murderer, and just about anything else evil he was big enough to be. Trappers had brought the elder Hankins back to the trading post and dumped him at Peter's feet, telling

143

him what had happened.

"Out here, boy," a mountain man told him. "You don't steal a man's horse. A lot of times, that's like givin' a man the death sentence. Your pa got what he deserved. Let it lie. You go after Preacher, and he'll kill you."

Peter Hankins drifted East and joined the Union Army at the start of the War Between the States. He had always been expert with a rifle, and he was made a sniper. He loved it. He loved to kill from a distance. He especially loved to kill Southerners. He'd won medals for it. When the war ended, he drifted back West, joined a gang of scum and ne'er-do-wells, and a few years later was caught up in a completely unexpected fight with Preacher and a young man named Smoke Jensen. Smoke got lead into him, although Peter doubted the young man knew it at the time. His hip still bothered him because of that fight. So after that, he shared his hatred of Preacher with hatred of Smoke Jensen.

Now he had a chance to kill him and make a couple thousand dollars in the process. It was too good to pass up.

As soon as he received the wire, he bought a train ticket and was on his way, sleeping in the car with his horse and his Sharps "English Model" 1877 .45-caliber rifle. Peter hand-loaded his own ammunition (2.6-inch casing) and knew almost to the inch what distance they would carry, and they would carry accurately for more than fifteen hundred yards, providing the wind was not kicking up.

Peter would kill man, woman, or child. He made no distinction. He was a man utterly without morals. And he was looking forward to this job.

Smoke stepped out of the house for a breath of night air after another of Sally and Jenny's excellent suppers. The men had staggered off to the bunkhouse, all of them full as ticks. Three days after the fight, and his hands were no longer sore or swollen. There had been no trouble from Biggers, Cosgrove, or Fat. Smoke was not expecting any from Club Bowers. Scoundrel that he was, he was also a man who had been around and could read signs. Smoke had him a hunch that Club would pull out of this fight given just the slightest opportunity.

Van Horn walked up and stood silent for a moment, rolling a cigarette. "When you figure they're gonna hit us, and how do you figure it?"

"Just as soon as they get everyone in here that's coming in."

"You know of a person name of Peter Hankins?"

"Peter Hankins?" Smoke mused. "Yes. I do. He's a long-distance shooter. He uses a special made Sharps .45. Sharps made the rifle for about a year, I think. Made it for target shooters. It had something to do with English marksmanship rules, I believe. I've never seen one. Hankins, huh? My mentor killed Hankins' father. Preacher caught him stealing horses and carved him up. That was years before I knew Preacher. I've known for a long time that Hankins hates me."

"How old a man would he be?"

"Probably in his early to mid-forties. He was a teenager when Preacher killed his father back in '55 or so. I have no idea what he looks like or where he lives. He's a loner. He comes in, bodies fall, he leaves. Usually without anyone ever seeing him. How'd you find out about him coming in?"

Van Horn smiled. "Oh, those sources of mine I told you about."

Smoke chuckled. "You mean the girls at the Golden Cherry, don't you?"

Van Horn laughed quietly. "Not much gets by you, does it, Smoke?"

"I can't afford to let much by me, Van. I have too many people who want to see me dead."

"I do know the feelin'," the old gunfighter said. "But if they attack this ranch, they're gonna be in for a tough fight of it. That's a salty bunch yonder in the bunkhouse."

"They'll attack. It's coming. That's why I sold off most of the cattle, except for the good breeding stock, and had you bunch the rest in that box. Will the girls tell you when Hankins gets into town?"

"Within the hour."

"Let me know. Tomorrow we all work close to the ranch. We've got to get ready for anything that might come our way."

"See you in the morning."

Smoke was up before dawn, as usual, and with coffee in hand, stepped outside to meet the dawning, about a half hour away. Wolf Parcell had been waiting on him.

"What's on your mind, Wolf?"

"Let's take the fight to them. Kill them all," the old mountain man said coldly and bluntly. "End it. Then the girl-child can live in peace."

Smoke smiled in the darkness. Mountain men were not known for their gentle loving nature toward anyone who had openly declared themselves an enemy. And for the most part, that philosophy was shared by Smoke. But he had learned to temper his baser urgings . . . to a degree. "Those days are just about gone, Wolf. Besides, we've got to keep public sentiment on our side."

The old man *harrumped* at that but said nothing in rebuttal for the moment. He drained his coffee cup and stuffed a wad of chewing tobacco into his mouth. He chomped and chewed and spat and finally said, "Two Injun friends of mine come to the bunkhouse last night. Told me a whole passel of gunslingers rode into town 'bout ten o'clock."

"I thought I heard something about one."

"Figured you would. Injuns asked about you. I told 'em you wasn't near 'bouts ugly as Preacher, and you was sizable bigger and somewhat smarter."

Smoke chuckled. And waited. He knew Wolf had more on his mind and would get to it in his own good time.

"Said they was a double handful of the gunslingers," Wolf said, after he spat. "They didn't know no names."

"The odds are getting longer, aren't they?"

"Yep. But we can handle them come the time. You'll cut your puma loose soon enough I reckon. And we'll be right there with you."

"You're looking forward to this, aren't you?"

"I'd be lyin' if I said I wasn't. That's a good girl in yonder. I like her. I ain't got no use for people who'd hurt a girl like that. Riles me up considerable. I take it personal. Bad Dog feels the same way. So's the rest of the fellers. When they come, Smoke, I ain't offerin' no quarter to none of them. I just want you to know that. I'm speakin' for me, Pasco, and Bad Dog. Cain't talk for none of the others."

"Try not to take scalps," Smoke said drily.

"I'll think about it." The old mountain man got up as silently as a stalking cat and moved into the darkness. He stopped and turned around. Smoke could see the faint smile on his lips. "You're a fine one to tell me not to take scalps, Smoke."

"That was a long time ago, Wolf."

Wolf chuckled. "You ain't old enough for it to be that long ago, boy. You got more of Preacher in you than you think. And I think this here fight's gonna turn real interestin'. For a fact I do."

Fourteen

Smoke saddled up, secured his bedroll, and rode out alone, taking a couple of sandwiches with him. He had told Sally, "I'll be back."

She did not question him. He might be back by noon, or he might return the next day. He might be back in three or four days. Sally knew they were in a fight to the death now, for her husband never tried to shield her from the truth. Hired guns were riding in from all over a three-state and territory area. By stage, by train, by horse. They were coming to Red Light to accept the fighting wages of Biggers, Fosburn, and Cosgrove. They were coming in to attempt to kill Smoke Jensen.

And this teenage girl, Sally added, cutting her eyes to the young girl standing at the kitchen counter, kneading dough for bread. They have no right to do that, Sally mused, her thoughts turning savage. She has harmed no one. She has a right to live on the ranch her mother left her, and to live in peace. Damn those men who would harm a child . . .

"When you finish with that, Jenny," Sally said, "get your guns. We're going to practice awhile."

"Yes, ma'am. Won't Uncle Smoke be alarmed at the gunfire?"

"No. I told him about it." Sally went to the front door and looked for Van Horn. The old gunfighter was by the corral, Wolf Parcell and Bad Dog with him. She walked down to him. He turned at her approach, taking off his hat.

"Jenny and I will be down by the creek for a time, shooting. I want Jimmy to come with us. I want to see how he handles a gun."

Van Horn smiled. "Yes, ma'am. I'll come down, too. Smoke say where he was goin'?"

"No. I didn't ask him. He'll be back when he finishes what he set out to do."

"I thought he was gettin' a mite riled when I spoke with him."

"He's given those who want this spread fair warning. In his own way. Now, I suspect, he's taking the fight to them."

"But he's all alone," Jimmy Hammon said, walking up.

"No, he ain't, boy," Wolf said. "He's got the spirits with him. Preacher's with him. And so is Griz and Nighthawk and all the rest of 'em. Five hundred years of fightin' and ridin' alone is with Smoke this day. Everything about survivin' that could be taught a man was taught to Smoke by them that took him as a kid and saw to his needs. Mayhaps we — and I was a part of lookin' after him — mayhaps we didn't do him right. Our time was endin' when Ol' Preacher took the boy under his wing. We didn't teach him no gentle ways. He'd done been taught that by his ma and pa. And they done a good job of it. Smoke's got a good mind to what is right and what is wrong. What we done was teach him the gun and the knife and the fight. I allow as to how it was fate that brought the boy to the High Lonesome and to us." He smiled down at young Jimmy. "I'd take you under my arm and tote you up to the High Lonesome, son, and I'd larn you the ways of the mountain men. But I'd be doin' you a disservice if I did. Them fancy-pants Eastern ways is rapid movin' out here. All talk and no action is the way it'll be in a few years. 'Fore long, any man'll be able to walk up to you and spit in your face. And if you gut him or shoot him, the law'll put you in prison for it. You mark my words: this country is in for a turrible time of it."

Sally put a hand on the boy's shoulder. "Jimmy will receive a formal education. Smoke and I will see to that."

"You mean I got to go to school?" Jimmy blurted.

"Yes," Sally said firmly. "You will go to school."

Van Horn looked at him. "Don't say nothin' 'ceptin' yes, ma'am, boy."

"Yes, ma'am, Miss Sally," Jimmy said.

Smoke sat his saddle on the north side of the fence, facing three of Jack Biggers' hands, who sat their saddles on the south side. The three had known it would someday come to this. They had

151

just hoped it would not be this soon.

"We ain't doin' you no harm, Jensen," one finally spoke. "And we're on our own range."

"That's right," Smoke replied. "And it is a mighty pretty place to be buried."

"Huh?" another said.

"What are you talkin' about?" the third asked.

"You ride for Jack Biggers. He's paying you seventy-five dollars a month and found for your guns. Jack Biggers has sworn to take my niece's ranch even if he has to kill her. That makes all of you an enemy of mine. So fill your hand or ride."

The three Triangle JB riders wanted to exchange glances, but they dared not take their eyes from Smoke Jensen. In a time when the average cowboy made about thirty-five dollars a month, that seventy-five Biggers had offered had looked awfully big. Now they weren't so sure of that.

"I'm giving you all a chance, boys," Smoke spoke softly but firmly. "Take a moment and think about it."

"Jensen," one said. "I'm gonna put both hands on this here apple and keep them there. Okay?"

"Fine. Do it."

The man carefully placed his gloved hands on the saddle horn and gripped it, one hand on top of the other, the reins under the hand holding the apple.

"Me, too," another said, and slowly followed suit.

"I'm not," the third hand said.

"Think about it, Jess," the first hand to show some sense told him.

"I ain't takin' water from Jensen."

"I am," the second man said. " 'Cause it's mighty scarce in Hell."

"Make your play, Jensen," Jess said.

"After you," Smoke told him.

Jess grabbed for iron and Smoke's .44 boomed. Jess fell backward out of the saddle. Neither of his buddies had taken their hands off the saddle horn. Jess tried to get up, the front of his shirt stained with blood. His gun had fallen from the holster.

"Ain't no human person that fast," Jess gasped, unable to get any further than to his knees.

"You boys take care of the burying and then ride out of this country. Get you a good job punching cattle and leave the gunfighting to someone else," Smoke told the remaining two.

Jess fell over to lie in the tall grass.

"Can we climb off these hurricane decks to see about him?" the first hand asked.

"Of course, you can. Just don't try anything stupid."

"Believe me, Mister Jensen, that didn't even cross my mind."

Jess cried out, "I'd like to live to see you get plugged, Jensen!"

"You'd be at the end of a long list," Smoke told him. "You'd best start making your peace with God and tell these boys where to send your saddle."

"You go to hell!" Jess said.

"Jess," one of his buddies said. "Hush now."

"You go to hell, too!" Jess told him. "As a matter of fact, both of you can just go to hell!"

Smoke watched as Highpockets Rycroft and Dick Miles rode up, both of them still looking sort of peaked from their last encounter with Smoke Jensen. Highpockets favored his left arm and Miles wore a pained expression on his face. Obviously, his stomach was still tender.

"What do you two want?" Smoke asked.

"We're on our side of the damn fence!" Highpockets protested. "We ain't botherin' you."

"I find you both offensive to look at," Smoke replied. "I don't want to see either of you again."

"Well, what are you gonna do if you do see us after this?" Dick asked.

"Shoot you."

"Shoot us?" Highpockets hollered. "Now, wait just a minute!"

"What about me?" Jess said.

"You done been shot!" Dick said. "Shut up."

"Or I might decide to hang you," Smoke added.

"Now, just hold on here," Highpockets protested. "We're just cowboys. We push beeves. And that's all. You got my word on that."

"Since when?" Dick blurted before he thought.

"Since right now!" his buddy told him. "And shut your damn mouth, you fool!"

Smoke lifted his .44 and cocked the hammer, pointing it at Dick.

"Whoa!" Dick bellered, throwing both hands into the air. "I ain't touched no gun, Smoke."

"You implied you hired out your gun against me," Smoke told him. "That's good enough for me."

"I didn't do no such a damn thing!" Dick yelled. "I don't even know what that means."

"I'm dyin' and don't nobody seem to care," Jess moaned.

"Well, do so quietly," Highpockets told him. "I got troubles of my own here."

"Shuck out of your gunbelts," Smoke told them.

"Huh?" Dick asked.

Highpockets looked at him. "Dick," he said, unbuckling his belt and letting it fall. "I always knowed you was slow, but you ain't gettin' me killed 'cause of it."

"Oh!" Dick said, and let his guns fall. "Uh, Mister Jensen — are you gonna kill us?"

"Nope. At least, not this time around. But I really think you boys should stop wearing guns. Now, that's not an order. But it *is* a suggestion. However," Smoke slowly let the hammer down on his .44 and all in front of it relaxed, "I might also suggest this." He looked at two standing over Jess. "What are your names?"

"Howie and Biff. I'm Howie. This is Biff."

"That . . . is reasonable," Smoke said. "All right, what I'm about to suggest goes for you two, as well."

"What about me?" Jess whispered.

"Shut up, Jess," Howie told him. "You're supposed to be dyin'."

"I want words spoke over me!" Jess said.

"Do I have to kick you in the head to shut you up?" Howie whispered. "Hush! You were sayin', Mister Jensen?"

"It might seem strange for you men to suddenly stop wearing guns. So if you decide to stay around here, you may wear your guns. But everytime you see me, you throw your hands in the air. If you don't, I'll just have to assume that you're unfriendly. And I'll shoot you."

"Throw . . . our hands in the air ever'time we see you?" Dick questioned.

"That's right. Can you do that?"

"I can do that!" Howie said. "Can you do that, Biff?"

"I can do that!" Biff said quickly. "Yes, sir."

Highpockets raised his hands. Swiftly. "Like this, Mister Jensen?"

"Just like that."

Dick threw his hands into the air. Biff and Howie did the same. They all looked kind of silly.

"We're just cowboys, Mister Jensen," Biff said. "That's all. We ain't gunfighters."

"Fine. When this is all over, if — *if* — you men behave and do like I tell you, you can all go to work for Miss Jenny. She is going to be the new owner of the Triangle JB."

"She is?" Highpockets asked.

"She is. Lower your hands. You'd like working for my niece. She keeps a tubful of doughnuts around all the time. And she bakes pies one day and cakes the next. She's a fine cook."

"I'm hungry now," Biff said.

"I'm dyin'!" Jess hollered. "Don't nobody care about me?"

"You want to take him into town?" Smoke asked.

"He wouldn't make it," Dick said. "He's about done for now."

"Oh, Lord!" Jess cried.

"You'd actually hire us to work for your niece after we rode for Biggers?" Highpockets asked.

"Sure. Just as long as you boys stick to punching cows and not punching or shooting at me," Smoke said with a grin.

"We're out of it," Howie said. "From now on. And that's a promise, Mister Smoke."

"Fine. See you boys." Smoke rode away.

"That's a nice feller there," Howie said. "I sure had him pegged wrong."

"He seemed right sure about Miss Jenny goin' to own the Triangle JB," Dick said.

"I damn sure believed him," Howie replied. "I am a changed man, boys. Believe it."

"What are we gonna do about Jess?" High-pockets asked.

Biff looked down at the would-be gunhand and shook his head. "Get a shovel."

Smoke rode toward the eastern slopes of the mountains that ringed the valley. He felt the men he had left alive by the fence would keep their word. He was a pretty fair hand at judging people, and those men had the appearance of being nothing more than good, working cowboys who'd had the misfortune to sign on with the wrong outfit.

He put the ranch out of his mind. Van Horn and the others would protect it — and Sally and Jenny — with their lives. Smoke had no doubts about that. For now, he had to concentrate on staying alive. He felt that those men by the fence were probably all the real working cowboys Jack Biggers had left on the payroll. All his other hands would be thugs, toughs, hired guns, or men who felt they were good with a gun. And there was a great deal of difference between the two.

Jess had found that out the hard way.

The terrain began to slope upward now, as the valley ended and Buck started the climb upward. The timber was thick here, and Smoke stayed in it. This was his type of country. It was here that he felt most at home and here that, if he had a choice, the fight would begin and end. Smoke was not called the last mountain man without good reason. He was hell on wheels in any type of fight, under any type of circumstances, in any terrain, but in the mountains, he was most effective. He understood the wilderness, the high country, and used it all to his advantage.

He swung down from the saddle, ground-reined Buck, and squatted for a time, building a cigarette and thinking, his eyes never stopping their searching for any sign of trouble.

He decided he'd given the Triangle JB people enough grief for the time being, climbed back in the saddle, and headed north, for Fosburn's spread. He'd see what kind of trouble he could get into up there.

Jess had been a hothead and not much of a cowboy. Jack Biggers summed up Jess's worth and then dismissed him. But it rankled him that Smoke had gunned down another of his men with the ease of stepping on a bug.

And Highpockets and Dick, Biff and Howie, were all behaving strangely since their return to the ranch. But Jack didn't want to chastise them too much; those four were the only real cowboys he had left, and somebody had to do some work around the place. Not that there was that much to do, especially this time of the year. The mountains provided a natural corral for the herds, and the Triangle JB's part of the valley was lush enough to sustain a herd three times the size.

But Jack wanted it all. He even wanted Fat's northern range, and he intended to get it.

What he didn't know was that Fat wanted Jack's part of the valley and Major Cosgrove wanted all of it. Each of the partners had their own little schemes all worked out. Or so they thought.

Jack got a fresh mug of coffee and walked out to sit on the front porch. He spotted High-pockets and Dick, Biff and Howie, and watched them for a moment. He frowned at them. What the hell were they doing?

The four men would walk a few steps, then stop and throw their hands into the air.

"Waco!" he called for his new foreman. His old foreman was one of those who had died in the street in front of the general store when the half dozen or so JB hands had come after Smoke.

"Boss?" Waco said, appearing by the side of the porch.

"What in the hell are those men doing over there by the bunkhouse?"

Waco looked, blinked, took off his hat and scratched his head, and took another look. The four men sure were acting strange. Looked like some sort of a dance to him. He'd never seen cowboys act like that before.

"Well, Boss . . . I can't say as I rightly know. Some of them saloons in town just got in a whole new batch of girls from St. Louis. Maybe that there's some sort of new eastern dance step those boys are tryin' out."

"Well, have them stop it immediately. They

look plumb foolish to me. Looks like a bunch of schoolgirls doin' the do-si-do. Silliest thing I ever seen."

"Yes, sir."

Waco waited until Jack had gone back into the house, then, after taking a slow, careful look all around him to be sure he was not observed, he took three steps, stopped, and threw up his hands. He was not aware that Whisperin' Langley and Val Davis were watching him from a bunkhouse window. "I kinda like it," Waco muttered.

"What the hell is that man doin' over yonder?" Whisperin' said.

"I don't know," Val replied. "But them four over there is doin' it, too."

"Didn't Biff and Howie go into town last night?"

"Yeah. To the saloon where them new gals from St. Louis is workin'. I heard 'em talkin' about it."

"It's a dance. That's what it is. Them gals done brought a new dance out here with 'em. Let's watch so's we can do it, too."

"I ain't much on dancin'."

"That looks easy to me."

Two of the West's most feared and formidable gunslingers looked around the bunkhouse. They were alone. Whisperin' took three steps forward, stopped, and threw up his hands.

"Try it, Val. It's easy."

Val, spurs jingling, took three steps forward,

stopped, and threw up his hands. "Yeah. It is, ain't it?"

Kit Silver had started into the bunkhouse. He paused at the doorway, stared for a moment, and then carefully backed out. He waved for Patmos to join him.

"What's up, Kit?"

"You better watch Whisperin' and Val," Kit warned. "I think they done fell in love. With each other!"

Fifteen

The man felt the rope settle around him and tighten, pinning his arms to his side. He didn't even have time to yell before he was jerked out of the saddle. He landed on his butt, on the ground, the wind ripped from him. He felt himself jerked to his boots and slammed against a tree, and the rope wound around him. When his head stopped spinning, his vision cleared, and he could see and comprehend what was happening, he knew he was in serious trouble.

"You like to make war on young girls, huh?" Smoke asked him.

"Not exactly," the rider gasped. "I just ride for the brand."

"You think you're going to continue doing that?"

"Not if you give me a chance to get gone."

"That might not be necessary," Smoke told him.

"Huh?"

"Did you hire out your guns or your skills with cows and horses?"

"I ain't no fast gun, Mister Jensen. Last time I tried that I damn near shot my foot off. I punch cows and mend fence and brand and . . ."

"I get the picture. How many working cow-boys on Fat's spread?"

"Me and two others. The rest is hired guns. My name's Luddy. My buddies is Dud and Parker."

"Lud and Dud?" Smoke said with a smile.

The cowboy tried to hide a grin. "We been to-gether since we was kids. Parker's all right, too."

Smoke loosened the rope and let it fall. As he was looping it back, he asked, "Step away from the tree. Keep your hand away from your gun."

"You can have it if you want it, Mister Jensen."

"Keep it. Is Fat paying you fighting wages?"

"No, sir. Thirty-five dollars a month and found. I could make more in the mines, but I ain't never liked caves and tunnels."

"Name some of the guns Fat hired."

"Tom Wilson, some guy named Chambers, Dan Segers, Russ Bailey. Then there's Al Jones, Paul Hunt, and some feller named Pell."

"Jim Pell?"

"Yes, sir. That's the one."

"First rate gun-handler. Anybody else?"

"About ten more. I don't know their names and stay out of their way. Then there's Bobby Jewel."

"He's a bad one, all right. Luddy, you tell your buddies to stay out of my way. The same goes for you until this mess is over. And it will be over, and then you can go to work for my niece."

"That's right nice of you, but her place ain't

big enough to support no whole bunch of punchers."

"It will be when *I'm* through."

There was something in Jensen's eyes that told
Luddy this man planned to take the whole damn
valley for his niece. Luddy figured he could do it,
too.

Smoke rode straight onto Fat Fosburn's
range, staying just out of the timber, but close
enough to reach it in a hurry, should the need
arise. He hadn't ridden a mile before he heard a
shout, and that was followed by a gunshot. He
stopped and wheeled Buck around. The fools
were shooting at him with pistols from about a
quarter of a mile away. Six of them. Smoke
waited for a moment, then turned Buck and rode
into the thick timber. He found a game trail and
stayed with it for a few minutes, until coming to
a tangle of brush. He circled around it, found a
place in the back where he could push through,
and swung down from the saddle, taking his rifle
and a bandolier of ammunition. He stripped the
saddle and bridle from Buck and let him freely
roam the small clearing. There was some graze
and a few puddles of rainwater gathered. Plenty
for as long as Smoke planned to be gone.

He took off his spurs and put them in his saddlebags, took a long drink of water, and slipped
out of the tangle, squatting and listening.

Smoke knew immediately these were not
manhunters. This bunch was blundering around

the woods, making enough noise to raise the dead.

"Over here, Willie!" one shouted.

Smoke sighed. Amateurs.

"What'd you find, George?"

"His trail. Come on. We'll get that bounty money and have us a high old time with the ladies."

George and Willie came a-blundering through the timber. Smoke slung his rifle and picked up a goodsized club and hefted it. Then he stepped behind a tree and waited. He didn't know whether it was George or Willie who came foggin' through the brush. Whichever it was got yanked out of the saddle and the club laid up alongside his head. Then he sighed once and went to sleep.

Smoke trussed him up and tossed him in the brush, then caught up the spooked horse and quieted it down, leading it off the dim trail and loosely tying the reins to a branch.

The second half of the pair came up as fast as he could in the brush and timber and yelled, "Where are you, George? Sing out, man!"

Smoke stepped out just behind and to one side and laid the club across the would-be tough's back. The blow knocked him clean out of the saddle and landed him on his face on the rocky ground. Smoke dragged him off the trail and trussed him up beside his careless friend.

"Jackie!" he heard the shout. "Here's Willie's horse. And I ain't seen hide nor hair of George since he shouted out. Ride back to the ranch for more men. We'll keep Jensen pinned down 'til you get back."

"Sure you will," Smoke muttered. "But only if I get careless and you get real lucky."

"Mister Fosburn says no bringin' him back alive," another voice drifted to Smoke. "He's to be cold dead. Then we hit the kid and them old wore-out bassards with her."

That's all I need to know, Smoke thought, then hauled out the two .45s he'd taken from George and let them bang. For a few seconds, the timber trembled with the sounds of rapid-fire pistols. Smoke heard one man holler, but didn't know if it was from a hit or a close slug.

Smoke quickly changed positions and unslung his rifle, earing back the hammer. He waited.

There had been six, maybe seven men who had spotted him. George and Willie were out of it. One had ridden back for reinforcements. Three or four hired guns left. He waited.

His cover was not the best, but Smoke stayed put. His clothing was earth-colored, blending in well with the surroundings. He moved only his eyes, knowing that any movement attracts more attention than small noises. His rifle was in a position where he could fire it one-handed, like a pistol, if need be.

His captive came to and began thrashing about and hollering. The guns of Smoke's pursuers roared and the thrashing ceased.

"You kilt George!" the voice screamed out

from where Smoke had left the pair trussed up. "Oh, my Lord, you blowed half his head off."

"Willie?"

"Yeah."

"You stay put, now. Don't move around none. More men's a-comin'."

Smoke spotted a flash of a red-and-white-checkered shirt and fired, instantly changing position. He heard a cry and the sounds of a man thudding into a tree or log. Smoke knew he'd made a righteous shot.

"I'm hard hit!" a man groaned. "Oh, God, he's shot me in the belly."

"Stay down and quiet. We'll get you out. The boys will be here in a little while."

But by then, I'll be gone, Smoke thought.

On his belly, Smoke began inching his way in a long, slow half circle. As he crawled, he listened to the voices calling back and forth in frustration.

"Cain't nobody see him?"

"I ain't seen him yet."

"I have!" Willie yelled. "Sort of. He's big as a mountain and meaner than a puma."

"He's just a man," another voice added, and this one was so close to where Smoke had crawled it startled him.

"Are you sure George is dead, Willie?"

"Sure? Hell, yes, I'm sure. Half his head is gone."

The man only a few yards from him grew impatient and shifted his weight. Through the thin brush, Smoke could see the man, half-turned away from him. He waited with the patience of a stalking Apache. The man turned his head and Smoke could see his profile. Lucky Harry, a gunfighter from California. Fat had imported some pretty good talent. Willie and George had chosen the wrong profession at the wrong time. But only one of them was left to question the choice . . . if question it he did.

Willie answered that. "I'm loose!" he hollered. "Damn you, Jensen. Me and George was pards. I'm gonna kill you, do you hear me?"

"Idiot," Lucky muttered. Then he was gone, moving silently and swiftly out of Smoke's sight.

Smoke knew that Lucky, and men like him, were as wary as an old wolf. They would take no unnecessary chances. That was why they had stayed alive after years in the man-hunting and gun-for-hire business.

"Damn your murderin', ambushin' heart!" Willie yelled, his voice filled with rage. "Stand up and fight me like a man, Jensen."

Nitwit! Smoke thought. You won't last in this business, boy.

"Git down, you damn fool!" a man called.

Smoke wasn't interested in putting lead in Willie; at least, not at this point. The other men were the dangerous ones, and they weren't going to make any rash moves. Only if Willie threatened him directly would he gun him down.

A slight movement caught Smoke's eyes. Slowly he lifted his rifle. A man's arm came into view. Smoke sighted in the arm and squeezed the trigger. The gunhand screamed in pain as the slug ruined his left elbow. He would go through life with limited use of the arm. Smoke rolled from his position as the lead started whining all around him.

He rolled down into a natural depression and stayed there until the lead stopped singing its deadly song. He groaned loud and long, knowing that surely no one would fall for that old ruse.

But Willie did.

"Got him, by God!" Willie shouted, jumping to his feet. "I'll gut-shoot that sorry no-good."

"Damn!" Smoke muttered, rolling over on his belly and peering over the lip of the depression.

Willie was running toward his position, a rifle in his hands and a wild look on his face.

Smoke knocked a leg out from under him, the slug striking the young man just above the knee and sending him crashing and hollering to the rocky ground. Willie's rifle clattered on the rocks as he grabbed at his leg with both hands. He scooted and hunched for cover, bleeding all the way.

"You better hunt you another line of work, boy," a man's voice called out from behind rocky cover. "You just ain't suited for this one."

Smoke stayed where he was, but shifted a few feet to get behind a bush, scant cover but better than nothing.

The man with the busted elbow could not contain a groan of pain. "I'm bleedin' bad," he called out. "And Boots is dead. This ain't no good."

"All right," the man who seemed to be the leader of this bunch called after a few seconds. "Start backin' down toward where we left the horses. Jensen can't get out. We'll just wait."

"Don't bet he can't get out, Walt," Lucky called. "You don't know Jensen like I do."

Has to be Walt May, Smoke thought. I put lead in him ten years ago. So this will be highly personal for Walt.

"I'm clear," Lucky called. "I got Chookie with me. Willie, you can ride Boots's horse. He ain't got no more use for it."

Chookie must be the one with the busted elbow, Smoke thought.

"I'm a-comin'," Willie called out. "I got to drag this busted leg. I'll kill you someday, Jensen!" he screamed out. "Damn you, I'll kill you."

Smoke reloaded his guns and waited. The sounds of galloping horses drifted to him and he slipped down and picked up the rifle Willie had dropped, taking it with him. He walked over to Boots and took his guns, slinging the gunbelt over one shoulder and picking up his rifle. He looked at the dead George. A slug had entered the man's head from the side, just above the temple area, and made a real mess when it exited.

Smoke saddled up and rode out, but he headed north, not south, staying in the timber.

171

Fat's ranch would be, for the most part, deserted, the men riding hard for the timber. Smoke would see just how much chaos he could cause there, and then ride into town to check on Jenny's "business" interests.

Smoke sat his saddle and watched the dozen or so men ride south, toward his last position. Smoke figured he had maybe thirty minutes, forty at the most, to do his mischief at Fat's ranch. Plenty of time. He loaded up all the pistols and kept the best rifle he'd picked up, discarding the other one.

"All right, Buck," he said. "Let's go be neighborly and pay a visit to Fat's spread."

He stayed on the ridges and in the timber until he was within a half mile of the ranch complex. He could see no one working or loafing around the buildings. Fat was not married, so there was no danger of any women or kids getting hurt. Biggers and Cosgrove were also bachelors. Smoke studied the layout for a few seconds, then smiled.

"Let's go, Buck," he said.

He walked Buck slowly down the ridge and onto the flats. A rider who did not appear to be in any rush attracted little attention. Just another wandering cowpoke riding the grub line.

Smoke swung down in front of the bunkhouse and was greeted by a man wearing a stained apron. "Howdy," the man said. "Coffee's hot and you can fix you a sandwich, if you like."

"That's neighborly of you. Folks down the

way told me to avoid this place. They said it was an unfriendly place."

"It is. That's why tomorrow's my last day. I got me a job down South. You best eat 'fore those no-'count riders Fat hired gets back. That's the surliest bunch I ever seen in all my life."

"Why not leave now?" Smoke suggested.

The man looked at Smoke for a long moment. "Oh, my God! You're . . ."

"That's right."

"I'll be packed and gone in five minutes!"

"You do that."

While Smoke was busy wrecking everything in the main house, the cook galloped away. Smoke dumped out and mixed flour and salt and sugar and coffee and beans. He smashed plates and threw pots and pans outside into the dirt. Using his knife, he slashed feather ticks and ruined blankets and easy chairs. He tore down drapes and curtains and threw them into the dirt of the front yard. Then he set about smashing every window in the house by tossing chairs and benches and footstools through them. He hadn't had so much fun since he was a kid. When there was nothing left in the ranchhouse to smash, break, turn over, or throw in the fireplace, Smoke set fire to the outhouses, tore down the corral and set the horses free, then tossed a flaming torch into the bunkhouse. He decided he might as well burn down the barn, too. So he checked the barn for animals, freed the horses from their stalls, and fired the place.

Back in the saddle, he surveyed all that he had done and sat his saddle for a moment, chuckling. There was going to be a lot of very irritated hired guns in about half an hour. And Fat was going to be as mad as a man could get.

Smoke decided he'd ride into the Golden Plum and have him a drink and something to eat.

He'd worked up quite an appetite, and it wasn't even noon yet.

Sixteen

Stopping just outside of town, Smoke washed up in a creek and brushed the last bits of flour and sugar and so forth from his shirt and jeans. He rode slowly up the twisty street and made sure Sheriff Bowers saw all the gunbelts hanging from his saddle. Bowers' eyes bugged out at the sight. He didn't need a professor to tell him that the men who had worn them would no longer be needing them.

"Morning, Sheriff," Smoke called cheerfully.

"It was," Club said sourly.

Smoke laughed and rode on. He stabled Buck and walked to the Golden Plum. He took a table at the rear of the place, his back to a wall. "A beer and something to eat, Jeff," he told the bartender.

"Right, Boss. Comin' up."

"How's business been?"

"Not good. Major Cosgrove ordered his men not to come in here."

"Did he now?"

"Yes, sir."

"You send your swamper to fetch Cosgrove. Tell him Smoke Jensen says for him to haul his big butt over here. Right now. If he doesn't, I'll come personally and drag it through the mud in the street."

Jeff grinned. "Right away, Boss. This I gotta see."

The swamper left at a trot, just as Club Bowers was walking up. He went to the bar and ordered a beer.

"You'd better not do that, Club," Smoke called. "Your master has forbidden all his slaves not to patronize this place."

Bowers turned around slowly. "Nobody tells me where I go, Jensen."

"Oh, well. If that's the case, by all means drink up and enjoy yourself. I just didn't want you to get into trouble with your lord and master."

"You're pushin', Jensen. Where'd you get all those guns hanging around your saddle?"

"I found them on the road. If their owners show up here, send them out to the ranch to claim them."

"You found them on the road, huh?"

"That's right. Just piled up there. Maybe they're broken. I haven't tried to fire any of them."

"You expect me to believe that?"

"Personally, Club, I don't much give a damn what you believe."

Club did not take exception to that. Smoke Jensen was a study to him. He knew Smoke's history and knew that Jensen was not a trouble-hunter — or had not been, up to this point. You had to push him and then he pushed back. But this time the man had ridden into Red Light pushing from the git-go. This kept up, Jensen would be taking scalps before it was all said and done. Club had heard that the man had done it before. He suppressed a shudder at the thought.

Club turned his back to Smoke and sipped at his beer.

Heavy bootsteps pounded on the boardwalk and the batwings were suddenly slammed open. Major Cosgrove's bulk filled the space. Club turned to look at the man. Major was madder than the sheriff had ever seen him. Jeff stood behind the bar, smiling. Major pointed a finger at Jensen. He was so angry his finger was shaking.

"You, Jensen," Cosgrove's words were almost a yell, "you do not give me orders. You do not send bums over to my office giving me ultimatums."

"You came, didn't you?" Smoke spoke softly.

Cosgrove cussed Smoke, calling the man every filthy word he could think of. Smoke smiled. He had finally succeeded in making the man blow his top.

Club watched Smoke. The smile baffled him. Jensen wanted a fight with Cosgrove. Not a gunfight, but a fistfight. Club was sure of that. But if Jensen thought Major would be easy, he'd best think again. Major Cosgrove was a skilled boxer, not a stupid mass of muscle like Mule Jackson. Jensen could probably whip Major, but both men would be a bloody mess when it was over.

"Major," Smoke said, after taking a sip of coffee. "You tell your workers they can patronize any business in this town they choose to. This is America, not some dictatorship. And you are not king in this town. Nor am I. But I'll tell you what I am. I'm a man who despises those who would make war against a young girl. Physically or financially. I'm going to stay in town until after the first shift ends at the mine. This place better fill up, Major. Because if it doesn't, I'm coming after you. And if I have to do that, one of us will be the guest of honor at a burying. Do you understand that?"

Major Cosgrove stood rock still for a moment. He was so angry he could not speak. He opened and closed his mouth half a dozen times, but no words came out. With an effort that was visible to all in attendance, he began calming himself. It was showdown time, and he knew it. And he could not afford to go into it so angry it overrode logic.

"Major . . ." Club started to protest, as he realized what the man was about to do. He cut his eyes at a movement on the second-floor landing. Moses stood there, a double-barreled sawed-off shotgun in his hands. At the other end of the landing, Clementine Feathers and several of her girls had gathered, all with rifles. Behind him and to his right, Jeff the bartender stood with a ten gauge sawed-off Greener.

Smoke still sat at his table, a strange smile on

178

his lips. Outside, the sounds of hard-ridden horse thundered up the street and the rider jumped off in front of the mayor's office.

"Mister Fosburn!" the shout was heard. "That damn Smoke Jensen done ruined your ranch and killed George and Boots. He wounded two, three more and burned down the barn and the bunkhouse and all the outhouses. He tore down the corral and scattered the horses all to hell and gone."

Major's face tightened and he clenched his big hands into big fists. Running boots were heard on the boardwalk and the batwings slammed open. Fat Fosburn stood there, his face red with anger. He spied Smoke.

"You! You . . . God damn you, Jensen. Club, I want that man arrested immediately."

Club got all tight and cold inside as Smoke cut his eyes to him. Now it was down to the nut-cuttin'.

"Did you hear me, Club?" Fat hollered.

"I heard you." Club was thinking hard. "Who saw Jensen do this?"

"Why . . ." That brought Fat up short. "Hell, I don't know. Somebody must have."

"Naw," the rider who brought the news said, standing just outside the batwings. "All the men was gone up on the ridges after Smoke. And the cook packed his kit and took off to Lord knows where."

"Well, why in the hell did you say it was Jensen, then, Parker?" Fat hollered.

" 'Cause he was the one the boys was after, that's why. I was out working cattle with Dud. I don't know where in the hell Luddy is. I seen the smoke from the fires come a-foggin'. Willie was there with a bullet in his leg, and Chookie's arm is busted."

"Then nobody saw Jensen do anything?" Club questioned, waves of relief washing over him. It was not fear of the man — just plain ol' common sense.

"I reckon not," Parker said, slipping in and walking to the end of the bar. He then got his first good look at Smoke Jensen. Lord, the man looked awesome.

Major removed his tie and collar and dramatically rolled up his sleeves.

Smoke stood up and took off his gunbelt.

Major did a couple of deep kneebends and fired some lefts and rights into the air. He held his arms out and shook them a time or two.

Smoke waited.

"Nobody gives me orders in this town, Jensen," Major said. "I run Red Light."

"Not after today," Smoke replied.

Major stopped his jumping around and shadow boxing. "I'm not Mule Jackson."

"You're going to resemble him when I'm through with you."

Fat Fosburn eased himself to the edge of the bar and stood beside Parker. He signaled to Jeff for a beer.

"Get it yourself," Jeff told him.

180

"No one will interfere in this," Major said, his voice firm. "You hear me, Club?"

"I hear you."

"Fat?"

"I hear you, Major."

He returned his eyes to Smoke. "Are we going to fight like gentlemen, Smoke?"

"Nope."

"I suppose it was foolish of me to expect that from someone of your caliber."

"You're not going to make me mad, either, Major. But if I were you, I wouldn't brag too much about how high-class you are. I've never made war against young girls."

Major flushed deeply, but he held any comments. This was a fight he had to have, and a fight he had to win. He had humiliated himself in front of several hundred people by shouting that he'd sue Smoke if the man struck him. That had been a foolish thing to do, since Major felt he was a much better boxer than Jensen, and infinitely more intelligent.

He was wrong on both counts.

Deputy Reed stepped in and quickly sized up the situation.

"Stand over here by me, Reed," Club said. "And don't interfere. Them's Mister Cosgrove's orders."

Smoke stood a step toward Major, pulling on riding gloves as he walked.

Major smiled. "No need for that if you soak your hands in brine, and I did back East when I

181

was a young prizefighter. And I was a very good prizefighter."

"You fight your way, I'll fight mine," Smoke told him. "But your hands look mighty soft to me."

"You'll soon find out they are not." Major Cosgrove lifted his fists and assumed the stance.

"Then come on, Major. Show me. Prove it. You're about to put me to sleep with all this talk. That's about the only way you could win it. Talk me to death."

Major tucked his chin down toward his shoulder and advanced. Smoke thought he looked ridiculous, one arm all stuck out and the other pulled back. And with his head jerked down like that, he looked all cockeyed.

Smoke laughed at the man. "You're about the silliest-looking thing I believe I ever did see."

Major lunged at him and tried to fake him out. Smoke didn't fall for it. Major snapped a left at him and Smoke flicked it away. Still he did not attempt to land a blow against Cosgrove.

The two big men circled each other. Smoke said, "I win, you call off the boycott against this saloon."

"Agreed," Major said, then swung a wicked right that just missed. "I win, you leave town."

"Agreed," Smoke said. "But don't get your hopes up too high." Then he knocked the living hell out of Major.

The blow seemed to come out of nowhere and staggered the big man backward. It was not unlike being kicked by a horse. The blow had caught him flush on the mouth and bloodied his lips, sending pain coursing through his head. Before he could get set, Smoke pressed and hit him four times, two lefts and two rights to the head that hurt.

Major Cosgrove felt his jaw beginning to swell and knew one eye would soon be closing from the terrible blow. He backed up, shaking his head. The blood flew with the effort.

Outside the saloon, a huge crowd had gathered, threatening to collapse the boardwalk. About fifty men had run around to the rear and entered through the back door of the saloon, lining the walls, most of them thinking that this was much better than a gunfight. It lasted longer.

Major Cosgrove knew now that he was in for the fight of his life. Smoke Jensen was no common brawler. The man had studied boxing and knew the moves.

Smoke certainly was no common brawler, although he could brawl with the best of them. He knew kick-and-gouge, boxing, rough-and-tumble, and Indian wrestling. And he was going to show Major Cosgrove a little bit of all of it.

Smoke pushed in and took a right to his head. The blow had power behind it and it hurt, splitting the skin. But it didn't slow him down. Ignoring a hastily thrown left from Cosgrove, Smoke plowed in, hooking a half dozen blows to the wind of the big man, bringing gasps of pain and backing him up. Major dropped his guard for just a second and Smoke seized the moment. He reared back and busted Major flush in the chops, scoring the first clear knockdown of the fight.

Major landed heavily on the floor and lay there for a moment, looking dazed and disbelieving that something like this could happen to him.

"Stay down and catch your wind!" Fat hollered.

Smoke backed up and gave the man a chance to climb to his boots.

Major glared balefully at the man. "I thought you weren't going to fight like a gentleman," he panted, blood dripping from his busted lips.

Smoke shrugged his shoulders and waited, letting his hands hang to his sides.

Major struggled to his boots. The entire front of his white shirt was now stained with blood. One eye was closing and his face was bruised.

Club picked up a pitcher of water from the bar and walked to Cosgrove, pouring it on his head. Major shook his head and bloody water flew in all directions. The men lining the saloon walls were silent.

"Thanks, Club," Cosgrove said. "That helped." He wiped his eyes on his sleeves of his shirt and lifted his fists. "I'm ready, Jensen."

"I'll call it off and we'll shake hands, Major," Smoke replied. "Then you leave Jenny alone and everybody will be friends. How about it?"

"I haven't even got my first wind yet, gunfighter," Major replied.

"Then that makes you a fool," Smoke flatly

told him. "I'll not give you another break."

"I know how you fight now," Cosgrove said.

Smoke smiled and lifted his fists. "Then come on, bigshot. Take your lickin' like a man."

With a curse and a roar, Major Cosgrove charged Smoke, both big fists windmilling.

Seventeen

Smoke was forced to back up under the savage, almost mindless onslaught. He caught two blows from the windmilling Major. One big fist struck him on the side of the head and knocked him back. Another slammed into his side and brought a grunt of pain from his lips. Smoke quickly recovered and ducked and sidestepped the wildly charging man, still shouting curses and dumping dire verbal threats on Smoke's head.

Smoke smacked Major on the jaw with a left and stopped him in his tracks with a right to the mouth that further pulped the man's lips and brought a dazed look to his eyes. Seizing the opportunity while it was available, Smoke set himself and hammered at Major's face. The blows drove the man back, his backward movement knocking over chairs and shoving tables aside.

Smoke pursued the man, relentless in his attack, while Cosgrove's supporters stood by and watched their boss get the crap kicked out of him, all of them well aware of the rifles and shotguns ready to crack and boom should they make any attempt to interfere.

Many of the miners in the town stood in the street and listened to the smacking of fists against flesh and the cracking of chair legs and made no attempt to hide their smiles. Most had no love for Major Cosgrove.

Major grabbed up a chair and splintered it over Smoke's shoulders. Smoke had turned just in time to prevent the chair from taking him in the face. So much for Major conducting himself as a gentleman. The chair had torn Smoke's shirt and bruised and cut the flesh on his shoulders and upper back.

Smoke backed up, picked up a chair, and hurled it at Cosgrove, the chair striking the man in the face and chest and knocking him off his feet. He hit the floor with a mighty crash that shook the walls and windows. Smoke backed off and let the man get up. Major was much slower getting to his feet this time. Blood dripped from his nose and mouth. His breathing was ragged. Each time he exhaled, he sprayed blood.

"Give it up, man," Smoke urged.

"To hell with you, gunfighter!" Major spat the words mixed with blood.

Smoke stepped in close and drove a big right fist through Major's guard that connected solidly with the man's jaw. Major swayed on his feet for a second and then called on his deep reserves of strength and recovered. He pressed in, stumbling as he came.

Smoke hit the man in the belly and drove a savage left hook into his ribs. Major cried out and turned. Smoke pounded his kidneys and Major crawfished back, his bloody face a mask of hurt.

Smoke did not let up. He pressed hard, driving both fists into Major's face, smashing his nose and further pulping his lips.

"Go down, Major!" Fat called out.

But Cosgrove only shook his battered head and stayed on his boots.

But not for long.

Smoke stepped up and swung a wicked right, the fist colliding against Major's jaw. Part of a tooth flew out of the man's mouth and he cried out as he went to his knees. Club Bowers winced at just the sound of the blow. The sheriff knew that after this fight, no one in his right mind would challenge Smoke Jensen to toe the line with fists. Mule Jackson still lay battered and broken in bed, and within moments, Major Cosgrove would probably be in the bed next to his foreman.

Major Cosgrove gripped the side of a sturdy table and slowly pulled himself to his feet. The man cannot be faulted for lack of courage, Smoke thought. On his boots, Major lifted his fists and advanced. His face was bruised and torn, and one eye was closed. The man's expensive shirt was in bloody tatters, his suspenders hanging down, ripped and flopping. His britches were torn and dusty from the floor of the saloon. Still he pressed on.

Smoke feigned and Major bought it. That was all Smoke needed. He smashed at the man with wicked blows to the face, driving Cosgrove back, stumbling and staggering. Smoke hit the man in the belly with everything he could put behind a punch, and Major doubled over, his face white with sickness. Smoke gave him a savage upper-cut that straightened Major up to his toes. Smoke stepped in and hooked to the side of the jaw, and Major went down. This time, he did not move.

Smoke stepped to the bar and picked up a pitcher of water, pouring it on his head. Jeff handed him a bar towel and Smoke dried his face. "Club, tell the men outside to come in and have a drink on me. This place is now open for business to all who want to come in."

Major Cosgrove did not show his face on the streets of Red Light until one week after the fight in the Golden Plum. Even then, his face was still mottled with fading bruises and marked with healing cuts. He walked slowly because of several still badly bruised ribs. His anger had now been replaced with a savage hatred for Smoke Jensen and everything and everybody connected with him. Which came as no surprise to Smoke when he was informed of it. He was well aware that men of Cosgrove's ilk are not rational people. He had given Cosgrove the opportunity to shake hands and live and let live. The man had refused it. Smoke knew now that the killing fields were fertile and would soon blossom blood-red with the flowers of death.

"You two do not leave the ranch," he told Sally and Jenny. "Cosgrove has got to make a move against us here. His long-distance shooter, Hankins, has been in this area for several days. Right now he's up on the ridges mapping out the best places to shoot from. Indians have spotted him and told Bad Dog. It's all down to the wire now."

Smoke walked the grounds of the ranch complex. All fire barrels were full. The area had been cleared of excess brush and anything else that might burn. Smoke had worked along the others, cutting the tall grass for several hundred yards all around the complex and then burning what was left down to the roots, leaving the area void of hiding places. Sneaking up on the ranch would be nearly impossible.

One week after the fight in the Golden Plum, Sally told Smoke they had to have supplies.

Smoke nodded his agreement. "I'll take Wolf, Bad Dog, and Barrie with me. We'll take two wagons. The rest of the men will stay here."

She stared up at him. "It's close to the end now, isn't it?"

"A few more weeks and it'll be over. Surely no more than a month. You know I've never held back from you, Sally. There'll be an all-out effort to kill me now."

"That's been tried before, honey."

"I seem to recall a few times, yes." Smoke kissed her. "You better see to bandages and alcohol and ointments and so forth. I have a hunch we're all going to get bloodied before this fight is over."

"Then why don't they come on out here and try to run me off?" Jenny said, considerable heat in her young voice.

Smoke and Sally turned. The youngster stood with a .45 belted around her waist and a rifle in her hands.

"Now you just calm down," Sally told her, walking to the girl's side.

"No, Aunt Sally. I won't calm down. My mother left this ranch to me. And the . . . businesses in town. I have a *right* to live here and be safe. I won't let Fosburn and Biggers and Cosgrove and their hoodlums interfere with my life another time. But I have no right to ask somebody else to fight and die for me." She walked to an open window. "Mister Van Horn!" she hollered.

Van Horn was standing just outside the window and nearly jumped out of his boots. "Yes, ma'am, Miss Jenny?"

"See that my horse is saddled. I am going to town and handle my own affairs."

"Yes, *ma'am!*"

Smoke tried to hide a grin but failed miserably. He wanted to tell his niece that it would be extremely dangerous for her to ride into town. But the girl had Jensen blood flowing in her veins, and to the best of his knowledge, no Jensens on his side of the family had ever shirked their duty, at least, as they saw it. Even his sister Janey, no-'count as she might have been, had done her best to raise a good girl and see to her

191

future. That counted for something.

Van Horn led a dainty-stepping paint pony up to the house. The mare was not a big horse, but it had a heart as big as any horse on the spread and it loved its master. Jenny had fallen in love with the paint at first sight and had gentled it herself.

Jenny went outside and booted her rifle and swung into the saddle. Sally looked at Smoke and together they laughed softly.

"She's a Jensen, all right," Sally said. "Well, I shall have a roast prepared for this evening's meal."

"With plenty of carrots and potatoes and a big bowl of thick gravy?" Smoke asked hopefully.

"Why, of course." She thumped his big chest with a small fist. "And if you're late, and supper gets cold, you will, Smoke Jensen, answer to *me!*"

"Yes, *ma'am!*" Smoke said.

Wolf and Bad Dog rode the wagons, Jenny rode beside Smoke at the head of the procession, and Barrie rode rear guard. The town-tamer had grown thinner in the few weeks since he'd signed on, and Smoke suspected the man was seriously ill and wanting to go out in a blaze of glory. Even though Barrie had not let up on his working around the ranch, Smoke had noticed he always kept a bottle of pain-killing laudanum handy.

"I'm going to ride back with Barrie for a time, Jenny," Smoke told his niece. "You lead this parade, okay?"

"Yes, sir."

Barrie looked at him as he swung back and fell in beside him on the bumpy road. "How far along is your cancer, Barrie?" Smoke asked.

Barrie grunted. "How'd you know?"

"Just a guess."

"Doc down in Butte said I might last out the summer. But that the end would be no way for a man to go. I don't intend to go out screamin' in pain."

"Not much I can say, is there?"

"Not a thing, Smoke. I'm just proud to have had the chance to ride with you and to help out that young lady up yonder. My own daughter would have been about three years older than her."

"Would have been?"

"Outlaws killed her when she was just a baby. And after they had their way with my wife, they killed her, too."

"I do know the feeling."

"Yeah. I know the story. Summer of '72, wasn't it?"

Smoke nodded, the memories rushing back.

"Something like that tears a man wide open," Barrie said. "It leaves a terrible invisible wound that don't never really heal. You got the ones who done it to your wife and baby. I got the ones who did it to mine. And now, you and me got the same opinion of outlaws."

"For a fact, we do. Does Van Horn know?"

"Oh, yeah. Me and that old *pistolero* go way back. He learned me about guns. I'd appreciate it if you wouldn't tell no one else."

"I won't."

"You know where that ol' lightnin'-blazed tree is up on the east slope, above that little spring?"

"Yes."

"Plant me there. I want to listen to the winds blow and the wolves howl. I always liked wolves. Never had no quarrel with them. I like to think they'll come down an' visit me from time to time. Jenny will come see me now and then, too. I know she will; she's a good girl. Makes a man feel good to know his final restin' place will have visitors ever' now and then."

"You sound like you're telling me good-bye, Barrie."

"Pain's gettin' worser. I can near 'bouts control it with laudanum, but I don't know for how much longer. I may not get another chance to say my farewells."

"I'd ride the river with you anytime, Barrie," Smoke said simply.

"That's mighty high praise, comin' from you, Smoke. Now you go back up yonder and ride beside that little niece of yours." He smiled. "She's got spunk, that one. She'll do. Van Horn thinks the world and all of her. So do I."

Smoke rode ahead to join Jenny. She looked at him. "Everything all right, Uncle Smoke?"

"It will be, baby. It will be."

Smoke knew they were in trouble the instant they rode into town. The boardwalk in front of every saloon, and gambling house was lined with strangers, each wearing one or two tied-down guns. Smoke knew some of them. Cosgrove, Biggers, and Fosburn had sent for the best they could find within a week's ride of the town. He spotted the man called Keno. Standing beside him was the Texas outlaw, Burt Nevins. Sitting down was Amos Mann, from over Nebraska way. Directly across the street were the King twins, Vern and Eddie. They smiled at Jenny and tipped their hats.

"Goddamn worthless trash!" Both Smoke and Jenny heard Wolf mutter hotly. "I hope they has the audacity to speak direct to that girl. I'll gut both of them."

Jenny grinned and looked back at him.

"Don't pay no nevermind to that pair of white trash, girl," Wolf said.

"Old man," Vern called, his face red from the remark. "You'd best watch your mouth before I take a notion to jerk you off that wagon and stomp your guts out."

Wolf whoaed the wagon and hopped down, leaving the wagon in the middle of the street. He walked over to the boardwalk, stepped up on it, and knocked the gunhand smooth off the boards and onto the ground. Turning, he smashed one huge, gnarled old fist into the gut of Eddie, doubling the man over and putting him gagging and puking on the boards. Vern crawled to his knees and tried to reach for a gun. With no more emotion than he'd feel stomping on a scorpion, Wolf kicked the man in the face, then reached down, pulled their guns from leather, and tossed them into a watering trough. Then, without looking back, he climbed back to the wagon seat and clucked the team.

Chuckling, Smoke lifted the reins and moved out. Jenny looked back and winked at Wolf.

The old mountain man blushed.

"Don't you be actin' brazen, now, girl," he called to her. "It ain't comely."

While others of their ilk were trying to get the King twins up on their wobbly feet, Smoke and the small procession were entering the next block on the twisty street. Smoke's eyes narrowed as he spotted Rod Ivey standing beside Lonesome Ted Lightfoot. On the other side of Lightfoot stood Sam Jackson, one of the most worthless men ever to pull on a pair of boots. Standing behind him was the Missouri Ridge-Runner, Clayton Charles.

"They're sure scrapin' the bottom of the barrel with this crowd, ain't they?" Wolf called.

"For a fact," Smoke called over his shoulder. "Back-shooters, the whole bunch of them."

"All these men gathered against us," Jenny said, her voice small. "I don't understand it."

Barrie had ridden up even with Bad Dog. "I have never seen so much human garbage in one place. Look there," he said, cutting his eyes. "Jesse Griffin and Kell Duffin. Those two are the scum of the earth."

Bad Dog nodded his head. "I saw Louie Devine and Ossie Burks, too. One thing bothers me, Barrie. If the men fighting this one very nice little girl have so much money they can afford to hire all this scum, why do they want one small spread?"

"Power, my friend," the dying town-tamer said.

"The white side of me understands that," the breed said. "The Indian side of me does not understand the yearning for more than a person needs to live comfortably."

"It's a mystery, for sure."

The wagons were pulled in behind the large general store. Smoke told Jenny, with a firmness to his words that the girl knew better to cross, to stay inside the store. He smiled at her to soften his words. "You pick out something pretty for Sally. Some cloth, maybe. Something. It's going to take a good hour to choose and load these supplies. Barrie will stay with you. I'll be about."

"Are you going to start something, Uncle Smoke?" the girl whispered.

"I might as well begin cutting the odds some, Jenny. Just remember this: all those men out there came here to kill you and me, and to help some very ruthless men to take something that doesn't belong to them. This is pure black and white, Jenny. There is no gray."

Smoke checked both guns and loaded up full. He walked behind the counter and took down a sawed-off double-barreled shotgun, broke it open, and loaded it up. He put a handful of shells in his jacket pocket. "Put this on my bill,"

197

he told the very nervous shopkeeper. He looked at Barrie. "Stay with Jenny. For sure they'll try to kill her this day."

"They got to go through me to do it," the town-tamer said. "And that ain't no easy task."

Smoke looked at the shopkeeper. "How do you stand in all this?"

"Neutral!"

"That figures." Smoke stepped out of the store and onto the boardwalk. He looked at Bad Dog, standing a few yards away. The man had found a chicken feather on the street and had stuck it in his hair. The halfbreed Cheyenne had a strange sense of humor.

"Count plenty coup today," Bad Dog spoke in broken English, a smile playing on his lip. "Take heap scalps." Then he laughed out loud.

"I happen to know that you graduated the eighth grade and had offers to go to college," Smoke said drily.

"Don't spread it around," Bad Dog said. "It would destroy the image I've worked so hard to cultivate."

"Right, Clarence."

Bad Dog groaned. "Especially don't let *that* get out. How did you discover my real name?"

The faint sounds of a trumpet reached the center of town. Within seconds, the booming of a bass drum came to them.

"Here come them damn Bible shouters," Wolf said, walking up. "Man over yonder at the assayer's office told me they was gonna hold a parade and a meetin' today."

The sounds of "Onward Christian Soldiers" rolled up the street.

"Wonder where the sheriff and his deputies are," Smoke said.

"They was all called out of town for some reason or the other."

"How nice for them."

The tooting and the drumming and the singing grew louder.

"Hey, old man!" Vern King shouted, walking up the boardwalk, his brother beside him. "This is your day to die, you son-of-a-bitch!"

The old mountain man didn't bat an eye or change expression. He just one-handedly lifted and leveled his Winchester model '73, .44-.40, thumbed the hammer back, and let it bang. The big slug caught the twin in the belly and doubled him over, dropping him screaming to the boards. His brother jumped for cover and the fight was on.

Vern rolled off the boards to land in the dirt, both hands holding his punctured belly.

Smoke saw a two-bit would-be tough who rode for Fat jerk both .45s from leather. He leveled the shotgun and gave the punk both barrels from across the narrow street. The charge lifted the thug off his boots and sent him crashing through a store window.

"Behind you, Uncle Smoke!" Jenny screamed from the store.

Smoke turned to see a wild-eyed man with a

knife in his hand coming up fast. He reversed the heavy shotgun and smashed the man's skull with the stock, splintering the wood and rendering the express gun useless. Smoke pulled iron and went to work.

Two of Cosgrove's toughs jumped onto the loading dock of the general store, rifles in their hands. They made it as far as the back door before running into Barrie. The town-tamer gave them .45-caliber frontier justice, the slugs knocking them back and sending them tumbling off the dock and onto the ground. Barrie twirled his .45s and waited.

Jenny lined up a rifleman on the roof of a store across the street and plugged him through the brisket with her short-barreled carbine. The sniper fell over the side, crashing through the awning and bouncing off the boardwalk.

Bad Dog took out two in just about as many seconds. His guns left the pair motionless in the street, both shot through the heart.

The temperance parade was briefly halted as the paraders jumped for cover, but the shouting and singing was only momentarily silenced. "Sing, brothers and sisters!" Violet shrieked from her station behind a horse trough. "Play, musicians!" she hollered.

The tooting and the drumming began. The choir was only a tad ragged.

Paul Hunt found Smoke Jensen and lined him up in his sights. Before he could pull the trigger he saw fire and smoke erupt from the muzzle of

Smoke's .44. A heavy blow struck him in the belly and he sat down hard, his .45 slipping from numb fingers. His last living thought was that this couldn't be happening to him. It just couldn't.

But it did.

Paul Hunt fell over in the dirt and closed his eyes for the last time.

"Help me, Eddie!" Vern hollered.

Eddie ran out to help his brother and jumped very quickly back behind cover as lead howled all around him. Wolf Parcell shoved cartridges into his .44-.40 and waited, crouched behind a barrel.

Pony Harris galloped his horse up the street, the reins in his teeth and both hands on pistols. Smoke shot him off his Triangle JB mount and the gun-for-hire rolled in the street. He rolled up onto the boardwalk and crashed through a window. He died in front of the receiving counter of Chung Lee's laundry, with Mister Lee shrieking Chinese curses at him.

Several Fosburn men charged the rear of the general store and were cut down by withering rifle and pistol fire from Jenny and Barrie. The young girl and the sick town-tamer stood side by side and stacked up the bodies. The shopkeeper and his wife had hit the floor behind the counter and stayed there.

Fat Fosburn, Jack Biggers, and Major Cosgrove lay on the floor of the mayor's office and wondered how the battle was going. Outnumbered fifty-to-one, surely Smoke and his crew and that damn snip of a girl would be dead before long.

The general store was across the street and just kitty-cornered from the mayor's office. Jenny had a wicked look in her eyes as she left Barrie to guard the rear and punched rounds into her carbine as she walked to the front of the store. She took down several rifles from the rack, loaded them all up, and stacked them beside her. Then she started methodically putting .44-caliber holes in the mayor's office.

"Jesus Christ!" Biggers hollered, as the lead began howling and shrieking all around them. A round struck the stove, whined off, and just missed Fosburn's head. Fosburn started hollering in fright. Major Cosgrove lay on his still-bruised belly and cursed the unknown rifleman.

Smoke was crouched in the alley between the general store and an empty building. He carefully chose his targets and seldom missed. Wolf Parcell and Bad Dog had chosen good cover and were making each round count.

Most of the hired guns had elected to stay out of this pitched battle. It had started out bad for their side and was getting worse. The singing and the drumming and tooting stayed constant from the far end of town.

The second block of Red Light was littered with the dead and the dying. The gunfire gradually died down, and then silence filled the street.

Cosgrove, Biggers, and Fosburn crawled to

their hands and knees and peered out the shattered window of the mayor's office. They stared in disbelief at the body-littered street. A few of the less severely wounded were attempting to crawl to the boardwalk. Doc White was in the street, along with some volunteers, picking up the wounded and carrying them off.

Smoke had reloaded and was walking down the center of the street. He stopped in front of the mayor's office. "Cosgrove! Biggers! Fosburn! Let's settle it now. The three of you against me alone. In the street. Come on, you yellow-bellied mice. You're eager to fight a seventeen-year-old girl. Try me. Here's your chance."

"Kill that son-of-a-bitch!" Cosgrove screamed from the office. "That's what you men are getting paid for."

Smoke jumped to one side and rolled into an alley as the street once more erupted in lead and gunsmoke.

Jenny took aim at the office and pulled the trigger, her slug sending wood splinters into Cosgrove's face. He hollered in pain and hit the floor, Biggers and Fosburn right behind him.

"Here come my boys!" Biggers yelled, as pounding hooves began echoing along the narrow street.

Fosburn peeked over the bullet-shattered window sill. "And my crew, too!" he hollered. "By God, it'll soon be over for Jensen now."

I'll believe it when I see it, Cosgrove thought. But he stayed on the floor. That damn girl over there in the general store was too good a shot.

Biggers had his hat blown off his head and he quickly joined Cosgrove on the glass-littered floor. Fosburn yelped in fright as one of his men was blown out of the saddle by a blast from a shotgun and the bloody body was flung onto the boardwalk. It rolled up to the bullet-shattered door, which was hanging by one hinge, and into the office. The blast had very nearly torn the man in two.

Across the street, Moses reloaded his Greener and let it bang. One of Biggers' men was tossed out of the saddle as if hit with a giant fist.

"Somebody kill that goddamn nigger!" Lonesome Ted Lightfoot yelled. He stood on the stoop of a dress shop.

Moses turned and pulled the trigger just as Lonesome hit the boards. The charge went over his head and blew a hole the size of a water bucket in the wall. Lonesome jumped into the dress shop and ran into a fully gowned manne-quin. Lonesome and the mannequin hit the floor, his spurs all tangled up in the gown. Miss Alice, owner of the shop, ran out of a back room just as Lonesome was getting to his feet. She hit him on the back of the head with a flatiron and Lonesome sighed and hit the floor. He was out of this fight.

Smoke and Bad Dog fired at the same time, the pistol slugs slamming a Triangle JB rider out of the saddle and to the ground. One of his own men rode a horse right over him.

Jenny screamed and Smoke dived through an open side window of the general store. Barrie was down, blood streaming from a cut on his head, and Jenny was grappling with Lucky Harry.

Lucky was grinning at her and holding both her hands in one of his, his other hand roaming over her body, touching her in places that made her face redden.

Lucky's luck was rapidly leaving him.

Smoke closed the distance, jerked Lucky from the girl, and savagely broke the man's right arm, popping it clean at the elbow. Lucky screamed from the pain and passed out. Smoke bodily picked him up and threw him through the one remaining store front window. The unconscious gunhand bounced off the boardwalk and fell into the path of a galloping horse.

Lucky's luck had run out.

The band had stopped playing and the singers ceased their singing and everyone had sought better cover. The temperance parade was over for that day.

Barrie's wound was not a serious one, and Smoke got him back on his feet while Jenny stopped the bleeding with a compress.

"Get in here!" Smoke called to Wolf and Bad Dog. "This thing is far from over."

The men dashed for the cover of the solidly built store.

"They got us cold, Smoke," Bad Dog said. "Must be fifty or sixty men still on their feet out there. They're all around the place."

The storekeeper and his wife had fled for the safety of another part of town.

"Are we trapped, Uncle Smoke?" Jenny asked.

Smoke's eyes had found several wooden crates stacked off to one side of the store. He smiled. "*They* think we are," he said.

Eighteen

"Out the back way, quickly!" Major said. "We can end this today if we seize the moment."

The three men behind the drive to kill Jenny Jensen and lay claim to her ranch and the gold that was in the mountains gathered a few of their most trusted hired guns and laid out their plans.

Inside the general store, every available rifle, pistol, and shotgun in stock was loaded up full and placed close to hand. Clemmie Feathers had gathered up her Soiled Doves and barricaded them on the second floor of the Golden Plum. They were armed with the rifles and pistols Moses had picked up from the fallen gunhands. Moses and Clemmie remained on the first floor of the saloon, along with Jeff the bartender and a few citizens who had the nerve to come out against Cosgrove, Biggers, and Fosburn.

The Red Light, Montana, Temperance League had wisely decided to give up their plans for a parade that day. When the shooting stopped, they had left their rather precarious cover and taken refuge in the livery, just down the twisty street from all the action.

In the general store, the small band of defenders had erected barricades of barrels and sacks of feed and Smoke had told everyone to grab something to eat while they had time. He was sitting on the sack of feed, calmly eating from a can of peaches.

Wolf Parcell shifted his wad of chewing tobacco and said, "This reminds me of the time me and Frenchy Ladue and Lobo and Powder Pete and Preacher was trapped in a cabin with about two hundred angry Kiowas outside. It got right chancy there for a time, but we held 'em off to a standstill. We had plenty of powder and shot and vittles. But we did get on each other's nerves there toward the end."

"How long were you trapped in there?" Jenny asked.

"Five days, as I recall," Wolf replied. "Them Kiowas finally just give up in disgust and rode off. We must have kilt a hundred of 'em."

Smoke tossed his empty peach can into a garbage barrel and stood up. Barrie and Bad Dog were defending the rear of the store. Smoke, Jenny, and Wolf stood by at the front.

"I can't believe they'll try a charge," Jenny said.

"They'll try one," Wolf said. "We ain't dealin' with the most intelligent folks in the world. Them's hired guns out yonder. Too damn lazy to work and too stupid to realize that ridin' the outlaw trail is harder work than near 'bouts anything else they might do. They're cowards, most of 'em. Almost all bullies is. But what worries me is, ain't none of us seen hide nor hair of that back-shooter, Hankins. He could be out at the ranch right now, worryin' the fool out of our people."

"I have a hunch that's exactly where he is," Smoke said, earing back the hammer on his Winchester and pulling the stock to his shoulder. "But that house is a fort, and he can't get much closer than five or six hundred yards. Besides, we'll be out of this bind in a few hours and back at the ranch an hour later." He sighted in and gently took up slack on the trigger. The Winchester barked and a man screamed a second after the slug shattered his ankle.

"You got a plan, Smoke?" Barrie carried, a bloody bandage around his head.

"Ten cases of dynamite over yonder in the corner," Smoke replied. "Plenty of caps and fuses. The street is narrow, and that makes for an easy toss. We'll liven up their day when the time is right and then make our break for it. One man with a rifle can hold off an army at the curve of the mountain road coming into town." He smiled. "Then I'll blow it closed and catch up with you before you reach the ranch."

Bad Dog chuckled his approval. "It is a good plan. But no," he contradicted. "I shall hold off the men and blow the pass. You need to be with Jenny and the wagons."

"He's right, Smoke," Barrie called.

"Suits me." Smoke listened for a moment. The street had grown very quiet.

"They're gettin' ready to make a charge,"

Wolf said. "They'll come all at once, front and back. Get set."

Smoke looked at Jenny. The teenager had tossed her hat to one side and tied a bandanna around her forehead. Her face was sooty from the gunsmoke, but her hands were steady holding the short-barreled carbine. A bandolier of cartridges was slung across her chest and she had belted a second gunbelt around her slender waist.

Wolf caught Smoke's eyes and grinned and nodded his shaggy head. Then he spat a stream of brown juice, stopping a scurrying roach cold on the floor, pulled his rifle to his shoulder, and said, "Here they come."

The men charged with a roar, and with a roar ten times as deadly, those inside the store fired, working the levers on their Winchesters as fast as they could. Smoke dropped his empty rifle and filled his hands with deadly .44s. Twelve rounds sounded as one long booming. When the shooting stopped, a dozen men lay dead, dying, or badly wounded in the street.

Reloading, Jenny asked, "Uncle Smoke? What will happen to Moses and Miss Clemmie and the girls once we leave?"

"Nothin', child," Wolf said. "All they've done so far is protect their interests. Right now, if news of them out yonder attackin' you was to reach the outside, they'd be five hundred Montana cowboys in here 'fore the week was over, all with knotted hang-ropes in their hands, lookin' for Biggers and Cosgrove and Fosburn. And not even the U.S. Army could stop 'em from stringin' them men up. Western justice is harsh at times and unfair at times. But out here, you lay anything but a gentle hand and a kind word on a woman, you're most likely dead."

"But they're Soiled Doves," Jenny said.

"That doesn't make any difference," Smoke said. "You own the establishment, so that makes it a war against you. They'll be all right."

"Let us drag our wounded in to tend to them!" the shout came from across the street.

"Go ahead," Smoke called out. "And while you're at it, check the buildings close by and make sure no women or kids are in danger, and then clear the street of any stray horses."

Several hired guns exchanged glances at that and silently came to the conclusion that that was a fair man over there in the general store. They holstered their guns and slipped away, heading for the livery. They wanted no more of this.

The others watched them go and thought them fools. But they kept their opinions to themselves.

While the street was being cleared of the wounded, Smoke and Wolf took that time to charge the sticks of dynamite.

"This is gonna come as a right nasty surprise to them ol' boys across the street," the old mountain man proclaimed, a wicked glint in his eyes.

"That's what I'm counting on. How about the

wagons and the supplies?"

"We got nearly all of it loaded," Barrie called. "The horses are still hitched up and all right. They're in the alley to my left."

"You mean we're actually going to take the wagons?" Bad Dog asked.

"Damn right," Smoke told him. "We came into town for supplies, didn't we?"

Wolf laughed in anticipation. "When we start tossing this giant powder, they'll be so much dust and confusion and crashin' of ruined buildin's and hollerin' and moanin' and groanin' it'll take those varmits over yonder ten minutes to figure out what the hell happened. By that time, we'll be clear of the pass and home free."

"Bad Dog, you and me to the second floor with the dynamite. We can get a better angle from up there. Jenny, to the back."

Bad Dog grabbed up a case of capped and fused dynamite and was gone up the stairs. Smoke turned to Wolf. "When I tap on the floor three times, you get the hell gone from the front of the store, Wolf. Just as soon as the dynamite blows, open up with rifle fire and get to the wagons. We'll blow the rear on our way out."

Wolf nodded and grinned.

Upstairs, Smoke went to work passing out the tied-together dynamite. Three sticks to a bundle.

"The street's all clear, Jensen," a man shouted. "No women or kids or animals close by."

Smoke did not reply, not wanting to give away

212

his new position overlooking the street. He tapped three times on the floor as he and Bad Dog were lighting the first bundles of dynamite.

"Clear," Wolf called.

Smoke and Bad Dog hurled the sputtering lethal charges. Just seconds before the center part of town started blowing up, someone yelled, "Jesus God! That's *dynamite!*"

In the rear of the store, four rifles started barking.

Then the mayor's office, a keno joint, one empty building, and Major Cosgrove's office erupted in a million pieces of mud, dust and dirt, splinters, bits of paper, busted spittoons, broken coffee pots, pieces of glass, the ragged remnants of four or five pairs of dirty long handles, shredded boots and shoes, and no small amount of various body parts.

Lester Laymon jumped up in the livery and flung out his hands. "It's the mighty hand of God!" he cried. "Bringing retribution to this earthly Sodom and Gomorrah."

Violet jabbed him in the butt with a pitchfork and Lester shrieked and jumped. "Sit down, you fool!" she admonished him. "That's Smoke Jensen blowing the crap out of the place with dynamite."

One entire wall had collapsed on Biggers and Cosgrove and Fosburn. They weren't badly hurt, just scared to the point of peeing in their underwear.

The dust was so thick it was like a foggy night

on the Barbary Coast. The dust was swirling around like whirlwinds. Smoke and Bad Dog each hurled another bundle of explosives, then got gone from the second floor of the general store, each carrying a bundle of dynamite to give to those hired guns out back.

But there was no need for that. Wolf and Barrie and Jenny had each tossed a charge and the back alley was a thick cloud of smoke and dust and hired guns lying unconscious on the ground.

The only building left intact in the center of the east side of the second block was Chung Lee's laundry. And Chung Lee was now, for the very first time, giving serious thought to returning to China. He was sure that feeling would pass . . . but not if this kept up.

Smoke and his party did not have to worry about blowing the pass. No one even heard them leave, much less pursued them as they rode and rattled down the back alleys and out of town. They came to the pass and Smoke signaled them on, staying behind for a moment or two. He sat his saddle and looked down at the town. The entire town was enveloped in a cloud of dust and smoke from a dozen small fires started by over-turned lanterns and cookstoves.

Chuckling at the chaos that must now be reigning in the center of Red Light, he turned his horse and headed after the wagons.

Jack Biggers had been blown out of one boot. He was staggering and limping around, and looked down, certain he had been crippled forever by the loss of a foot.

Fosburn's pants had caught on fire and he just managed to put out the flames before they reached a critical part of his body. He was now standing outside the ruin of what had been his office, clad in very short pants and a shirt with no sleeves, wearing a very dazed look on his face.

Major Cosgrove crawled out of the rubble, his clothes sooty rags. He sat on the edge of what remained of the boardwalk in front of one of his several offices. He looked around him at all the carnage. He had never seen anything like it. There were men with broken arms and broken legs and busted heads and hands, and men lying dead in grotesquely twisted positions.

He felt like crying.

Then he saw Biggers limping around with a worried look on his face, and Fosburn standing in the middle of the street in short pants.

"Fosburn," he called. "Will you, for Christ's sake, put on some damn pants?"

Lonesome Ted Lightfoot staggered out of the dress shop, holding his aching head, the knot on his noggin compliments of Miss Alice and her flatiron. He pulled up short at the smoke and dust and fire and devastation before him. He thought for a moment he was dead and had gone to Hell.

Patmos sat down on the busted boardwalk beside Major. "Nineteen dead and twelve wounded," he told the man.

"How many of the wounded expected to live?" Cosgrove asked.

"Not very many."

"Make that twenty dead," Kit Silver said, walking up and sitting down. He took out the makings and started building a cigarette.

"What other wonderful news do you have to tell me?" Cosgrove asked bitterly.

"Five men pulled out during the lull in the fightin'. They were top guns, too."

"Why did they pull out?"

"A personal opinion?" Kit said, thumbing a match into flame and lighting up.

"Go ahead."

"I can send out the word and have you a hundred men in here in a week's time . . ."

"Do it!" Cosgrove said savagely.

". . . But no more than ten or twelve of them will be top-notch men," Kit went on as if the man had not spoken. "Fightin' Smoke Jensen has become known as a losin' proposition. And if you're half as smart as you think you are, you know why after this."

"He's just a man, goddamnit! He's just a flesh-and-blood man. That's all!"

"Sure," Kit said sarcastically. "Sure. Just a man who can crawl up into a wolves' den and go to sleep cuddled up against a big ol' mama wolf. A man who had pumas for pets as a kid. A man who can call eagles to him. A man who when he lays down to rest has wild hawks guardin' him . . ."

"That's nonsense!" Cosgrove snapped.

"Some of it is, some of it isn't, believe me. I've been west of the Missouri all my life. I ain't never seen no human man like Smoke Jensen. And to tell the truth, neither has nobody else, either. I'll get your men in here for you, Cosgrove. But if you think this last bunch was scabby and no-'count, just wait until you see what'll come in now. Hiders and bounty hunters and wore-out buffalo hunters, all of them stinkin' and with fleas jumpin' on them."

"I don't care what they look like, just as long as they can do the job."

"Has anybody seen my pants?" Fosburn asked.

And in the valley, Smoke pushed open the door and smiled at Sally. "I told you I'd be back in time for supper."

Nineteen

"We have to move fast," Major Cosgrove said, one day after the fight on Main Street. "Several families have moved out of Red Light. They're sure to talk about this situation, and that will attract the attention of the territorial governor. He'll send people in here. We can't have that."

"We've already confirmed that Jensen is a real U.S. Marshal," Fosburn said. "He could legally arrest all of us for attempted murder, extortion, and God only knows what else. Why hasn't he done so?"

Biggers smiled grimly, a cruel twisting of the lips. "Jensen doesn't want to do this the legal way, that's why. Jensen doesn't pay much attention to written law. He wants us dead. All of us." He mumbled an obscenity.

"Kit says he can have gunhands in here," Cosgrove said. "I told him to go ahead. He left yesterday, right after the fight. By now he's sent the wires out and men are on the way. My God!" The man stood up from behind his new desk in his new office. "We're losing a fight against nine men, one woman, and two teenagers. To date our combined losses are about twenty-five dead and just about twenty wounded. Tough, top gunslingers are pulling out of this fight. Most didn't even wait around to get paid."

"I say we hit the ranch," Biggers said.

Club Bowers looked at the man, but offered no comment. Hitting the ranch would be suicide, in his opinion. One of his deputies had ridden out that way and reported back that the ranch looked more like a heavily fortified Army post than a working ranch complex. The land around the complex had been cleared and burned for hundreds of yards. Peter Hankins had finally checked back in after several days in the field and said there was no way he could get a shot at anyone on the ranch. Time was on the side of Smoke Jensen and family, and Club knew it.

Maybe it was time to pull out . . . he'd been giving that some serious thought.

"You have an opinion on any of this, Club?" Cosgrove asked.

"Yeah," the sheriff said. "Give it up and live and let live."

"Have you lost your mind?" Biggers almost shouted the words. "We *can't* give it up. We've got too much money invested in this fight. The gold in those mountains is worth a fortune!"

Club stood up and walked to the door. He put his hat on his head and turned to look at the men. "Is it worth your lives?" He stepped outside and walked to his office. There, he sat on the bench on the boardwalk and looked at the work crews clearing out the wreckage from the

219

dynamite. Cosgrove had sent men from the mines to clear the mess and they were almost through. Now all that was left of very nearly a block was a great empty space in the center of town.

The man and woman who owned the general store had flatly told Cosgrove that either he paid for repairing the store and replacing the damaged goods or they would sue him and make certain every newspaper west of the Mississippi knew about it. At the prompt advice of Lawyer Dunham, Cosgrove told his men to go to work and told the store owner to order replacement goods and send the bill to him.

Club knew that Cosgrove had lost the upper hand in Red Light. The merchants had banded together and told Club they would no longer pay protection money to him. They all went armed now, and his deputies were very nervous. On this very morning, Club had told his men to enforce the law and that was it. They took orders from him, not from Major Cosgrove, Jack Biggers, or Fat Fosburn. The Big Three didn't much like that, but Club Bowers really didn't much care.

Deputy Modoc sat down behind him on the bench. "It's over, ain't it, Club?"

Club nodded his head. "Yeah, it is, Doc. The money men over yonder don't know it yet, but it's over. They'll be a lot more shootin', and a lot of killin', but it's over. It's like I told you boys this mornin'. From now on we enforce the law. We arrest whoever breaks it."

"Even them over yonder in the office?"

"Even them. I'm ridin' out to Miss Jenny's ranch and makin' peace with them folks and tellin' them how it's gonna be from now on. I'll see you later."

"Rider comin', Mister Smoke!" Jimmy yelled from his lookout position in the barn loft. "I think it's Club Bowers. He's alone."

Smoke stepped out of the house, buckling his gun-belt around him. He stood in the yard and waited. Club held up a hand. "I'm peaceful, Smoke. Can I step down?"

"Sure. Come on in the house and have some pie and coffee."

With coffee poured and thick wedges of pie cut, Club said, "From this day on, Smoke, me and my deputies enforce the law as it is written. You break the law, I'll arrest you, or go down tryin'. The same thing goes for Cosgrove, Biggers, Fosburn, or any of these no-'counts they're bringin' in. My office no longer takes protection money from any merchant. They say you can't teach an old dog new tricks. Well, I'm an old dog, and I think I can change. At least, I'm going to give it one hell of a try. Excuse my language, Miss Sally, Miss Jenny."

Smoke held out a hand and Club shook it. "Welcome to the right side of the fence, Sheriff."

Club smiled. "I think I like it over here, Smoke."

"How are things in town, Sheriff Bowers?"

Jenny asked innocently.

Club chuckled. "Settlin' down, Miss Jenny. Been an awful lot of funerals, though. Boot Hill's rapidly fillin' up."

"How did Cosgrove take your decision?" Sally asked.

"I think he seen it comin', Miss Sally. Didn't none of them kick about it too much. I been uneasy about the situation in town ever since Miss Janey passed on."

"Did any of the Big Three have anything to do with my sister's death?" Smoke asked.

Club shook his head. "No. She died of the fever . . . or complications brought on by the fever. I know that. Van Horn held on to the ranch until Miss Jenny could get out here. That old man is randy to the core, let me tell you. You know there's gold up in the mountains?"

"I guessed as much," Smoke said.

"Worth a fortune, so Cosgrove says. I'll tell you what I think. I think Biggers wants Fosburn's spread, Fosburn wants Biggers' spread, and Cosgrove wants it all. These guns that's comin' in . . . well, I think they'll follow the orders of the man who offers them the most money, no matter which one of the Big Three they might be workin' for at the time. That's what I think."

"How about the townspeople?" Sally asked.

"They want things to settle down. They're tired of Cosgrove and all the trouble. And they've told him so. Still tellin' him so when I

222

left. Chung Lee told him that if any more trouble happens, he was gonna starch his longhandles so stiff they'd look like a suit of armor standin' in the corner. Then he called him some things in Chinese that I'm pretty sure wasn't very complimentary."

"What's his next move, Club?"

"I wish I knew. All I know is that Kit Silver is wirin' for more gunhands to come in. And even Kit admits they'll be the scum of the earth. There is no law, yet, about two men settlin' their differences in the street. I can't interfere in that. But I am going to keep the peace in Red Light, Smoke. I mean that."

"Good. I won't push inside the town limits, Club. But I won't be pushed, either."

"That's fair enough. You know that damn backshootin' Hankins has been snoopin' around here, don't you?"

"I suspected it. And some of the boys cut his sign yesterday."

Club ate the last of his pie, drained his coffee cup, and walked to the door. Just before he plopped his hat on his head and stepped outside, he smiled and said, "But on the other hand, it would be a real shame if somebody called that damn Hankins out into the street, now, wouldn't it?"

The fire in his belly had been so strong that Barrie had taken his blankets outside the bunkhouse and slept under the stars so the other men would not hear the occasional muffled moan of pain that passed his lips. He finished a bottle of laudanum and the pain eased, then went away. Breathing easier for the first time in hours, the town-tamer looked up and stared long at the stars in God's heavens and suddenly thought: this is my last time to see them. It has to be. I'm not goin' out layin' in some damn bed screamin' in pain, unable to control myself. That ain't no way for a man to go out. A man ought to have the right to pick and choose his time and place of dyin'. And I'm gonna do just that.

It had been a week since that fine time in town with Smoke and Bad Dog and Wolf and the girl. What a little gal Jenny was. Barrie smiled under the canopy of stars. He liked to think that his daughter would have been just like her. Couldn't ask for no finer.

And Barrie knew that Smoke had gotten word from Clemmie Feathers that the town was over-flowing with two-bit gunhands on the payroll of the Big Three.

Barrie made up his mind. At four that morning, he was bathing in the creek and shaving as carefully as possible in what light there was. He'd had his black suit done up nice by Chung Lee and his handmade boots, which he seldom wore, polished to a high sheen. He put on a spar-kling-clean white shirt and black string tie. He saddled up silently and strapped on his matched .45s, sticking two more .45s behind his gunbelt. He had made out his will during the first week he was at Jenny's spread and given it to Van Horn.

Van Horn, meanwhile, was sitting in his private quarters at the south end of the bunkhouse, drinking coffee and watching his old friend get ready to ride into Red Light and die. He longed to go with him, but knew that Barrie would resent it. Knew that the town-tamer wanted it this way. But there was something he could do. He smiled thinking about it.

Barrie had no sooner left the yard than Van Horn slipped out of the bunkhouse, saddled up, and took a shortcut to town. He could make damn sure that Club Bowers and his deputies didn't interfere.

Smoke lay beside Sally and heard both men leave. He knew what Barrie was going to do, and had a strong suspicion what Van Horn was going to do.

"Good-bye, Barrie," he whispered. "You're a good man."

"Did you say something, honey?" Sally whispered.

"No, dear. You must have been dreaming. Go back to sleep."

"Whahsiit?" the old man at the livery stable mumbled, still half asleep.

"I've rid hard to get here, old-timer," Van Horn said, gruffing up his voice. "Here's a dollar. Get over to the sheriff's office and tell him they's been a stage holdup at Red Creek Crossing. It's real bad. Dead folks all over the place.

The outlaws took off up Devil's Pass. Move, man!"

Van Horn slipped back into the darkness, pretending to be seeing to his horse. The rummy-eyed old hostler beat it over to Club's place and within fifteen minutes, Club and his deputies were riding out for Red Creek. It would be a good five to six hours before they returned. By that time, Van Horn thought with a smile, it'll all be over.

All but the buryin'.

Van Horn walked over to Clemmie's and sat on the porch with Moses, who had just gotten up to stoke up the fire. The men sipped coffee as the sky grew silver in the east.

Barrie had a fine breakfast of biscuits and gravy and good strong hot black coffee. And then he bought a genuine five-cent cigar from the counterman. On the boards, he lit up and puffed contentedly. Man can't ask for much more, he thought. The fire in his belly was gone, and Barrie knew it would never return. He brushed his coat back, exposing the butts of his .45s, then went for a little walk. He stopped for a time to pet a stray dog. The dog licked his hand and Barrie was pleased. He'd always liked animals. He never trusted a man who disliked dogs . . . serious character flaw there.

Then he saw a knot of gunhands come walking out of the South End Hotel, on their way to breakfast. One of the men was Luther Cone, and with him was his sidekick, equally no-'count Jim

Parish. Barrie had run both of them out of at least two towns that he could recall. After two suspicious killings.

"Might as well start here and now," he muttered. He stepped out into the street. "Cone!" he called. "Parish!"

The men stopped and turned to face Barrie. "Well, well," Cone said. "Would you look at this, Parish. It's old Barrie hisself. You ridin' the grub line, Barrie?"

"No," Barrie called. "I'm ridin' the killin' line."

"Huh? What you mean, the killin' line?"

"You workin' for Biggers, Fosburn, or Cosgrove?"

"All three, if it's any of your damn business."

"You come to make war against a fine little teenage girl, huh?"

"If you're talkin' about Janey's daughter, she's just like her momma, a slutty little two-bit whoor!"

"You'll not talk like that about her, Cone. Fill your hand, you scummy bastard!"

Cone and Parish drew — or tried to. Barrie's right hand flashed and his .45 roared. Cone and Parish went down in the dirt, both of them gut-shot. Barrie stepped two paces to one side and plugged a third man, a no-'count who fancied himself a gunhand and called himself the Arizona Kid. The Kid should have stayed on the farm, milking cows. Barrie shot him through the heart and then stepped back across the narrow street and into the alleyway as a hail of bullets came at him. One tugged at his sleeve, another clipped the brim of his hat, and another kicked dirt on his polished boots. Barrie knocked a leg out from under the man who dusted up his boots.

"Gettin' real interestin' up yonder," Van Horn said to Moses. "I think I'll just mosey up that way."

"I'll get my hat and join you," Moses said. "And my rifle."

Very few of the older, more experienced gunhands in the employ of the Big Three took any part in the shootout with Barrie. Word had spread throughout the camps of the gunhands, and when those with rooms in the town's several hotels heard about the town-tamer coming in all dressed to the nines and with polished boots and totin' at least four pistols, they figured what was coming.

The gunfighters put all that together and reached the conclusion that Barrie had come to town to die . . . but only after making sure a whole bunch of others got sent down that same dark road.

And a man like that would be hard to stop.

Barrie ran around the rear of a saddle and leather shop and slipped back up to the street, walking between it and a gaming house. He saw Dev White, a Utah gunslick peeping around the corner of a hastily vacated cafe. Barrie sighted him in and the bullet knocked the man sprawling and hollering. A rifle roared and splinters tore into Barrie's right cheek. He ignored the bleeding and dropped to one knee, leveling his .45. A New Mexico punk was sent howling to the ground, his belly punctured by town-tamer lead.

Jody Thomas, a North Dakota kid who was wanted for murder, came running out of the Eagles Nest Hotel, his hands filled with .44s. Moses and Van Horn fired as one and Jody was knocked off his boots and went crashing through a window, back into the lobby.

"You're bleedin' all over the carpet!" the desk clerk hollered at the dying gunman.

Jody had no rebuttal to that. He simply closed his eyes and died.

"Stay out of this, you old goat!" Barrie hollered up the street at his longtime friend.

"We'll try to keep it fair," Van Horn yelled.

"Fair, hell!" Barrie said, reloading. "I got 'em outnumbered."

"Get that crazy fool!" Cosgrove yelled from the upstairs window of his new apartment over his mining office.

The street filled with guns-for-hire.

Barrie stepped to the other side of the alley, both hands filled with .45s, and yelled, "Here I am, boys. I'm half puma, half wolf, and Gloryland bound. So step up here and I'll punch your ticket to Hell!"

Then he opened fire.

Twenty

Larry Brown, Johnny Newman, and two gun-slicks from Texas stepped off the boards and onto the street and Barrie put them on the hellbound train, punching their tickets with .45 slugs.

A bullet clipped Barrie's ear and another one burned his shoulder. He didn't feel a thing. "Here's another for Miss Jenny and Smoke Jensen!" he yelled, jamming his empty guns into leather and jerking out two old long-barreled Peacemakers from behind his belt. He cocked and fired so fast the sound was one continuous roll of deadly thunder.

When Barrie ducked back into the early morning shadows of the alley, the street in front of the hotel was littered with wounded and dead.

He ran around the gaming joint and a man opened the rear door and stuck out a sawed-off ten-gauge and a small sack of shells. "You don't remember me, Barrie. But I was bartender in a little mining town in Colorado you cleaned up. Give them no-goods hell, ol' hoss."

Before Barrie could thank the man, the door closed.

Barrie checked both barrels for blockage and loaded the Greener up. He began walking toward the corner of the building. Cosgrove was still shouting from the window, joined by Fosburn, standing in the door of his mayor's office.

The left side of Barrie's suit coat was drenched with blood from his mangled ear, and he had taken lead in his right leg. He limped on, ignoring the pain. He'd endured a hell of a lot worse from the pain in his belly.

Dave Stockton and John Robinson came racing around the corner of the keno joint. Barrie smiled at them and gave the pair both barrels from the sawed-off express gun. The worthless pair was flung back, nearly cut in two from the heavy charge.

Barrie stepped into the narrow passageway between buildings and saw Cosgrove, standing in his window, yelling and screaming and shouting orders. The range was far too great to do much damage with the shotgun, but Barrie gave the man both barrels to keep him honest. The shot had lost most of its punch when it reached Cosgrove, but it bloodied his neck and face and sent him hollering to the floor, certain he'd been mortally wounded.

At the ranch, Jenny sat down at the table with Smoke and Sally and the hands and asked, "Where are Mister Barrie and Mister Van Horn?"

"Barrie went into town to even the odds a little bit, Honey," Wolf told her. "I 'spect Van Horn went in to watch the show."

"You mean . . ."

"Barrie is dying, Jenny," Smoke told her. "This is the way he wanted to go out. After breakfast, Cooper, hitch up a team. Some of us will go in to bring the body back. Pasco, you and Ladd get shovels and ride up to the east slope, by that lightning-blazed tree above the spring. Dig a deep hole."

"Right, Boss," Pasco said.

"And be careful, that damn Hankins is probably prowling around. He'll shoot anybody he sees on this range. If you see him, drop him."

"With pleasure," Ladd said, pouring syrup over his huge stack of flapjacks.

"I shore would like to be in town for this mornin's show," Wolf said. "When Barrie gets goin,' he's plumb hell with a short gun."

"I'll take that damned ol' has-been," a young man who called himself Rusty said, hitching at his fancy rig. He pulled both guns and stepped out of the saloon, where he'd spent the night, drinking and gambling and whoring. With both hands wrapped around the butts of .45s, Rusty marched right down the center of the narrow street.

"He'll last one minute," Kit Silver said, pouring a mug of coffee.

"Thirty seconds," Ned Harden shortened it.

"Hey, turd-face!" Van Horn called to Rusty.

"Ten seconds," Dan Segers said. "Van Horn just bought into it."

"Rusty's dead, then," Les Spivey said.

232

Rusty whirled around and took a shot at Van Horn, standing in the gloom under an awning. Rusty's shot went wide. Van Horn's aim was deadly. Rusty sat down hard in the street and commenced to bellering, his guns in the dirt and both hands holding his stomach.

"You should have stayed to home, boy," Van Horn said, punching out the empty and filling the slot.

Ray Houston stood up in the hotel lobby and started toward the stairs.

"Where you goin'?" Kit Silver asked.

"I'm through," Ray said. "This deal's done gone sour. They got a range war shapin' up down in New Mexico. I'm headin' for there."

"Hold up," Nevada Jones said. "I'll ride with you."

Ron Patrick picked up his rifle and said, "That makes three of us. This war ain't for the likes of me."

Barrie's wounded leg was about to buckle on him and some lucky gunhand he'd not even seen had shot him in the side. "Time to end it," he muttered. He called out, "In the street, boys! Me agin you all. Holster your guns and meet me eyeball to eyeball. Who's got the sand to do it?"

Moses lifted his rifle and Van Horn put a gnarled hand on the barrel. "We're out of it unless they pull something sneaky, Moses. This is Barrie's show from now on."

Perry Sheridan, a tough from Oregon, stepped out onto the boards. "I'll meet you, Barrie."

"Well, come on, then," Barrie shouted, standing tall and bloody in the street. "I ain't got all the time in the world, you know."

Andre McMahon joined Perry, as did four others. The older, wiser gunnies stayed put.

"Fools," Kit said. "Can't they see that Barrie ain't got nothin' to lose?"

"Fifty dollars says they'll git him," a young squirt tossed the bet out.

"Oh, they'll get him," Kit said. "But they won't none of them be alive to brag about it. That's too high a price to pay for ten seconds of glory."

"If you want to call killin' a dyin' man something glorious," a lanky gunfighter said. "Hell with this. I'm haulin' my ashes out of here. Cosgrove and Biggers and Fosburn ain't fit to polish that Jenny girl's boots."

"That ain't what I'd like to polish about her," a brute of a man said with an evil grin on his dirty and unshaven face.

The lanky gunhawk lifted a .44 and shot him between the eyes, knocking him out of the chair. The gunhawk looked around the room. "Anybody else got anything nasty they want to say about that little girl?" No one did.

"I don't like makin' war agin kids," Shady Bryant said, standing up. "I'll ride out with you, Slim."

Kit Silver poured a shot glass of whiskey into his hot coffee and stirred in a spoonful of sugar. "I tried to tell them money men this wouldn't work. It might take time, but the right cause near 'bouts always wins. And that kid's in the right. I'm out of this. I'm gonna stick around, but I ain't rightly sure what side I'm gonna be on."

"Then you better get clear of my sight," Curtis Brown said.

"You want to try an' make me?" Kit said softly.

"I think I'll stick around, too," Slim said. "I'm with you, Kit."

"And me," Shady said.

"I don't hear no shootin' out there," Brown changed the subject.

"Barrie's just standin' in the street, laughin' at them fools. He's sayin' something."

"Can you make it out?"

"Naw."

"What a pitiful lookin' sight," Barrie said to the men facing him in the street.

"You're the pitiful one," Andre called. "Man, you're bleeding bad."

"I'll live long enough to kill you," Barrie told him.

Andre flushed, cussed, and grabbed iron. Barrie shot him in the chest and then dropped to one knee as he cleared leather with his lefthand .45. When the smoke cleared, Andre, Rusty, and their friends were down and hard hit. Barrie staggered to his boots, blood leaking from two more bullet holes. He almost fell climbing up onto the boardwalk, but managed to stay on his feet and reload just as Eddie King stepped out from the doctor's office.

"My brother, Vern, just died, you son-of-a-bitch!" he shouted across the way.

Barrie turned. "Good," he said. "One less punk on the face of the earth." Then he lifted his Peacemaker and drilled Eddie right through the brisket.

A would-be tough and fulltime bully leaned out of a second-story window and sighted Barrie in with a rifle.

"Not that way," Kit Silver said, standing on the boards. "He's too good a man to go that way." He palmed his gun and put a hole in the bully's head.

Leaning up against a post, Barrie looked at the man, questions in his eyes.

Kit shrugged. "It's a free country, town-tamer. I can change sides if I want to."

Barrie smiled as his mouth filled with blood. "That Jenny gal, she'll do, Kit."

"I'll see to it personal, ol' son. You save me a place where you're goin'. I figure this for my last fight."

Shady Bryant and Slim Waters stepped out to join Kit. "Count us in, too, Barrie," Slim said.

"Good men," Barrie said weakly. "All of you. You make me proud. I told all of you more than once there was a streak of good in you. Even when I was runnin' you out of some damn two-bit town. You just proved me right. Now point me toward a nest of snakes whilst I still got the strength to do some stompin'."

"Second door to your left," Shady said. "But

they're waitin' on you, Barrie."

Barrie smiled his bloody smile. "I wouldn't have it any other way." The town-tamer staggered to the door, kicked it in, and walked in shooting.

Smoke halted the wagon about a mile from town. Van Horn and three of Cosgrove's men were heading his way, leading Barrie's horse. Barrie, wrapped in a blanket, was tied across the saddle.

"These ol' boys here," Van Horn explained, "decided they didn't like the idea of makin' war against a young girl. Before he died, Barrie vouched for them. He said they might need a bath, but they was good boys."

"That's good enough for me," Smoke said, swinging down from the saddle. "Welcome to the spread, boys. I can guarantee you the finest food you ever ate."

"Miss Jenny and your Missus really make tubfuls of doughnuts?" Slim asked.

"Every day."

"Lord! I've found a home."

The men placed the bloodsoaked blanket containing Barrie into the hay-filled wagonbed. Cooper, holding the reins, looked back at the body. "I liked that man," he said.

"We all did, boy," Kit said. "Hadn't a been for him, I'd a been ridin' the outlaw trail. All three of us would. I ain't sayin' we're angels. But I ain't robbed nobody or done harm to a woman.

And I ain't gonna start now."

"You should have seen him work, Smoke," Van Horn said. "He either outright killed or got mortal lead in twenty-six men this morning."

"Twenty-six!" Smoke said, clearly startled.

"That about passes your record, don't it, Smoke?" Slim asked.

"Certainly does."

"And them figures is right on the mark," Shady vouched for the number. "Barrie had nine slugs in him 'fore he finally give up the ghost. But he went out with a smile on his lips, knowin' he done a good thing. Cosgrove and Fosburn was in shock, I think. The undertaker was so happy he was rubbin' his hands and smilin' to beat the band. Finally, ol' Fat Fosburn, he got to makin' threats about this and that and Shady, he went up to him and punched him in the mouth. Knocked him down in a big mud puddle. Cosgrove, he run off back to his office. There really ain't much to them men. Biggers neither, I'm thinkin'."

"Barrie went out gentle, talkin' about Jenny," Van Horn said. "I really think he started out likin' the girl and in a short time grew to love her like she was his own. Jenny's gonna take this hard."

"She knows why he left," Smoke said. "I told her, and Sally's with her now. They're all up on the east slope. Kit, would you boys mind staying at the ranch and looking after things while we have the funeral?"

"We'd be honored to, Smoke. And the ranch and everything on the place will be just like you left it. Or the three of us will be dead in the yard," he added grimly.

Twenty-one

The burial procession left Slim, Kit, and Shady at the ranch, each man with a basket filled with doughnuts and a rifle by his side.

"I'd be plumb filled with ire if someone was to disturb me while I'm eatin' these," Slim said. "I might get so put out I'd have to kill somebody."

"If you do," Van Horn said, "I hope it's Hankins."

Slim shuddered. "I don't like that feller. He gives me the creeps. I can't abide a sneak, and that's what he is. I believe in meetin' a man eye-to-eye."

Wolf drove the wagon as far as it could go, and then Barrie was carried up the ridge overlooking the bubbling little spring. They'd dressed him up in clean clothes and wrapped his boots and spurs and guns in the blanket with him.

Pasco and Ladd had dug a deep hole and gathered rocks to shelter the mound once Barrie was covered.

Van Horn spoke a few words, Smoke read from the Bible, and then Jenny sang "O Valiant Hearts" and Sally sang "What a Friend We Have in Jesus." There was a lot of nose-blowing and eye-wiping. Even Ol' Wolf Parcell kept wiping his eyes and complaining about the "damn dust a-blowin' ever' which a-way."

If Hankins was around, he had missed the funeral procession from the ranch and no long-range shots were fired. Which was wise on Hankins' part. Considering the mood of this gathering, had he tried a shot, the men would have tracked him into town and hanged him . . . along with Cosgrove, Fosburn, Biggers, and anybody else who might have gotten in their way.

The last words of the farewell prayer, offered by Sally, were just echoing away as the sun went down. Far in the distance, a big timber wolf howled.

"Look in on him from time to time, my brother Wolf," Bad Dog said, lifting his head, his eyes searching the horizon. "He would like that."

"Amen," Wolf Parcell said, and the service was over in the last fading light of the day.

Cosgrove, Biggers, and Fosburn were clearly in a state of shock over the killing or wounding of twenty-six newly hired gunhands and the defection of three top guns.

"One man," Biggers said, looking down into his coffee cup. "One sick and dying man breezes into town and we bury twenty-one men."

"And four out of the five who survived are not going to make it," Fosburn added.

Cosgrove was silent. He sat by the window of

his office and stared out at the town that had once been his. Now he wielded no power. None. Once he could have snapped his fingers and the townspeople would have jumped. Now they just looked at him through eyes that held nothing but contempt. Mule Jackson had left Doc Blaine's small clinic and boarded the stage for God knows where. The man had picked up his wages and left. Still in pain and still badly shaken by the horrible beating laid on him by Smoke Jensen, Mule was only a shell of his former self.

Mule Jackson would drop out of sight, not to be heard from for a long, long time.

The town was still filled to overflowing with hired guns, but even they walked light around the citizens and caused no problems. Not after one had lipped off to a citizen and tried to bully a young boy. The boy's father, upon hearing the news, went home, got his shotgun, and shot the thug dead in the street. Club Bowers made no arrest. He had told Cosgrove, "Keep your pet hyenas on a short leash, Major. I can't be responsible for what these citizens might take it in their minds to do."

Cosgrove sat and listened with only half a mind to the talk around him. He knew what he ought to do: tend to his mining operations, fire all the gun-hands, and live quietly and luxuriously with his considerable wealth.

He should do that, but he knew he wouldn't.

Major Cosgrove had never been beaten, in

business or in a fistfight. Now, since Smoke Jensen had arrived, he'd been publicly humiliated, stomped on, and thwarted at every turn, and he'd had the entire town turn against him. Nearly all of his really good gunhands had left him. Hankins had not been able to get a clear shot at Smoke Jensen. Cosgrove could not understand that, could not understand that Hankins, while he hated Jensen, was deathly afraid of the man. With Smoke Jensen, you only get one shot. Miss or wound the man, and Jensen would spend the rest of his life tracking you down and ultimately killing you.

One simply did not play deadly games with Smoke Jensen. Not ever.

Even Lawyer Dunham was keeping a very low profile, and gradually distancing himself from the Big Three.

"What are we goin' to do, Major?" Jack Biggers asked, breaking into Cosgrove's dark thoughts.

"Counting all hands, how many men can we muster?"

"Right at fifty," the rancher replied. "But if you're thinkin' 'bout attacking Jenny's ranch, forget it. That place is a fort. Since Smoke sold off most of the cattle, 'ceptin' for some of the finest bulls and heifers I ever seen, the hands ain't done nothin' 'cept work around the complex. Smoke sent a hand down south and brought a damn wagontrain of supplies back. They got enough supplies out there to last a damn year. You can't get within a mile of the ranch — day or night — without being spotted. They started out by clearing two or three hundred yards. Now it's up to about three-quarters of a mile. Jenny's got ten first-rate men out there, not countin' Smoke and Sally. And you better not discount Sally Jensen."

"Tell me about it," Major muttered. The buckshot that Barrie had fired at the man had done little damage, but a few pellets — and rusty nails and so forth — had scarred his face, and Major Cosgrove was a vain man when it came to his personal appearance. All the more reason for hating the Jensens.

Cosgrove stood up from his windowseat and paced the office. He could no longer count on Sheriff Bowers or any of his men. Club was a changed man and the citizens were warming to him. He had pared down his deputies by firing Reed and Junior. If a general election were held this day, Bowers would be reelected by a landslide.

Everything, *everything* he had worked for was vanishing all around him. Most of his power was gone, and with it the prestige he had basked in.

Goddamn Smoke Jensen!

"Movement on the west side of the range," Slim said, handing Smoke the field glasses he'd been using up in the barn loft. "I think it's Hankins, and I think he's camped up there somewhere."

"Tonight I'll take the game to Hankins," Smoke said. "We've got to get rid of him. Once that's done, we can all breathe a little easier."

"You got a plan?"

"Yes," Smoke said, standing up. "Kill him."

Peter Hankins thought he had it all figured out. He had picked and then rejected two dozen different locations from which to shoot. Then he spotted one that was so obvious he had missed it from the outset. It was going to be a long shot, but he felt he could do it. He'd made shots from that distance before, but only during his many long hours of practice. He figured the distance at just under three-quarters of a mile. He could do it, he knew he could. And when he killed the legendary Smoke Jensen, from that moment on, Peter Hankins could name his own price, and men of a certain ilk would pay it.

Come night, he would work his way into position and wait.

Smoke dressed in dark clothing and slipped his feet into moccasins. He blackened his face with soot and tied a black bandanna around his forehead. He took a knife and his rifle only. He knew that this work would either be very close in, or long distance. There would be no in-between.

He did not underestimate the abilities of Peter Hankins. The man was a hunter and one of the best.

Smoke had napped through the hours of the

afternoon, getting ready for the long night hours that lay ahead of him. Then he ate a good supper and slipped some jerky into his pocket. Jerky was swiftly going out of vogue in the early eighties but not with Smoke. He did not take a canteen. The area was dotted with springs, and he knew where they were.

He also thought he knew where Hankins had settled in for the night, patiently waiting for his morning shot.

Conversation at the supper table was sparse, with the men only picking at their food. None of them liked the idea of Smoke going out after Hankins alone.

"It oughta be me goin' out yonder after Hankins," Wolf Parcell grumbled. "I spent more years in the wilderness than you been alive, boy."

"You boys look after Jenny," Smoke had told them. He patted Sally's hand and slipped out into the darkness. He would rub his skin and his clothing with various types of grass and then dirt on top of that to mask the human smell.

Bad Dog chuckled as the door closed.

"What's so funny, *amigo?*" Pasco asked.

"Biggers, Cosgrove, and Fosburn have about fifty men on their combined payrolls at this time, right?"

" 'Bout that. Why?" Kit asked.

"They will have somewhat less than that by this time tomorrow, I am thinking. That was not Smoke's regular Bowie he was carrying for this night's work."

"What was it, then?" Slim asked.

Bad Dog met Sally's amused eyes. Mrs. Jensen said, "A Cheyenne scalping knife."

It took Smoke the better part of three hours to cover just over a mile. Twice coyotes trotted past him, unaware of his presence. Once a skunk came close to him and Smoke said a very sincere and silent prayer for the little animal to pad right on along and leave him alone.

Then the wind shifted and Smoke caught the unmistakable smell of hair oil. Oh, vanity, he thought. It's going to get you killed, Hankins.

Ever so gently and soundlessly, Smoke eased around until he was pointing toward the smell of barbershop hair oil. With the wind blowing toward him, and the breeze freshening, there was no chance Hankins could smell him, and little chance of him hearing his approach.

Hankins stiffened at a slight unnatural noise and looked all around him, only the top of his head and his eyes poking out of the slight depression. He could see nothing out of the ordinary and he did not hear the noise again.

Hankins settled back into the natural hole, his rifle across his knees, and relaxed himself. It was silly of him to think that any cowboy was going to be able to slip unseen across a mile of burned-over ground without enough cover to hide a quail. He had seen those coyotes, hadn't he? And a man was a whole lot larger than a coyote.

Hankins longed for a hot cup of coffee and a

247

warm bed. But he warmed himself internally by thinking of seeing Smoke Jensen fall dead with a bullet in his chest or back. Chest would be better, Hankins concluded. What a shot this would be. He would be talked about over campfires for the rest of his life.

If Hankins had any idea how short the rest of his life was, he would have been praying instead of mentally building monuments to himself.

Hankins almost peed in his underwear when someone tapped him on the shoulder. He tried to twist around, jerk up his rifle, and jump up at the same time. All he succeeded in doing was falling down in the hole and losing the grip on his rifle. He came up with a pistol in his hand and felt a powerful hand clamp around his wrist and jerk. Hankins went flying to land against the side of the earth depression, the wind knocked out of him.

The last thing he remembered seeing through his panic-filled eyes was the dark, menacing shape of Smoke Jensen, a knife in his hand.

Sheriff Club Bowers thought he heard a horse walking slowly up the street of the town. With half-closed eyes, he could see the wall clock. Two o'clock in the morning. Must have been his imagination. He rolled over, pulled the blanket up to his shoulders, and went back to sleep.

He was awakened by a frantic banging on his door. "Sheriff!" a man hollered. "Come quick, Sheriff. Cosgrove and the mayor is about to have a conniption-fit. Get your britches on, man. Hurry, now."

Cussing, Club pulled on his pants and boots. It wasn't even daylight out yet. "This had better be good," he muttered. "I sure was sleepin' sound."

A crowd of men had gathered around a horse, tied to the hitchrail in front of Major Cosgrove's offices. He recognized the animal as one that worthless back-shooting Peter Hankins had been riding.

Cosgrove and Fosburn were backed up against the outside wall of the building, both of them pale and looking like they wanted to puke.

Hankins' rifle was in the special-made saddle boot, and something was tied to it. Club pulled up short when he saw what it was.

A scalp.

Hankins' scalp. The man's blond hair was unmistakable.

"You reckon we're about to be attacked by wild Indians, Sheriff?" a man who was new to the West asked, nervousness in his voice.

"No. Hell, no, Adkins. Just calm down. The only Indians around here are tame ones, for the most part. Besides, Indians didn't do this."

"How do you know?" Adkins pressed.

"Indians keep the scalps, man. No Indian would have tied the top knot to this expensive rifle and turned this fine horse loose." This was the horse I heard walking up the street last night, Club thought. Oh, Jensen, you ballsy bastard.

You got more guts than any ten men combined.

Cosgrove pointed a finger at the scalp flapping in the cool early morning breeze. "That's . . . something only a damn *heathen* would do!" His voice trembled as badly as his finger.

"Yep," Club said, rolling a cigarette. "For a white man to do this is almost as bad as a growed-up man who would try to steal a young girl's ranch and kill her in the process."

"I demand you go arrest Smoke Jensen!" Fosburn hollered. "I order you to arrest him!"

"You don't order me to do a damn thing, Fat." Club cupped his hand around the match flame and lit up. "And how do you know Smoke Jensen done this? Was you there? Did you see it?"

"Why . . . ah, no. Of course not."

"Well, shut your mouth then."

"You're all against me!" Cosgrove suddenly screamed out. "Every damn one of you. Well . . . well . . . by God, we'll see who wins this fight. I *own* this town. It was my money that helped *build* this town. No two-bit gunfighter is going to cheat me out of what is rightfully mine. I'll hire a hundred, a thousand gunfighters to kill that damn Smoke Jensen. You all hear me? And I'll have you all groveling at my feet, begging me to forgive you for turning against me. I . . ."

Lawyer Dunham had walked down from his quarters to see what the commotion was all about. "Mister Cosgrove, as the man handling your affairs, I would suggest, in the strongest possible terms, that you shut your damn mouth before you develop what is known as a buffalo mouth and a hummingbird ass."

"You're *fired!*" Cosgrove screamed.

"Suits me," Dunham said. He looked at the flapping scalp and grimaced. "My word! I was going to the Grand Hotel for breakfast. I think I'll settle for coffee."

"I'll join you," Club said.

"What about that . . . scalp?" Fosburn hollered.

"He worked for you," Club told him. "You bury it."

Twenty-two

Before the citizens of Red Light had settled down to breakfast that morning, twelve hired guns stuffed their saddlebags, rolled up blankets in ground sheets, saddled up, and pulled out. Many of the residents of the boom town stood silently on the boardwalks and watched them leave.

Lawyer Dunham stood with Sheriff Bowers. "I have been such a fool," the attorney said. "The big money offered me by Cosgrove, Fosburn, and Biggers dazzled me. It blinded me to what is right and wrong and sent me down the wrong path."

"I been on the wrong path near 'bouts all my growed up life," Club said. "I do know what you're talkin' about. But ain't it a nice feelin' once you know you're back on track?"

"Yes. I started experiencing that sensation about a week ago. I feel as though a great weight has been lifted from me. Sheriff? I would like to handle Miss Jenny Jensen's affairs. And I won't even charge her for my services. Do you suppose I could safely ride out to her ranch without Smoke shooting me?"

Club chuckled. "Mister Dunham, you'll be surprised at how forgivin' Smoke is. I've spoke at length with half a dozen or more cowboys who right now still work for Biggers or Fosburn. They all, to a man, told me that Smoke could have easily killed them out on the range and had plenty of cause to do just that. Instead, he offered them a job on Miss Jenny's ranch once this fracas was over. Yeah. Really. I'd bet my last dollar — most of it, until lately, ill-gotten —" he admitted, "that you ride out there and they'll invite you in, give you coffee and pie, and everybody will shake hands and forget and forgive the past. Smoke has offered the same deal to the Big Three more than once, and they turned it down. He'll not offer it again. Come on. I'll ride out to the ranch with you."

As the sheriff and the lawyer were riding out one end of town, Jack Biggers and his entire crew, including the cook — an old outlaw wanted for murder in three states and two territories — were riding into town from the other end. Within five minutes, the hired-gun crew of Fat Fosburn came thundering in. Shopkeepers and store owners began closing and locking their doors. The Golden Cherry and the Golden Plum shut down. The town began bracing for a showdown the citizens knew was probably only hours away.

People called pet dogs and cats inside and tied them up or caged them. They began moving their horses out of the livery stables of Red Light and into corrals outside of town, out of bullet range. Thirty minutes after the heavily armed gunslicks rode into town, the long main street of Red Light was void of any decent person. Only the horses of the gunhands stood at the hitchrails. The hired guns sat in various saloons and waited for word to start the war.

"I will control this town," Cosgrove said, his eyes blazing with anger and approaching madness. "This is my town, and I give the orders."

Both Biggers and Fosburn felt it was their town, too; but they didn't bring that up at this time. Major Cosgrove had strapped on a gunbelt and had a rifle and a bandolier of ammunition on his desk.

The mine had shut down and the town was eerily silent. The miners were staying close to their tents and shacks on the slopes above Red Light. Whoever won, they would still have a job. They played cards, drank coffee, and waited.

On the Fosburn ranch, Luddy, Parker, and Dud packed up their few possessions and saddled their personal mounts. They stood for a moment, looking across the saddles at each other.

"Ain't nobody yet said where it is we're goin'," Parker broke the silence.

"I ain't no gunhand and never called myself one," Luddy said. "But I reckon it's time we seen if Miss Jenny Jensen might need some hands over to her place."

"I'll go along with that," Dud said.

The men swung into the saddle and put the Fosburn ranch behind them.

On the Triangle JB, Highpockets, Dick, Biff, and Howie saddled up and mounted up.

"I damn sure ain't leavin' no regrets behind," Biff said, picking up the reins.

"Me, neither," Highpockets said. "You reckon Smoke really scalped that back-shootin' Hankins like Biggers heard he done?"

"You want to ride into town and ask some-one?" Howie looked at him.

"Hell, no! I don't want to get within ten miles of Red Light. That town's fixin' to explode."

"You know," Dick said, "Jack Biggers ain't got no family nowhere. They's gonna be a lot of work to be done around here once he's in the ground. And Smoke *did* say we could go to work for Miss Jenny."

"She's gonna own this place for sure," Biff said. "Let's ride over to her place and ask if we could please have a cup of coffee and a dough-nut."

Lawyer Dunham sat in the lovely living room in Jenny Jensen's ranchhouse and drank excel-lent coffee and enjoyed some of the finest doughnuts he'd ever put in his mouth. He had gotten over his astonishment at the nice recep-tion he'd received and was now talking legal business with Smoke, Sally and Miss Jenny. Smoke had told him to put any past differences between them behind him. All that was in the past and best forgotten.

Lawyer Dunham was greatly relieved to do just that. Being hurled out of a second-story window was an experience he did not wish to relive.

"Rider comin'!" the lookout in the barn loft hollered. "It's young Billy Leonard from town."

The young man jumped from his horse and ran up to Sheriff Bowers, who had just stepped outside. "Deputy Brandt says to come quick, Sheriff. All the gunfighters has gathered in town. The men you fired, Reed and Junior, are workin' for Cosgrove. All the people in town are takin' sides, and they's gonna be a face-off before dark. It's bad, Sheriff. Real bad."

"More riders comin' in," the lookout called. "From north and south. I recognize Highpockets and Luddy."

"They've left the Big Three," Club said. "I spoke to them only a few days ago. They're good boys. I trust them to keep their word."

"So do I," Van Horn said.

Highpockets rode up to the front porch and tossed his hands into the air. The others did the same.

"What the hell . . . ?" Club said.

Smoke laughed at the men. "No need for that, boys. But I must say you have it down pat. You boys looking for work?"

"Punchin' cows and breakin' horses, yes, sir," Highpockets said. "We ain't hirin' out our guns. But we'll fight for the brand if attacked."

"That's all anyone could ask. Put your stuff in the bunkhouse and the barn. When this mess is over, we'll rebuild the bunkhouses on Fat's place and over on the Triangle JB."

"But the bunkhouse on the JB is in pretty good shape," Dick said.

Smoke smiled at him. "It probably won't be when all this is over." He looked over at Van Horn. "Pick the men who stay here, Van."

"Ladd, you, Ford, Cooper, and Jimmy stay here at the ranch. Highpockets, you boys leavin' any saddle pals behind?"

"Not a one, Mister Van Horn. And I can speak for all of us. They all drifted when the gunslicks started comin' in. If you're worried about us tossin' lead at anyone who attacked this ranch, you can put your mind to rest. Y'all didn't start this war. Biggers and Fosburn and Cosgrove is in the wrong, and so is any who ride for them."

"That's good enough for me. You men stay here and protect the ranch."

"You new men," Sally called from the kitchen window. "Jenny and I just fixed a huge tub of doughnuts and the coffee is hot and fresh. Stow your gear and come on back here . . . if you're hungry, that is."

The seven of them almost broke their necks getting to the barn and the bunkhouse.

Smoke looked at the gathering of men. "Whoever is riding into town with me, get geared up for a fight. We'll pull out in half an hour."

Smoke stepped back inside and looked at Sally. "Keep some of those doughnuts handy, honey. The boys and me will be hungry when we get back."

Eight men saddled up and rode out, heading for Red Light and a showdown with five or six times their number. Smoke headed the column. In addition to his matched .44s, he carried two more .44s tucked down behind his belt and his old Colt revolving shotgun slung by a strap over one shoulder, a bandolier of shells across his chest.

Beside him rode Van Horn, the legendary old gunfighter still ramrod straight and leather tough, his Remingtons loaded up full and ready to bang. Like Smoke, he had shoved two spare six-shooters behind his belt.

Behind Smoke and Van Horn rode Wolf Parcell and Bad Dog, both heavily armed, both carrying bows and a quiver of arrows.

Third in the column rode Pasco and Kit Silver. Behind them rode Slim Waters and Shady Bryant. Kit Silver felt in his guts this would be his last fight. He had carried that feeling with him since the day he rode into Red Light. But if it was true, he would go out on the right side, and that gave him comfort.

The men pulled up at the pass and bunched. "You can bet they're waiting for us," Smoke said. "We'll go into town in pairs, two minutes apart. Just as soon as they open the dance . . ." He looked at Wolf, grinning at that remark. "Or, whoever opens the dance, we don't stop until it's over. I'll see the deputies first and give them Club's message. They'll clear out of town in jig time, you can bet on that. Club's giving us all a break by ordering his deputies out and by staying at the ranch until an hour before sundown. So it better be over by then. By now, with the fresh horse we gave him, Billy Leonard has delivered my message to the Big Three and found himself a safe hole. I want to thank you men . . ." Smoke paused, unable to find the right words.

Wolf said, "Just 'cause you was partly raised by that ol' windbag, Preacher, don't start actin' like him by makin' no long-winded speeches. You and that creaky, ancient ol' reprobate with you just ride on into town and get set. Me and the boys will be right behind you. I think it'd be best if we leave our horses at the crick, out of danger. Time the gun-smoke settles, this town will be tame and Miss Jenny won't be bothered no more. Now git!"

"Creaky ol' reprobate!" Van Horn hollered.

"Hee, hee, hee!" Wolf giggled, and the others smiled at the antics of the randy old mountain man, who was still tough enough to take on a grizzly bear . . . and would, if the opportunity presented itself.

"I'm gonna put a knot on your head when I get back," Van Horn warned Wolf.

Wolf laughed and slapped Van Horn's horse on the rump. "Go git 'em, Van!"

Van Horn and Smoke reined up at the creek, stripped saddle and bridle off their horses, and hobbled them. They checked their guns and exchanged glances.

"See you at the other end of the street, young feller," Van Horn said, then hopped across the little creek and began working his way up behind the first line of houses and buildings.

Smoke took the other side. But he stayed on the boardwalks, at least for now.

There was not one living creature visible on the streets or boardwalks of the town. Not a dog, cat, chicken, horse, or man, woman, or child.

Smoke looked back. Wolf and Bad Dog were swinging down from the saddle at the creek. He walked on until he came to an empty building at the end of the first block of stores. All the stores that he could see were closed and locked.

Far up the street came the sound of a tinny piano and the high, shrill, false laughter of a hurdy-gurdy girl. Smoke looked across the street at the alleyway. Van Horn was standing there. He looked over at Smoke, shrugged his shoulders, and walked on.

Smoke paused, his eyes searching the second-story windows to his right. He was certain men with rifles had been posted along the way, but he could spot nothing that would give away their location. He resumed his slow walking.

The town was filled with gunfighters on the payrolls of Biggers, Fosburn, and Cosgrove; but where the hell were they? All scattered out in the town's many saloons? Some of them, yes. But he rather doubted that all of them were in the bars. Smoke stopped his walking. They had to be in the stores, all spread out along the narrow, twist-ing streets.

Smoke slipped off the boardwalk and stepped into the coolness of a shadowed alley. He slipped one of the spare .44s from behind his belt and jacked the hammer back as he walked toward the rear of the buildings. At the alley's opening, he looked back left, toward the Golden Cherry. Clemmie waved to him from a window on the second floor. Smoke returned the wave and walked on. By now, Wolf and Bad Dog would be a block behind him and Pasco and Kit would be hobbling their horses at the creek. The hired guns would know their quarry was in town. So why didn't they make a move?

That question was answered when a young man who looked to be in his early twenties sud-denly stepped out from behind the rear of a building, both hands hovering over the butts of his guns. "Leather that six-shooter, Jensen, and face me like a man. I've come to kill you."

"Don't be a fool, man," Smoke told him, the cocked .44 in his right hand. "I've got no quarrel with you. Give this up and go on back home."

"Yellow, that's what you are!" the young man sneered.

"I'm offering you your life, partner," Smoke reminded the young man. "Take the offer. Don't die for nothing."

"You ain't gonna holster that gun and try your luck with me?"

"Not a chance, kid. This is not a game. Give it

up, go home, and live."

The would-be gunslinger stood for a moment, cussing Smoke. Then, with a strange cry of desperation, his hands closed around the butts of his guns and Smoke fired, knocking a leg out from under the young man. The young tough hollered in pain, both hands grabbing at his shattered knee. Smoke walked up to him and took his guns from leather, noticing that one was a .44 and the other a .45. He kept the .44 and threw the .45 into the bushes.

He looked down at the young man, writhing in pain on the bottle- and can-littered ground. "Boy, if I ever see you again and you're carrying iron, I'll kill you on the spot. Do you understand all that?"

"Yes . . . sir," the young man groaned out the words. "I swear to God I'll never tote no gun again. But Jesus, I hurt something awful."

"Pain is good for a man. It's a reminder that you're still alive." Smoke walked on.

His shot had been the only one thus far. Smoke felt that was about to change. Now the hired guns knew where he was and they surely would be coming after him.

He heard a pistol bark and a man scream. That was followed by a crash of breaking glass and the thud of a body after falling a distance. Van Horn had nailed one of those on a second floor . . . or a rooftop.

He heard running boots and stopped, filling his left hand with a .44. Two men sprang out of a narrow passageway between buildings and pulled up short, spotting Smoke. Smoke did not recall ever seeing the men before. But they cursed him, their guns lifting. Smoke had no choice but to open fire. He fired four times, the slugs taking the hired guns in belly and chest as the muzzles lifted. They spun around and jerked their way into the rapidly enveloping darkness of death.

Behind him and to his right he heard a curse, a shot, and a short cry of pain. He turned his head for a second, spotting Ol' Wolf some distance behind him, both hands filled with guns.

Smoke walked on, now slipping into the dark and narrow passageway the hired guns had sprung out of. He stopped just short of the street, listening.

"I'll give a sack of gold for every dead Jensen supporter!" he heard Cosgrove scream. "A sack of gold, men, do you hear me? A sack of gold." The voice was slightly muffled, so Smoke figured Cosgrove was safely behind walls.

Boots sounded on the boardwalk and the entrance was suddenly filled with men from the Triangle JB.

"Is it a good day to die, boys?" Smoke threw out the question a second before he opened fire.

Twenty-three

The booming of the .44s was enormous in the narrow space, and the alley became thick with gunsmoke. Smoke dropped to his belly and crawled under a building, leaving the Triangle JB men moaning and groaning on the ground. He inched his way toward the street, stopping just before he reached the high boardwalk in front of a saloon that he knew belonged to Fat Fosburn. Above him, the floor was heavy with pacing boots. He rolled over on his back and listened to the muffled talk.

"Goddamnit, there ain't but seven or eight of them. What the hell are we waitin' for?"

"I just caught me a glimpse of Kit," another said. "Damn turncoat! I can't figure what got into him."

The voice came from right above Smoke. He emptied one .44 into the floor above him, then swiftly rolled to his left, screams of anguish ripping from several men inside the saloon. Smoke was to the rear of the building and running up the littered way before the men in the saloon could gather their senses and start pouring lead into the floor.

He forced open the door to a barbershop, closing and locking it behind him, then ran to the front of the establishment. The door was bolted and the shades drawn halfway down. Kneeling down by the front and peeping out, Smoke quickly reloaded and caught his breath.

By now, all those backing him up would be in town and ready to force the hands of the Big Three. Smoke and Van Horn had cut the odds down some, but those supporting Jenny were still badly outnumbered . . . by how much was something none of them with Smoke knew.

Smoke had inflicted some damage by shooting through the floor back at the saloon. Maybe one or two men had caught lead. But so far, no class gun-hand had showed himself, and there were about a dozen or so of them still on the payroll of Fosburn, Cosgrove, and Biggers.

Back of Wong's Chinese Cafe, Pasco came face to face with a slick who called himself the Lordsburg Kid. He'd killed a couple of Mexican sheepherders and raped one Mexican girl. The Kid thought he was hell on wheels with a gun.

"Damn greaser!" the Kid hissed at Pasco. "Anybody who'd work with sheep is scum."

"Oh?" Pasco said easily. "My cousin, Carbone, used to herd sheep as a boy. I do not think you would say that to him. If he's still alive, that is," he added.

"You ain't Carbone."

"This is true. I am better than my cousin, *amigo*. Faster, and a much more accurate shot."

"You're a damn greasy liar!"

265

Pasco drove the Kid's center shirt button all the way out his backbone with one slug. The Kid never even cleared leather. Pasco stood over the body and shook his head. "You should have learned some manners from your *madre* and *padre, amigo.* Now it is too late."

He walked on.

"Jenkins!" Van Horn called to a particularly vicious gunhand he remembered had said some terrible things about Miss Jenny.

Jenkins turned and grinned at Van Horn, his teeth yellow and rotted. "Why, you damned old wrinkled-up worthless coot! I doubt you even got the strength to pull them wore out old Remingtons from leather. Will them things still fire?"

"Why don't you try me and see, Jenkins?"

Jenkins laughed at him and grabbed for iron. Van Horn shot him twice in the belly and left him dying in the alley. "Some folks nowadays just ain't got no respect for their elders and betters," Van Horn grumbled. "No tellin' what it'll be like a hundred years from now."

Wolf Parcell clamped a gnarled old hand on the neck of a Biggers' rider and drove his head against the outside wall of a building. Several times. On the fourth try, the gunhand's head drove clear through the wood and Wolf left him dangling there by the neck, the toes of his boots dragging the ground.

"Either that was rotten wood or that boy's shore got a hard head," Wolf muttered.

Bad Dog just couldn't resist it. He had spotted a man on the roof of a hardware and guns store and quietly notched an arrow. The man finally presented him with the target he wanted, and Bad Dog let the arrow fly. It embedded about six inches into the left cheeks of the man's big ass. The gunslick dropped his rifle and went to bellerin' loud enough to wake the dead. A man ran out the back of Darlin' Lill's Saloon, both hands filled with guns, and Bad Dog gave him a Cheyenne present. The man dropped silently, an arrow through the heart.

The gunhand on the roof was trying to climb down, hollering and squalling each time he moved his left leg. Bad Dog put an arrow into his right leg and the man fell off the ladder to land hard in the alley. He did not move.

Slim Waters stepped into the rear of the Cards and Wheels Club, both hands filled with guns. He toed open the door leading from the main room to the storage area and stepped inside.

"This here's for Miss Jenny, boys," he announced, and started shooting.

Kit Silver stood facing five men, the class gunslick Val Davis among them.

"You're a fool, Kit," Val told him.

"Maybe," Kit replied. "But you're dead." Kit smiled and grabbed iron.

Shady Bryant faced three top guns, his hands by his side. "Well, boys," he told them, "I reckon this is my last hurrah. Let's make it a good one." Then he laughed, jerked his guns, and went to work, this time, on the right side.

Smoke heard the roaring reports of guns and knew it was root hog or die time. He smashed out the window of the barbershop — remembering that he must be sure to use some Big Three money to replace it — and yelled, "Here I am, boys. You want that sack full of gold, come get me!"

Smoke ran out the back of the shop and around the corner just as men ran out of buildings and sought cover where they could find it and started pumping lead into the barbershop.

Standing by the corner of a building, Smoke dropped two before the men realized he wasn't in the barbershop and started throwing lead at him.

By that time, Smoke had crawled under a building and was working his way toward daylight on the other side of the establishment.

He paused to reload, shoved the Colts behind his belt, and pulled the sawed-off revolving shotgun from his shoulder. He checked the barrel for blockage. At short range, the ten-gauge was an awesome weapon. Smoke crawled out from under the building and looked at the backs of three men, Ned Harden and Haywood among the group — two of the more odious gunhandlers Smoke had ever had the misfortune to encounter. They would do anything, to anybody, at anytime. All that was about to stop — abruptly.

"You boys looking for me?" Smoke called, getting a good grip on the sawed-off, for its recoil could rip it from the grasp if a man wasn't ready for it.

The trio spun around, eyes wide and mouths open. "Jesus God!" Harden yelled, spotting the cut-down revolving shotgun.

There was about fifteen feet between them. Smoke started pulling and cocking and blasting. It was a good ten feet from the corner of the alleyway to the mud and dirt of the street, and that's where all three landed. Or what was left of them.

Smoke reloaded the hand cannon and listened for a few seconds. The shooting had stopped from inside the Cards and Wheels Club and from behind the apothecary shop. He had no way of knowing the outcome.

Kit Silver had taken five out with him. The gunfighter sat with his back to a building, four slugs in him; but he was not dead yet. He smiled at Val Davis, who lay mortally wounded, looking at him. The others with him were dead.

"Why'd . . . you do it, Kit?" Val asked.

"Felt like it. Felt good, too. Sorry you'll never get to know what it's like to do something right for a change."

"You've killed me!"

"Sure looks like it, don't it?"

Val put his head on the ground and died.

Kit shook his head. "I hope I live long enough to die among better company than this," he said.

The interior of the Cards and Wheels Club looked like a slaughterhouse when Pasco backtracked and entered the place. Slim was still alive, but just barely.

"I won't lie to you, Slim," Pasco said. "It's bad."

"Yeah, I know. In the side pocket of my jacket. A napkin. Get it for me, will you?"

"A napkin?"

"Got . . . something wrapped up in it."

Pasco opened the napkin. One of Jenny's doughnuts. Slim held out his hand and grinned, the blood leaking from one corner of his mouth. He took a bite and chewed contentedly. "Mighty good, Pasco. Mighty good." He swallowed, closed his eyes, and his head lolled to one side.

"Damn!" Pasco said.

Shady Bryant lay with his hands still gripping the butts of his guns. Three dead gunhands lay in front of him. A young man who called himself the Red River Kid and fancied himself a fast gun stood looking at the scene. He shook his head and took off his gunbelt, slinging it over one shoulder. He started walking toward where their horses were picketed. The farm back in East Texas looked real good to him right now.

"Is that you, Red River?" a man called, sitting on the ground, his back to the outside wall of a privy. Bullets had broken both his legs.

"Never heard of him," the kid called over his shoulder, and kept right on walking. "My name's Frank Sparks."

"I'd a shot him yesterday," the wounded gun-fighter spoke to the slight breeze that wound around the buildings of Red Light. "But if I'd a done what he's doin' twenty years ago, I damn sure wouldn't be in this fix now." The wounded gunslick watched the young man walk across the meadow. "Good luck, kid," he called weakly. "And to hell with this," he muttered. He pulled his guns from leather and tossed them into the tall grass.

Smoke walked into the Golden Plum, through the back door, and said, "Give me a beer, Jeff. I do believe I've worked up something of a thirst."

Jeff looked at him. "You're hit, Mister Jensen."

"Bullets burned my arm and scratched my side. Nothing serious."

Wolf and Bad Dog stomped in from the back, followed by Van Horn, who was supporting the badly wounded Kit Silver.

"Slim and Shady's dead," the old gunfighter announced. "It's down to us, now."

"No, it isn't," the voice came from the rear of the saloon, which was getting quite a bit of traffic. Moses stood there holding a rifle, a pistol belted around his waist. Clemmie and her girls stood behind him, all of them armed with various types of weapons.

"You put that ornery Silver on a pallet over here, Van Horn," Clemmie said, looking at Kit. "Me and that rounder go 'way back together. He's too damn mean to die."

Kit grinned at the madam as he was placed on a hurriedly made pallet of blankets.

271

Chung and Wong were next, both of them armed with long-barreled, ten-gauge goose guns. Wong said, "So sorry I could not bring some good Chinese food." He held up the shotgun. "Could not carry this and food at the same time."

Chung said, "Battle lines have been drawn, Mister Smoke Jensen. We are now all on this side of street, enemies on other side."

"Have drink of rye, Mister Jeff," Wong said. "Like cowboys do."

"You ain't never had a drink of rye in all the time I've known you. And you sure ain't gonna like it," Jeff warned.

Wong broke over the goose gun and loaded it up. "Warm belly, though. Might not get another chance for some time."

"He certainly has a point there," Smoke agreed.

Jeff smiled and set out shot glasses and bottles. "Serve yourselves, boys. I've got to get my guns!"

Twenty-four

Above the town, on the slopes and ridges leading to the mine, the townspeople waited, watched, and listened. Most families had packed picnic lunches, and several of the saloon owners had transported barrels of beer and cases of whiskey and set up makeshift bars for the thirsty. No loving creature not directly involved in the fight had been left behind in the town. Pet cats were in boxes or crates, and dogs were on leashes. Chickens were in coops. Hens went right on laying eggs.

Across the narrow street, Cosgrove, Biggers, and Fosburn crouched behind the heavily barricaded front of the mayor's office and tried to make some sense out of what had happened and what was happening. All three had finally gotten it through their heads that this day was going to be the turning point in their lives — one way or the other.

Fosburn sat with his back to a wall. He had two guns strapped around his tubby waist and a rifle across his knees. His hair was disheveled and his face was dirty. His eyes seemed to have lost their sparkle. Of the three, Fosburn had turned realist.

273

"We were too greedy," the mayor spoke in quiet tones. "We had it all but wanted more. Now look where that's got us."

"Shut up," Jack Biggers snarled at him.

"Oh, he's right," Major Cosgrove said. "I don't have to like what he says, but I'm forced to agree with him. I do have to add this: none of us counted on Smoke Jensen."

"Make a deal with him," Fat said.

"I don't think that is possible at this stage," Major said. "The three of us have but two options left us — win or die."

"Jesus Christ!" Biggers almost shouted the words. "There can't be more than seven or eight of them over there. They're all in the saloon. We've still got about thirty-five hardcases and we have them surrounded. Why are we talking about dying and making deals?"

Fosburn stood up and walked to the shattered front window. "Smoke Jensen?" he called.

"I hear you," Smoke's voice rang out.

"I'll make a deal with you."

"What kind of deal?"

"You let me ride out with my money from the bank. I'll sell you my ranch at a fair price. You'll never hear from me again."

"You don't have a ranch," Smoke's words were loud and clear. "None of you do."

The Big Three exchanged glances. Fosburn shouted, "What the hell are you talking about, Jensen?"

"You men stole the land you're running cattle

on. You killed the original land owners or ran them off. But you never properly filed on the land you stole. The quit claim and other deeds were forged. And bad ones at that. My wife has had two dozen lawyers and Pinkertons seeking out survivors and relatives. She bought the land from them. It's all legal. Your interests in the mine will go to the survivors and relatives of those you killed or ran out. Law suits are being filed now. U.S. Marshals are on the way here now with warrants and other legal papers. Neither you nor Biggers have a pot to piss in or a window to throw it out of. You're both dead broke. No deals."

Biggers and Fosburn were too astonished to speak. They stared at one another open mouthed.

"But I'm still rich, you bastard!" Major hollered. "You men working for me hear that? I've still got sacks and sacks of gold. And there's gold on Jenny Jensen's ranch. Up in the mountains. The richest vein in all of Montana. I'm giving it to you hired guns. You hear me? I'm writing out papers now. But you've got to kill the Jensens and all associated with them to get it. You'll all be worth millions if you do that. Think about it. You'll never have to work again. Never again have to sleep on the ground or worry about where your next meal or next dollar is coming from. You'll have fancy food and the best drinks and the fanciest women. For the rest of your lives!" he screamed.

"That's right, boys," the calm voice of Van

Horn drifted out of the Golden Plum. "And all you got to do to earn it is kill me, Pasco, Bad Dog, Wolf Parcel, Kit Silver, and Smoke Jensen. Then you got to kill all the men out at Miss Jenny's ranch, and that includes Little Jimmy Hammon. Them's some bad ol' boys out yonder. And then you got to kill Miss Sally and Miss Jenny. And after that, you got to explain to the judges and the lawyers and the Pinkertons and the U.S. Marshals what happened to us all. Think about that."

"That's nothing!" Major yelled. "Without bodies, no one can prove a thing. Take the saloon, men. Take it, and be worth millions, or ride out with holes in your drawers and patches on your boots."

"They's still the townspeople," Patmos said to Whisperin' Langley.

"Kill 'em all and dump their bodies down a mineshaft and blow it closed," Whisperin' whispered.

"Hell," Bobby Jewel said. "They's five hundred or so people in this town."

"So what?" Jim Pell said. "We take the saloon, then the ranch, and have some fun with the women out there, then we kill Biggers, Fosburn, and Cosgrove, and we have it *all!*"

"Yeah," Sam Jackson said. "Let's do it."

"Pass the word," Whisperin' said. "We take the saloon. Now!"

"They're fools," Wolf said from his position in the saloon. "There ain't enough of them left to overpower us. We'll stack them up like cordwood out yonder in the street and back there in the alley."

"But they'll try," Smoke said. "They've got big money in their eyes now."

"Even if they should succeed," Kit said from the pallet, his voice weak, but his guns were loaded up and by his side, "they'll turn on Biggers and Fosburn and Cosgrove and kill them, too. All the real gunfighters has gone. Them with any honor at all has left or changed sides. That's pure scum out there now. Half of those bums out yonder have killed their own mothers and fathers and brothers and sisters for one reason or another. A horse turd has more value than all them out there put together."

Wong lifted his long-barreled goose gun, sighted in, and pulled the trigger. The charge blew the entire window out of its frame and tore the head off the rifleman who was getting set to snipe at the saloon. The headless body fell backward, bounced off a wall, and came catapulting out of the shattered frame, to crash through an awning and lie on the boardwalk.

Fosburn looked at the bloody, horrible sight about two feet from him and shuddered.

Wong picked himself up off the floor and reloaded the empty chamber.

Moses, Chung, Jeff, and the Soiled Doves from the Golden Cherry stationed themselves at the rear of the saloon, ready to repel any intruders. Clemmie stayed by the side of the wounded Kit Silver.

Stormclouds had been gathering all morning, and now a light rain began to fall. Lightning licked around the high peaks of the mountains that rimmed the mining town.

"That'll keep them from burning us out," Wolf remarked, chewing on a sandwich from the free lunch table.

Smoke nodded and lifted his rifle. A very small part of a leg was exposed across the street, the man behind a horse trough. Smoke sighted in and pulled the trigger and the man howled as the bullet shattered a shin. He staggered to his feet and turned to try to limp away, and Pasco nailed him from his position on the second floor of the saloon. The hired gun fell into the horse trough.

"Remind me to have that water changed," Smoke said. "I wouldn't want to poison a good horse."

There was a lull in the fighting while both sides tended to wounded, caught their breath, and had a drink, and while those aligned with the Big Three plotted unspeakable evil against fellow human beings.

Those in the Golden Plum waited as the rain picked up.

"I don't trust these men," Fat whispered. "I think they'd as soon kill us as anybody else."

"Where's your foreman, Waco?" Major asked Biggers.

"Gone," Biggers said sourly. "Pulled out last

night. Said he didn't sign on to fight girls and women and to associate with the likes of them I got on the payroll. Man turned Christian on me or something. Wouldn't surprise me none to see him pop up over at Jenny's ranch."

Waco was at that moment riding toward Red Light, with a dozen of the area's small ranchers and farmers who had had quite enough of Cosgrove, Fosburn, and Biggers. Now that someone had finally gotten the ball rolling, they were in the game, root hog or die. From the edge of town, the men reined up, staring at the several hundred men, women, kids, and animals all gathered together at the mine complex.

"Must be hell in the streets of Red Light," Waco observed. "Let's go down and even up the odds a little bit for them on the side of Jensen."

Up on the mountain, the local Temperance League had gotten cranked up and there was preaching, singing, tooting, oom-pahing, and drumming.

Out at the Circle Cherry, Club and his deputies were playing poker with Sally and losing nearly every hand. "Ma'am," Deputy Brandt asked. "Who taught you to play poker?"

"Louis Longmont," Sally said sweetly. "The bet is five dollars to you."

The sheriff and his deputies tossed their cards on the table. Louis Longmont was the most famous gambler in all of America, plus a noted gunfighter and a man worth millions and millions of dollars. "I believe we'll just get a breath of fresh air, ma'am," Club said.

Sally smiled and raked in her winnings. "Come here, Jenny," she said. "I'll teach you about cold-decking and palming."

Club and his deputies shook their heads and walked outside, Club saying, "That there, boys, is one hell of a woman. Can you believe that Smoke Jensen actually dries the dishes?"

Modoc looked at him. "Wouldn't you?"

"Riders coming into town, Smoke," Pasco called from the second floor. "It's Waco, and he's bringin' in a bunch of small ranchers and farmers."

"Waco's all right," Kit said. His voice seemed to be a little stronger. "I figured he'd get a gutful of Jack Biggers and leave." He started chuckling, and the others looked at him strangely. "It just dawned on me what Highpockets and Biff and them others was doin' that day at the ranch. Walkin' around, stoppin', then throwin' their hands up into the air. We all thought it was a new dance step. Then, when I seen Whisperin' and Val doin' it in the bunkhouse, I thought they had changed sides and was in love with one another!"

Clemmie started giggling at the very thought of Val Davis and Whisperin' dancing together, and it was highly infectious. Soon everybody in the saloon was roaring with laughter. Pasco had been sitting on the landing, looking out the window, and he almost fell down the steps, he was laughing so hard. Wolf Parcell was roaring with high mirth. The laughter reached those in the buildings directly across the street.

"What in billy-hell is so damn funny?" Jim Pell snarled the words.

"They must know something we don't," Al Jones said.

"Yeah," Dusty Higgens said, entering from the back door. "Believe me, they do. Like Waco and about twelve or fifteen men just rode into town and took up positions all around us. We got Smoke and them others surrounded in the saloon, and now we're surrounded in here!"

"Not with no twelve or fifteen men," Chambers said.

Dick Whitten stood up to look out the window and a rancher drilled him clean between the eyes with a .30-.30.

"You wanna bet?" Dusty asked.

Twenty-five

"I've had it," a hired gun said to his buddy. They crouched behind the shattered windows on the second floor of a dry goods store. "I don't know what them others plan on doin', but I'm out of it."

"Me, too, Les," his friend replied. "I'm sorry I ever got into this awful situation."

Les took off his bandanna and tied it around the muzzle of his rifle, just behind the front sight. He stuck the barrel out of the window and waved it back and forth. Then he left the rifle balanced on the sill. The men took off their belts and laid them beside their rifles, in plain sight of anyone on the second floor across the street.

"Two of them giving it up," Pasco announced. "Second floor across the street and to our right."

In the rear of the saloon, four gunhands covering the back talked it over and decided they'd had enough of this town. They darted from cover to cover while those in the rear of the saloon held their fire and watched them leave. The gunhands made their horses and rode off. None of them looked back.

Moses slipped to the storage room door and called, "The back is clear, Smoke. The gunnies gave it up and rode off."

"The ones with any brains at all, and that ain't many of them, have sensed it's over," Kit said. "I figure you give some others the chance to ride clear and they'll go. That'll leave about twenty at most."

"Waco?" Smoke yelled.

"Right here, Mister Jensen!" the ex-Triangle JB foreman hollered.

"Hold your fire. Let's see if any want to ride out. If they do, let them have safe passage out of town."

"Will do."

"You men across the street!" Smoke yelled. "You heard it. Any who want to ride can do so in safety. Just clear out of this area and stay clear. It's up to you."

A moment passed before the call sprang from a building. "We're ridin' out, Jensen! They's eight of us. Hold your fire. You'll not see none of us again."

"Ride out, then!"

"Damn you all to hell!" Biggers shouted. "You're all dirty cowards!"

One of the retreating gunnies yelled out, telling Biggers where he could go and what he could do to himself while he was on the way. A couple more of those leaving yelled out some options for Biggers.

"That would certainly be an interesting sight to see," Clemmie muttered.

"Twenty-four or twenty-five left," Kit said, loud enough for Smoke to hear. "Maybe two or

283

three less than that. But I could probably name those who stayed. They're the bad ones, Smoke. They'll not give up."

"Then they'll die," Wolf grumbled.

"They know that, too," Kit said. "They're worthless trash and sorry human bein's, but they ain't cowards. They just ain't got good judgment."

Five hired guns rushed the front of the saloon. Rifles and pistols boomed and cracked from inside the Golden Plum. Five bodies lay still on the muddy street, the rain washing their blood into the wagon wheel ruts.

"How many?" Kit called.

"Five," Smoke told him, punching out the empties and reloading.

"Ruined," Fat Fosburn muttered from his position on the floor. "We had it all and now we have nothing. Jensen stripped us down to the bare bones. Even if we survive this, we're all looking at long prison terms or a hangman's noose. Too many people heard our offer to the gunfighters. I been to prison. I just ain't goin' back." He stuck the muzzle of his rifle into his mouth and pulled the trigger, blowing out the back of his head and splattering his brains on the wall.

Jack Biggers looked at the mess and swallowed hard. He cut his eyes to Major Cosgrove. "Now what?"

Cosgrove shook his head. "I don't know. There's only one way out of this damn town, and it's blocked by Waco and those men with him. All my gold is up at the mine. I've got to get it. It's all I have left. It's a fortune, Jack. Come on. We can't ride out, but we can walk out through the mountains. We can follow the ravines up to the rear of the mine office without being seen. All the townspeople have taken shelter from the rain in the sheds and the mouth of the pits. The gold is concealed under the office floor."

"We can't carry all that gold, man!"

"There are burros up there. They can go where a horse or mule can't go. They can tote the gold. We got no choice, Jack."

"If the gunhands see us leaving, they'll kill us."

"You have a better idea?"

Jack shook his head. "No," he said softly.

Jack Biggers and Major Cosgrove slipped out the rear of the office and stood in the hard-pouring rain for a few seconds. The rain would help conceal their movements. The pair pushed off, running hard and staying low.

Since the abortive attempt to rush the saloon, no shots had been fired from either side. The bodies in the street gave mute testimony to the secure position of those inside the Golden Plum. It was a standoff, but a standoff that the gunhands knew they could not win.

"Whisperin'?" the hoarse call came from the outside, just loud enough to be heard by those in the front room.

Whisperin' moved to the busted window and

285

looked out. Russ Bailey stood in the rain, pressed up close to the building. "Yeah?"

"Fat Fosburn is dead in the office. Looks like he blowed his own head off. It's a real mess, I tell you. Cosgrove and Biggers is gone."

Whisperin' mouthed an extremely ugly word several times. "We been sold out, boys," he told those in the room. "Cosgrove and Biggers has run. They got to be headin' for the mine. I suspect that's where he's hid all that gold he talked about."

"But there ain't no way out of that place!"

"Yeah, there is. Mule knew a way through and told some of the boys 'fore he left. There's a horse ranch just over the pass."

"Just over the pass means *walkin'* through them damn mountains, totin' the gold by hand."

"We can do it. At least, we can carry some of it. Come on, let's start slippin' out one at a time. Don't tell the others. Hell with them."

"Not me," Tom Wilson said. "I was caught in a thunderstorm in the mountains one time. If you ain't never seen it, you don't want to be in it. There's lightnin' dancin' and poppin' everywhere. They was three of us down in Colorado when we got caught. I was the only one who made it out. You ever seen a man hit by lightnin'?" He shuddered. "I have. Johnny's eyeballs popped out of his head. I'm stayin' right here."

"Somebody do something!" Russ said. "I'm

freezin' to death out here in the damn rain!"

"Let's go."

Five men slipped out the rear of the building to join Russ in the rain. Lonesome was the last to leave. Tom Wilson stayed where he was, all right. Lonesome Ted Lightfoot had cut his throat to ensure the man's silence. They were all a real nice bunch of folks.

"Smoke!" Pasco called from the landing. "I thought at first I was seeing things. But now I'm sure. There's some men heading for the mine. I saw two about three or four minutes ago. Then about four or five more."

"That's it? No more?"

"Not yet. What do you think is up?"

"Rats desertin' the ship," Kit called.

"Probably," Smoke said. He checked his pistols and picked up a rifle, making certain it was loaded up full. "Hold it here, people. I'm heading for the mine."

"You want some company?" Van Horn called.

"No. You can be sure they're keeping a good eye behind them. One man alone will be much harder to spot. Besides, I think you're going to have your hands full with those still across the street. See you shortly."

Smoke was gone out the back door, running hard for the mine, keeping to the alley and out of sight of those across the street. At the mine road that angled off from the edge of town, Smoke darted across the crushed rock road and took the hard and long way up to the mine, clambering over huge rocks and jumping young rivers of water that would vanish when the rain stopped. Since this route was very nearly impossible for a man to climb, Smoke knew it would be the last place those above him would look.

Once, when he paused to catch his breath, he studied the long stairs that led from ground level to the main offices. Since the mine was not working this day, the mule-drawn hoist was not being used and he could see two men just entering the offices, high above him. The big one was Cosgrove and the other one looked like Jack Biggers. It sure wasn't Fat Fosburn. The size was all wrong.

The angled steps had four landings, five if you counted the landing at the top. It was a good three hundred feet off the ground.

Then Smoke saw a knot of men running up the steps. Five, no, six of them. They paused for breath at the first landing. Unless you were accustomed to it, this high up was no place to be running, and it could sap your strength quickly.

Smoke climbed on while the storm raged, lightning dancing all around the high peaks above him. He had slung his rifle, muzzle down, and made sure his pistols were snug in their holsters and thonged down tight.

He was winded when he reached the top, but as far as he knew, no one had spotted him. The temperance band had stopped tooting and oompahing and drumming, and the singing had stopped. The townspeople had taken refuge wherever they could find it, and none were in sight.

Smoke studied the situation. There was no way he was going to risk climbing those steps; he'd be a very conspicuous target. Unless . . .

He studied the sheer wall of the cliff behind the steps, where the hoist was located. He could probably climb up a couple of hundred feet of dry cable, but damned if he was going to try it in a drenching rain.

Then he realized there was a road leading up to the mine proper. Naturally, dummy! he berated himself. How else could they build the damn complex way up there? The rain had obscured the narrow road, just wide enough for a wagon with a skilled driver at the reins and a stout rope or chain hooked to the rear of the wagon with the other end attached to a heavy-duty spoked gearbox of some type in case the wagon brakes failed.

Smoke left his dubious shelter and ran for the road. With his clothing soaked, he blended in against the gray water-soaked rock of the cliff the road had been carved out of.

Jack Biggers suddenly appeared on the top landing and started shooting at the men who were now at the second landing. The men returned the fire, driving the rancher back into the building.

Interesting, Smoke thought, as he squatted under a small overhang very near the mouth of the mine, which was on a level with the top landing. More steps led from the mine to the office. He unslung his rifle and wiped it as dry as he could, thinking: I'll just stay here out of the rain and if I'm lucky, maybe they'll kill each other.

No such luck. Patmos turned, spotted Smoke, and opened his mouth to shout out the warning. Before he could yell, Smoke drilled the gunfighter clean and Patmos went down on the slick landing. The shot was lost in the roar of rain, the howl of wind, and the crash of thunder.

For a few seconds — enough time for Smoke to leap out and run for a small foreman's hut — those on the landing with Patmos thought he had lost his footing and slipped. Whisperin' knelt down beside him and got the word from the badly wounded killer-for-hire. From his hiding place behind the hut, Smoke watched Whisperin' look wildly all around the spot where Patmos had pointed. Then the gunhand had to jump for safety as both Cosgrove and Biggers opened fire from above them, driving the gunfighters back. Whisperin' leaped away, leaving Patmos exposed on the landing. Patmos's body jerked in pain as half a dozen rounds were fired into him. He feebly lifted one hand, then the arm fell to the landing and he did not move again.

"That sure is a loyal bunch," Smoke muttered. "Certainly true to one another."

As he leaned against the hut, a thought came to him. Wherever miners are, there is bound to be dynamite. Smoke picked up a broken ax handle and used it to tear off a couple of boards from the rear of the hut. He smiled. The place was filled with cases of dynamite. Then he lost his smile as he realized what a lousy place he'd picked to hide behind. If a stray bullet hit the right spot, there wouldn't be enough left of him to pick up. Not even with a spoon and shovel.

He grabbed a dozen sticks and some caps and fuses and vacated the area immediately.

While those on the middle landing were being sniped at by Cosgrove and Biggers, unable either to return the fire or do much looking for Smoke, Smoke edged closer and capped and fused his dynamite. He lit a bundle and gave it a flip. The bundle of explosives bounced on the landing and went sailing off into space, exploding harmlessly in midair.

"What the hell?" Smoke heard Biggers holler from above him.

"You bastards!" Whisperin' yelled at the pair on the top landing.

"That wasn't us!" Cosgrove shouted.

There was only the howl of the wind, the rush of the rain, the snap and cracking of lightning, and the booming of thunder for a full half minute, as the men above and below each other gave that some thought.

"Oh, hell!" Lonesome Ted Lightfoot muttered. Then he raised his voice to a shout. "Cosgrove, Biggers! We better work together, boys. Smoke Jensen is up here with us."

"Hell with you!" Biggers shouted. "You look out for your own butt, gunfighter."

Smoke tossed another bundle of dynamite. It landed flat and stayed put on the slick boards. When it blew, it took about half the landing and forced the remaining gunfighters to press up against the face of the cliff. Patmos's body rolled off the shattered landing and fell to the rocky ground below.

Cosgrove and Biggers laughed at the men below them. Smoke stopped their laughter by tying a bundle of explosives to the broken ax or pick handle and hurling it up to the top landing.

"Jesus Christ!" Cosgrove yelled, as he and Biggers jumped for the dubious safety of the office building.

The charge blew off half the safety railing, tore a great hole in the floor of the landing, and shattered all the front windows in the office building. It also rattled the hell out of the office building constructed against the face of the cliff.

"That's it," Whisperin' said. "That's all for me. We can't get out, boys. We got the vigilantes below us, Cosgrove and Biggers above us, and Jensen over yonder someplace. I'm done."

"Might as well," Jim Pell said. The others nodded their agreement.

"Jensen!" Whisperin' shouted. "Can you hear me over all this damn stormin'?"

"I hear you," Smoke called.

"Can you see us?"

Smoke shifted positions behind crates and broken wagon wheels and other discarded debris. "I can see you."

"We're done, Smoke. You hear me? It's all over for us. We yield."

"Throw all your guns over the side. All of you. Unbuckle and toss everything over the side."

The men chucked it all over the side of the shattered landing. They even reached down into boots and behind their belts in the small of the backs and pulled out hideaway guns and knives. Everything went over the side.

"Now stay where you are. Press up against the face of the cliff. Cosgrove and Biggers can't see you or hit you with gunfire. Is there a back way out of that office building?"

"No," Dusty called. "They got to use this landing or the road you're on. They're trapped." Just like us, he thought.

Far below him, Smoke could see men gathering, taking up positions behind rocks and boulders and wagons and rail cars. Two dozen rifles or more were now trained on the office building. He could make out Waco and Wolf and Pasco and several others on his side. The storm had blocked the sounds of the final fight in Red Light. The outlaws were licked.

Almost.

Twenty-six

"It's all over, Cosgrove, Biggers," Smoke yelled from below the office building. "You have no more men. Give it up."

"Hell with you!" Major Cosgrove yelled. "Come and get us."

"Don't be fools! Look below you. There are two or three dozen rifles pointed at you right now. We can shoot that office building to bits. Give it up."

Cosgrove and Biggers chanced a look below them. Jensen sure wasn't lying.

"I hate Smoke Jensen," Major Cosgrove said. "I despise that man more than anything on the face of this earth. How the hell was I to know that Jenny was the blood kin of the last mountain man?" Then, out of sheer desperation, hate, fury, and frustration, he lifted his rifle and began firing at the men assembled far below the office building.

No one knows exactly what happened after that. And no one ever really will. The most popular theory is that Cosgrove had cases of dynamite stored in the building and the returning rifle fire touched it off. But still others say they saw a hideous flash of blue lightning strike the building.

Whatever the reason, one second the office building was there, and in the next instant it was gone, debris flying in all directions and raining down to the ground below.

But not one trace of Major Cosgrove or Jack Biggers was ever found. And neither was any of the gold. Some say there was a rear exit to the building, a natural cave that was sealed by the massive explosion. Some say they escaped.

All anybody knew for sure was that when Whisperin' Langely, Dusty Higgens, Jim Pell, Lonesome Ted Lightfoot, and Russ Bailey were finally rescued from the landing, they had to change underwear. The explosion must have given them quite a fright.

Sheriff Club Bowers and his deputies rode into town just in time to witness the explosion. U.S. Marshals had ridden into Red Light only seconds before the huge wall of flame blew out of the cliff.

Reverend Lester Laymon said it was the heavy hand of God that done it.

Violet said her husband was an idiot . . . as usual.

When all was said and done, all the legal papers served and filed and settled, the citizens of Red Light were the new owners of the mine and Jenny Jensen owned the entire valley of lush graze and flowing creeks and gushing springs . . . and the gold up in the towering mountains. That was never mined. All records of where the huge vein was located had gone up in the explosion and only Smoke Jensen knew the exact location, and he wasn't talking.

The gold is still there. Untouched.

Jenny's range stretched for miles, north to south. It's still in the family, and still producing some of the finest beef on the market.

Red Light was soon dropped and the town's name was changed. Kit Silver married Clementine Feathers and settled down. Club Bowers was honestly elected sheriff of the county and was sheriff until his death, well into the next century. Wolf Parcell vanished back into the mountains. But he kept a close eye on Jenny, until she got married a few years later. Van Horn remained foreman of the ranch until his death, years after the big fight in Red Light, Montana. Wolves still visit the grave of Barrie on the lonesome ridge above the little spring. All the hands stayed on and a hundred years later, the crosses in the cemetery on the ranch bear the names of Pasco, Clarence Bad Dog, Jim Hammon, Cooper, Ford, Ladd, and all the others who fought for and with Jenny Jensen and her Uncle Smoke.

Smoke and Sally stayed around long enough to see that Jenny would be all right, and then they mounted up for the long ride back to the Sugarloaf in Colorado.

Smoke would be back to check on Jenny from time to time. But that's another story . . . about the last mountain man.